WARM NOVEMBER

By the Author

Awake Unto Me

Forsaking All Others

A Spark of Heavenly Fire

Warm November

Visit us at www.boldstrokesbooks.com

Warm November

by
Kathleen Knowles

2015

WARM NOVEMBER
© 2015 By Kathleen Knowles. All Rights Reserved.

ISBN 13: 978-1-62639-366-0

This Trade Paperback Original Is Published By
Bold Strokes Books, Inc.
P.O. Box 249
Valley Falls, NY 12185

First Edition: August 2015

THIS IS A WORK OF FICTION. NAMES, CHARACTERS, PLACES, AND INCIDENTS ARE THE PRODUCT OF THE AUTHOR'S IMAGINATION OR ARE USED FICTITIOUSLY. ANY RESEMBLANCE TO ACTUAL PERSONS, LIVING OR DEAD, BUSINESS ESTABLISHMENTS, EVENTS, OR LOCALES IS ENTIRELY COINCIDENTAL.

THIS BOOK, OR PARTS THEREOF, MAY NOT BE REPRODUCED IN ANY FORM WITHOUT PERMISSION.

Credits
Editor: Shelley Thrasher
Production Design: Stacia Seaman
Cover Design by Sheri (graphicartist2020@hotmail.com)

Acknowledgments

I want to thank Judith for taking the time to tell me about her transition as a late-in-life lesbian. I'm also grateful to Yvette for friendship and insight.

My spouse, Jeanette, performed her usual duty as combination muse, beta reader, critic, and cheerleader. My friend Kent was always there to hear about how "the book" was going. Love and gratitude go to my sister Karin for pretty much everything.

Last but not least, thanks to all the friends of Bill for the last thirty years, one day at a time.

For Jeanette, who's always in my corner
and always tells me exactly what she thinks. ILY

Chapter One

Merle Craig was a realist, a clear-eyed, clearheaded, facer-of-facts person. She'd been that way ever since she'd gotten sober at the age of thirty-seven after twenty years of hard drinking. She'd rid herself of the alcoholic haze that had enveloped her brain and learned to face life on its terms. In spite of her hard-won perspective, she still didn't much like surprises.

She came home after her routine Saturday-morning AA meeting to find Kay, her lover of ten years, sitting at the kitchen table staring into space.

Merle poured herself another cup of coffee and sat down. She stared at Kay, trying to discern what might be up with her.

"Hi, love. Do you want me to start with laundry, and you can take care of the living room and dining room?"

Kay didn't move or respond for an unusually long time. Then she looked up and at Merle, her expression unreadable. "I think we should break up."

Merle's throat closed and she had a hard time swallowing her coffee. Her shoulders seized with anxiety. Things weren't great between them, but she hadn't thought they were that bad.

"Okay." She drew the word out carefully. "Could we talk about this? Why do you think we should break up?" She kept a close eye on Kay like she was a dicey lab experiment that might fail at any moment. Merle was one of those people who masked her inner turmoil by becoming quieter and calmer the more upset she was.

"I'm not happy. Surely you've noticed."

Merle *had* noticed. She knew Kay was unhappy but didn't think Kay was unhappy with *her*. At least Kay had never said she was.

"Yes. I've thought that. Would you tell me about it?"

Kay had been laid off two years before. Her mother had died. Those events could surely take their toll on Kay's psyche but still…

"I don't know if I can. I feel like we're missing something." Kay stared off into space. She could be annoyingly vague sometimes.

"I need some more detail. Is there something you want to do? Something you want me to change?"

"It's not you. It's me."

Merle's chin dropped to her chest. "You want to flush ten years down the toilet. Just like that?"

"I don't *want* to."

"Would you give therapy a try?"

"Sure. We could." She shrugged.

"But would you participate?"

"Yes. Of course I would."

So off they went to a therapist, and Merle tried hard to believe they weren't going to therapy just so they could break up.

After she'd gotten sober, she'd waited a long time to get involved with someone. She wasn't sure it would ever happen, and when she'd met Kay, she was convinced she was the right woman. She wasn't prepared to be wrong or to go down without a fight.

❖

They sat in their twin armchairs facing their therapist, Aja. They described how, when, and where they met, and their most recent history.

Aja fixed them with sharp, dark eyes that belied her benign expression and asked, "So. Are the two of you still having sex?"

They looked at each other, then back at their therapist, and neither said anything.

"Don't both of you try and talk at once now," Aja said drily.

"No." Kay spoke first. "I'm just not into it."

"Oh?" Aja raised an eyebrow. "Could you say a little more about that?"

And sure enough, Kay said more.

Merle grew to hate Aja's prodding. It made Kay spew stuff Merle had no idea was in her brain. She'd known all along that Kay was codependent and a big procrastinator and a laggardly decision-maker. Merle often had to work to get Kay to say what she was thinking or to do something or decide something. She thought Kay had gotten over the codependence. Kay's failure to tell Merle ninety percent of what was on her mind was the worst procrastination *ever*. Years of Kay's thoughts came tumbling out.

In between therapy visits they talked and argued and processed.

"It's getting better, isn't it?" Merle asked after a few months.

"Maybe, we'll see," Kay said.

When the Supreme Court invalidated Section Two of DOMA and finally voided Proposition 8, Merle asked Kay if she was ready to get married. In 2008, Kay hadn't wanted to get married, citing the uncertainty of Prop 8 and the upcoming election and the fact that they wouldn't have full equality because of DOMA. It had made sense to Merle at the time. Kay's difficulty making decisions made any whiff of ambiguity or uncertainty stop her cold.

"You want to get married *now*?" Kay asked. "We're trying to get through therapy and don't know if we're going to stay together."

"That's the point of marriage! It's supposed to help you stay together. I love you. I want to stay with you. I want us to stay together! We've got this house."

"Oh. You know. Marriage isn't really a gay thing. It's a straight thing. Who needs it? We don't." Kay waved her hand, dismissing the possibility.

Merle shut her mouth. She was ready to pay any price to keep them together. The therapy continued and she waited for the miracle to happen. It didn't.

At last, on one bright April day, Kay invited Merle to join her on the living-room couch.

Kay uncharacteristically sat close to Merle, took both of her hands, and said, "I've tried. I really have, for your sake. But we can't do this anymore."

Merle held back her tears. She wanted to say many things, but the only thing she could articulate was, "What are we going to do with the house? You can't buy me out. You're going to walk away from your equity?"

"The house was always your thing, sweetheart. You can stay here and buy *me* out. I'd give you lots of time." And she smiled, sadly.

It was true. Merle had wanted to buy the 1930s Craftsman with a front porch on Bernal Hill's south side the second she saw it. Kay thought it was dull looking and too expensive. They'd argued about that too, of course. Not only would she have to pay the mortgage herself, but she'd have to repay Kay thousands of dollars. Anger piled on top of sadness and fear.

It took a full year, but Kay finally made the decision to leave and Merle had to accept it.

For someone who wasn't especially well organized about life, Kay was coldly efficient about removing all traces of herself from their home.

On the day Kay was to move, Merle's friends made many offers of sanctuary to her and warned her to not be there, but Merle didn't listen. Kay could change her mind. That wasn't unprecedented. Merle didn't want to miss it in case it happened again.

Kay had rented a U-Haul and somehow acquired a nondescript young man to help her move. According to the old joke, the answer to the question of "What does a lesbian bring to the second date?" was "a U-Haul." Turned out she brought the same U-Haul when the whole thing ended.

Merle found that amusing in a sickening way. Her friends were right; she should have stayed away. The whole scenario was surreally unpleasant.

She stood in the driveway with her yellow Labrador retriever, Arthur, at her side. Where had the moving boy come from? Some son of one of Kay's friends, no doubt. Kay hated to pay for stuff she could get for free.

She felt rather than saw Kay's presence at her side, likely for the very last time.

"Well, that's it," she said. At least she had the grace to look sad. For the last year of the endless therapy and processing and back and forth, she'd had two modes: acting peeved or showing fake solicitousness.

"Yep." Merle didn't trust herself to say more.

"Here's my key." Kay dropped her house key into Merle's hand. Merle looked at it for a second, then closed her fingers and stared at Kay. She was still pretty, with her long reddish-brown hair, gray eyes, and faraway expression. Long ago, Merle had thought she looked ethereal, like a born-again hippie. These days, she had worry lines and a twitch in her left eyebrow. They'd both aged.

"So you'll let me know when you get the title changed? You'll do that right away?" Kay asked. Except it wasn't really a question. It was an order couched as a question.

"Sure."

"Take care." Kay jumped up into the cab of the U-Haul. Merle watched her practice her familiar ritual of settling herself: she straightened her clothes, flipped her hair, and buckled her seat belt. The U-Haul drove away.

Arthur leaned against Merle in his affectionate big-dog way. She touched his head and he nosed her hand. Arthur's bulky body against her leg made her feel a little better.

"Well, that's that, buddy. Just you and me now." And after all the drama, the trauma, the endless discussions, it was done. She hadn't the foggiest idea what was next. She closed her eyes and recited the Serenity Prayer.

God, grant me the serenity to accept the things I cannot change, the courage to change the things I can, and the wisdom to know the difference.

She turned and went into the house.

❖

A light fog drizzle was falling as Merle walked to the Full Moon Café after the Bernal New Day AA meeting with her friends Sigrid and Clea. They kept the conversation general and light until they got their food and sat down near the front window. Kay had left a couple of weeks ago.

"So, Mer. How're you holding up?" Clea asked. She and Sigrid had been Merle's closest friends in the program in recent years. They were there when she'd started. They'd lost touch and then reconnected a couple years after she met and courted Kay. They'd been a couple since before Merle had met them.

"I'm okay. I guess."

"Not a very convincing answer." Sigrid glanced at Clea but then returned her attention to Merle, who took a drink of coffee.

"It's like she's still there. I keep looking up and expecting her to walk into the room."

"I hear that's what happens when someone dies," Clea said, her tone arch.

"She's very much *not* dead, thanks. Though she might as well be." Merle stared at the ceiling, hands in pockets, and sighed.

"You're moping." Sigrid was stern though not cruel. Her tone was kind rather than snarky. Merle still didn't want to hear her observation, though it was true.

Merle shifted in her chair and frowned. Where were her two supportive friends? Today she was mired in sorrow and wanted at least to have them acknowledge her loss. She wanted a little compassion.

Clea and Sigrid had always been noncommittal about Kay. Not critical but not effusive. She didn't ask them for much information. Maybe she hadn't wanted to hear what they really thought. "They" was the correct pronoun because she never heard them express anything but agreement with each other.

"Can't I mope a little? I lost my lover, for Christ's sake. Give me a break. I'm not drinking, I'm not suicidal. I'm not even stuffing sugar into my face. How about allowing me just a touch of self-pity to make me feel better?"

She put her thumb and forefinger close together and grinned then, and they laughed.

"Like someone with a terminal disease, I have good days and bad days. This is a bad day. Let me enjoy it."

Sigrid nodded. "Go right ahead, sweetie, but tomorrow, you've got to snap out of it."

She patted Merle's cheek. "You'll be fine. Your sense of humor appears intact. Yes, of course you're allowed to mourn the loss."

"So tell me, now that she's gone, what did you really think of her all that time?" It was time to find out what she'd avoided asking about.

Kay had always said, "You can have your AA friends. I don't need to be part of that." And Merle had agreed. Clea and Sigrid had never pressed the issue.

"It's not important what we thought," Clea said, "but what *you* thought."

"Oh no. You're not getting off that easy."

"What does it matter now?" Sigrid asked. "She's out of the picture. You're going to find someone else. Someone better." Sigrid looked away when she said that, and Merle's curiosity perked up.

"Aha. So come on. Tell me." Sigrid looked at her spouse. Clea shook her head, making her hair-weaves sway.

"Go ahead on. She's not going to let it go. Girlfriend's like a pit bull when she gets going."

"We thought she was self-absorbed," Sigrid said. "She was okay. But well. It was always all about her."

"Don't you think we're all self-absorbed?" Merle asked, knowing Sigrid was right but wanting to argue anyhow. "But that explains why we never got together as a foursome. Why we didn't 'couple date.'"

"She was emotionally withdrawn," Clea said.

"Hard to pin down," Sigrid said.

"Wishy-washy," Clea said.

"Narcissistic." Sigrid said the word as though that was the final straw.

"She had issues, I agree, but—"

"That's an understatement."

"That time she left you at Tim's party because she was bored." Sigrid rolled her blue eyes heavenward. "Or when she refused to go with you to your dad's funeral. You said she said it was too inconvenient and you'd be better without her."

"That was likely true. Kay in a bad mood on a trip?" She shivered, recalling a few occasions.

Sigrid pursed her lips. Her attitude indicated that Kay's actions were a grave violation of relationship commandments. Maybe they were. At the time, Merle hadn't thought about it, but now she wondered. *Everything* was called into question. Had she spent ten years making excuses? Had she simply ignored her own needs because she knew Kay wouldn't be able to meet them? She was pretty self-sufficient. She'd never wanted to be in a clingy relationship. She and Kay had made fun of other lesbians who were inseparable, attached at the hip, dressed alike, and so forth. *Not us*, they'd agreed.

On the other hand, Merle was in awe of her two friends and their relationship. Sigrid was a Scandinavian with white-blond hair, and Clea was a very dark-skinned black woman. They were opposites in looks but were always in agreement emotionally, spiritually, and intellectually. They had minor disagreements, but they either worked through them or agreed to disagree. That was what made them work, she supposed. Where it counted, they agreed. They were in sync. They flowed.

She and Kay had almost always struggled with some sort of issue. Merle was analytical so she accepted their constant discussions about the least little thing as normal. That might have been just another sign she'd missed. When did a minor difference of opinion become a reason to break up?

"Whoa. So how come you never said anything about any of this?"

"What would be the point?" Clea asked.

"You needed to figure it out for yourself," Sigrid said,

"I suppose I wouldn't have received any criticism of Kay very well."

"You never bad-mouthed her or complained about her. You're very loyal that way. And you loved her," Clea said.

"You had to figure it out for yourself. You know how we are." Sigrid meant that no one could tell someone else to do something. Humans would just go ahead and do the opposite. Or they would do it and then resent you for telling them. That was probably what Kay's shtick really was. She would agree when it suited her or she sensed Merle had reached her limit. It was a depressing characteristic of the human psyche.

Merle stared at the table, then at the ceiling again. She pulled her legs in and straightened her spine.

"I *did* love her. I was enamored of her. I thought she was beautiful. I still think so. And intelligent and kind. I just thought we were going through what all couples go through."

"Honey, it's a fine line between working through your problems and just letting the other person get away with BS," Clea said.

Merle winced.

"She was all those things, sweetheart." Sigrid spoke kindly. "But she was a lot of other things as well, including massively dishonest. So here you are."

"Here I am."

"What are you going to do now?" Clea asked, her dark eyes probing her.

"What do you mean what am I going to do now? Nothing, I guess. What *should* I do?"

They glanced at one another and then back at Merle.

Sigrid said, "For the moment, nothing is likely a good choice. Give yourself some time."

"Are you okay for money?" Clea asked.

"Yes. Why would you ask that?" Merle felt suspicious and defensive in spite of herself.

"Well, you just lost half of your household income. And you've got a mortgage to pay. We thought—"

"I'm fine for now." Merle had worked for many years as a lab manager for a fairly well-known researcher at UCSF. "But I'm going to have to get a roommate soon to help with the mortgage. I have to buy Kay out of the house, though she said I could have a lot of time."

"Okay. Just asking. That was nice of her, at least. This whole thing is pretty traumatic and disjointing. You shouldn't minimize it."

"I'm not."

"We know, sweetie, and we were just teasing. You can sure enjoy some self-pity. Then you need to pull yourself together and move forward. No wallowing." Clea shook her finger at Merle and laughed, which made Merle laugh, because she knew what they meant. No alcoholic or drug addict, no matter how long she was clean and sober, could afford to let self-pity take over. That way lay madness, then possible relapse. Both, probably.

"We could go on a little vacation." Sigrid looked thoughtful. "Maybe a few days in Mendocino? How does that sound?"

"Sure. That would be good." The idea intrigued Merle. A vacation with just Sigrid and Clea. No Kay. She might as well experience as many situations as possible without Kay just to get used to the new reality. Going on vacation with her friends ought to help the process along.

❖

Mendocino was a three-and-a-half-hour drive up Highway 1, so that left plenty of opportunity for talking about Kay. Merle didn't want to bore her two friends, but they listened and made sympathetic comments. Merle realized why they hadn't spent that much time together as a foursome. And why Sigrid and Clea had said very little about Kay. They didn't much like her.

Kay no doubt had picked up some kind of vibe from them and didn't ever suggest they get together. It had become clear to Merle just how many vital thoughts Kay had kept to herself.

Merle said, "I want to pound the side of my head and yell, 'How could I have been so stupid!'"

Clea was driving, but Sigrid turned around and patted Merle's leg. "Merle, honey, you don't have to beat yourself up."

"You're right. It's pointless. I loved her, I chose her. It's not my fault I didn't get what I paid for. So to speak. She was damned good at manufacturing a façade of actually caring for me."

"She likely *did* care for you, but she's a codependent monster who wouldn't know the truth about herself if it came up and kicked her in the teeth."

"So Sigrid, tell me what you *really* think." Merle enjoyed the Kay-bashing now. If it had happened before the breakup, she might have done some teeth-kicking herself. Now it was funny and ego-boosting.

Clea squinted ahead as she negotiated the curvy, narrow two-lane highway and growled. "That child was a selfish twit. You were a saint."

Sigrid turned around and cocked her head. "You were very patient with Kay."

"Let's talk about how I was a saint some more." Merle was enjoying the conversation. It was handy to have her posse on her side.

"Not so fast, chickie," Clea said. "I was being sarcastic." She checked her rearview mirror.

"Stop tailgating me, bro," Clea said to no one in particular.

"Aw, crap. I want to be a saint for a while." Merle pretended to pout. "I know, I know. What was *my* part?" She asked the not-quite-rhetorical question everyone in recovery had to ask themselves when things went south. Nothing could be wholly blamed on someone else. Responsibility must be assumed. She wasn't sure she was ready for that part. But she wanted to ask the question before either Sigrid or Clea asked it.

"So, Merle dear, what *is* the answer?" Sigrid was serious. No more sarcasm.

"I was kind of pussy whipped." To her surprise, that statement popped into her head pretty quick.

"Oh no, we don't want to hear about that." Sigrid put her hands over her ears.

Merle leaned forward and put her hands on the back of Sigrid's car seat.

"No, really. I had it for her bad, I always did. I think that worked for her for a while. Until it didn't. She would be lovey-dovey every once in a while, but then it went away all together. I just thought I wanted sex more than she did. *That* it was my fault."

"Wanting sex is not a fault, girl," Clea said. "Not being honest is a fault."

Merle knew what she meant. Her part in this debacle: she refused to see the truth even if Kay wasn't speaking it. It was there for her to discover and she refused to see it.

"I was in denial. You know how that goes. Hey, pull over there," Merle said all of a sudden. They'd reached one of her favorite spots on Highway 1.

Clea obeyed, and the three of them climbed out of the car. They were near Jenner and at the top of a mountain, it seemed. The hill was behind them, with Highway 1 snaking its way through canyons and around hills. The Russian River estuary lay just below them. The sun glittered on the Pacific. A lone fishing boat chugged north. From their height, it looked like a toy boat. They could see but not hear the white water that was so much a part of the coast of Sonoma County.

"This is the best part of being a Californian," Sigrid said. "The scenery is so dramatic."

"It sure as heck is." Merle's thoughts were drifting. *Be grateful. Be happy. It's over. She's gone. Time to get on with the rest of your life. Your friends love you. You have a good life. And she's not coming back.* Merle was going to have to repeat that to herself a lot.

They stood at the overlook for a few minutes without speaking, then turned as one and got back in the car to continue their journey north.

❖

They stayed at a B&B in Fort Bragg, the scruffier, more working-class town just north of Mendocino. They visited the upscale shopping mecca during the day or hiked in the state park. Clea was the bigger shopasaurus, so while she was indulging that side of herself, Merle and Sigrid went off together. They watched seabirds swoop over the cliffs and walked along the myriad paths just outside of the village of Mendocino. Spring was more to Merle's liking than summer because Mendocino suffered from summer overcrowding. If only Kay had broken up with her a little sooner. Ah well. It was still good to be away from the city for a bit. Mendocino was lovely even with all the summer crowds. At least there weren't too many kids. It was definitely not a kid-friendly place.

Merle and Sigrid settled on one of the benches on the bluffs just south of the town. It was Merle's favorite time of day, the late afternoon. The sun was still out, but the fog was moving in and a bracing chill filled the air.

She looked at Sigrid in profile, her head back and her eyes closed. She had a purple muffler wrapped around her neck. Her curly golden hair moved in the breeze.

Sigrid said, "Sometimes I like to just feel a place like this rather than *see* it."

"I like to engage all my senses."

"True."

Merle studied Sigrid, wondering if she should ask the question. Would it destroy Sigrid's holiday reverie? Maybe, maybe not. She didn't want to torture her two friends with constant chatter about Kay. She had something different in mind, though, than rehashing the debacle with Kay.

"Why do you and Clea stay together?"

"What?" Sigrid's blue eyes flew open and she looked alarmed.

"That didn't come out quite right. I meant, what makes you work? I believe you do. I see that you do, but what I want to know is why."

"Oh." Sigrid sat back and looked thoughtfully out over the cove to their left where an arch in the rocks funneled the waves in an interesting way. "I think what you want to know is why you and Kay *didn't* work."

"Nooo. I think I know now."

"Tell me."

"Kay was so wonderful for the first few years. She was lovable and attentive and present and sexy and all of that. I was gaga about her. We bought the house, we got Sadie. We planted the garden."

"You were only missing the white picket fence."

"Yeah, we had it in spirit. So we're going along, everything just fine. Then things got a little less smooth. I got laid off from that one lab. Kay got mono. I thought we were just weathering a few rough spots. Somehow, as time went by, she became, I don't know, less attentive? I was the same. I felt the same. She said she was fine but she wasn't. The withdrawal was so gradual, I didn't even see it. I thought *I* was too demanding."

"You weren't. She wasn't giving enough. And you were too nice. Too supportive."

"Yeah, I suppose so. How could I have been so dumb?"

"There's no way to answer that, sweetheart. That's somewhat like asking 'Why?' And 'why?' is not a spiritual question." Sigrid smiled as she repeated the AA wisdom.

Merle fell silent for a moment. Sigrid touched her shoulder.

"Mer. Don't think that you should have known better, that you're too 'recovered' to have this happen."

Sigrid was saying aloud what Merle couldn't let penetrate her consciousness but had been there nonetheless. Hearing Sigrid say what she hadn't wanted to think about was painful but somehow comforting.

"How did you know that was what I was thinking? *I* didn't know that was what I was thinking."

"Because we all think that. We think because we've worked those steps and gone to those meetings and haven't drunk or used drugs for a kazillion years that somehow that confers some special wisdom on us. That we shouldn't make mistakes and behave inappropriately. It's bullshit."

"Yeah. It is. I know. I'm no different from anyone else."

"Nope. You and I and all of us are just fallible human beings. Nothing more and nothing less. This breakup shouldn't discourage you. It can show you what to look out for next time. You can and will get the woman you deserve. I'm sure of it." Sigrid hugged her, and Merle got a little teary, but she felt better.

"I want to hear how it's supposed to work. This love thing."

"I'm not sure I can explain that."

"Oh, come on. You and Clea, you've got a great relationship. As far as I can see."

"I see. Well. I only know what works for us."

"That's good enough for me. Talk." Merle propped her head on her elbow and composed her mind to listen.

"I believe," Sigrid paused, looking for the right words, "that Clea is the one person in the world I truly can depend on. She will never fail me. I have absolute trust in her. She's my rock."

"Aww. That's sweet."

"Spare me. There's nothing sweet about trying to survive life. You need one person in your corner." Sigrid turned around to be face-to-face with Merle again.

"You can't be constantly wondering what she's thinking. You don't always know, of course. We aren't mind readers. Nor would I want to be. But you must be convinced that you can trust your lover. No matter what. That includes trusting her to tell you what you need to know even if it isn't what you want to hear."

Merle nodded, remembering all the energy she'd expended trying to figure out where Kay stood or what she was thinking. It seemed even when Kay actually did verbalize something, it might have been a lie.

"Tell me. When you think you've found the next one—and I'm positive there'll be another one—what will you do differently? We're not at the stage of life where we can make many Kay-like mistakes." It wasn't the first time Merle heard the steel and the reproach in Sigrid's voice about something. For all her physical softness, she was mentally more hard-edged than Clea, who was a softie from way back, even though she talked tough. It was probably Sigrid's Scandinavian heritage. Merle thought *she* was a realist, but she had nothing on Sigrid.

"I guess you think I've recovered enough to hear that."

"I would think so. I'm not trying to make you feel bad, Mer, but I want you to take a really good look at why you stayed with someone who wasn't right for you. I know you're not stupid and you've got a great recovery. You missed the signals that we could see. I used to tell Clea, 'Oh gosh, I really worry about Merle and Kay. I don't think it's working.'"

"I wanted to believe. I loved her so much. When she was there, she was there. Then she wasn't. The last few years, she kind of just disengaged. I'd ask her, but all she would do would be to make excuses. 'I'm tired. I have to work this weekend.' 'Can't you go to a meeting or something? You're nagging me.' And so forth."

"Do you think she was cheating?"

"Kay?" That just wasn't anything that made sense. Kay always talked about how much she admired her parents' happy fifty-year marriage and wanted to emulate it.

Sigrid looked at her closely, waiting for an answer.

"Nope. I can't imagine that. Why? What do you think?"

"I really can't say, sweetie. I was never close to Kay. I think she had plenty of other faults without that one." Sigrid snorted. She was a sardonic one.

"Yeah. She used to go crazy when I left the top off the toothpaste. She had all these little things she was super rigid and controlling about. Then she'd be totally disengaged. I never knew what to expect."

"You put up with it," Sigrid pointed out.

"Yup." Merle sighed. "I know. I wanted to keep things going. Keep the peace."

"Someone else was a little codependent."

Merle smiled, acknowledging the truth.

"And your next lover? What will you do different?" Sigrid tilted her head. "What has this experience taught you?" That was one of Sigrid's big things—experience mattered. Sigrid always said, "I can and do have opinions on everything. We all do. Tell me your experience and I might listen."

"She'll have to meet certain goals." Merle laughed.

"Such as want to have sex with you? Not care if you don't cap the toothpaste?"

"Very funny, but that'd be a good start. But more, she's got to be right out there with her feelings. I want to know what she's thinking. I don't want to have to drag it out of her or, as in the case of Kay, be misled."

"She did mislead you, didn't she, though she may not have meant to. I don't believe she had any idea what she really wanted."

"Nope, and my next girl is going to be very, very sure what she wants and who she wants. Me. Marriage. Forever. The whole ball of wax. I'll get that out of the way right away."

"And when will you ask her to marry you? I'd wait until the third date…"

Merle shoved Sigrid just a bit, but not hard enough to make her fall off the bench. At that moment, Clea appeared.

"Hey, if you want to throw her off the cliff, the answer is no. Only I get to do that."

Sigrid turned around, and Clea bent her head and they kissed tenderly.

Sigrid eyed the packages and bags Clea carried. "Darling, is there anything left to buy in Mendocino?"

"Oh, honey, you best believe they're never gonna run out of junk for tourists to spend money on. I've only made a little-bitty dent."

"I'll bet." Sigrid patted her cheek. "Well, ladies, I think we've reached an important decision point. What's for dinner?"

Merle said, "How about more seafood?"

"There'll never ever be enough seafood for me," Sigrid said with a theatrical flourish.

"That's a fact. She's spoken. So let's go drive back to Fort Bragg and head to Noyo Harbor to that little place right at the end of the road under the bridge and practically *in* the ocean. We can watch the boats cruise in."

"Fabulous!" Merle said. "I vote for that."

Merle thought about Sigrid's crack about "Kay-like mistakes." It was true, and she would most definitely not rush into anything. She wasn't even thinking about looking anyhow; she was still too raw. It would take some time to shake off the toxic emotional residue left over from Kay. She could be like someone newly sober. The traditional advice to those folks was to not make any big changes for at least a year. That would neatly apply to this breakup. There was no rush. She wouldn't find another girl for a long time.

Chapter Two

The week after she returned from the Mendocino trip, Merle stepped out her front door with Arthur, straightened her shoulders, and took a deep breath. To her left, just beyond the downtown skyline, the San Francisco Bay was a sheet of blue, no whitecaps disturbing its surface. To her right, the path up to the summit of Bernal Hill beckoned her to climb. This scene had sealed the deal for her when she and Kay had first seen the house.

Kay had complained that it cost too much and wasn't close enough to public transit. Merle had argued for the other amenities of the neighborhood: its beauty and village-like atmosphere. It wasn't gentrified but was still funky in a sweet way, not in a dangerous way, and it was full of lesbians. And there were lots of dogs. Merle had always wanted a dog and to live in a place where it would be pleasant to walk with one. In retrospect, she'd gotten everything she wanted and perhaps Kay hadn't. Well, Kay had agreed to buy the house and that was that.

During the time they'd lived in Bernal, she'd lost track of the number of failed relationships she and Kay had heard of. If lesbians loved to couple, they also tended to uncouple at a high rate. She remembered another old joke, "It takes lesbians two days to move in (via U-Haul, naturally) and ten years to break up." Apparently it was true.

She circled the bottom of Bernal Hill, steeling herself. She hadn't walked up to the main congregation spot on the south side of the hill since Kay had moved out because she simply didn't want to have to face their acquaintances and neighbors and tell the truth. The dog-owning lesbians in the Bernal Heights 'hood were a tight-knit, gossipy bunch.

But she had to do it sooner or later, and it might as well be on this sunny June Saturday afternoon. She walked to the end of her block and onto the well-worn path up the hill. A few feet above her home, the path intersected with the access road that encircled Bernal Hill called, appropriately, Bernal Heights Boulevard. It was blocked to car traffic past the houses so she and Arthur zigzagged back and forth on the wide road. He loved to investigate the smells of his neighborhood and mark them.

Merle waved at a few people she knew but didn't stop to talk. They reached the parking lot where the biggest crowd gathered. When she stopped to let Arthur drink at the fountain she felt a tap on her shoulder and turned around to face Miley, one of her least favorite neighbors. Miley was a major gossip and had always seemed to flirt with Kay whenever they met. Not that Kay had walked much with their dogs. She'd usually come up with some reason she couldn't, so Merle gave up asking her. She liked her walks with their dogs.

"Hey, Merle. Haven't seen you in a while."

Merle forced a friendly grin and watched Arthur slurp water. He could take forever sometimes and she'd be stuck talking to Miley.

"Yeah. Been busy. Out of town for a few days. You know."

"I hear you. How's Kay? She didn't want to walk today?" Miley was either being dumb or had a very short memory.

Merle didn't want to lie. That would come back somehow and smack her in the face.

"Yeah. Well. We split."

Miley stared and her eyebrows flew up.

"Really? No kidding. That's too bad. I'm sorry to hear that." Surprisingly enough, she even sounded sincere.

"Oh. Well. Thanks." Arthur finally finished his drink, shook himself, and looked at her expectantly. "Got to get moving. The big guy needs to walk." She turned toward the path.

"Oh. I'll go with you." Miley gave her dog's leash a tug. Her boxer, Tucker, followed her. Merle would have to make conversation now. She'd wanted sympathy from Clea and Sigrid, and she'd processed the break with them. She didn't want to discuss anything with Miley, let alone her split from Kay.

Merle tried to set a fast pace, but Miley kept up with her. That was the problem. Everyone in Bernal Heights was fit from all the walking and hill climbing, and she wasn't going to be able to lose Miley by moving faster.

"So what happened? Do you mind my asking?"

"Oh. The usual, I guess, drifting apart, different needs."

"I know, I know. You can't depend on anything. I always thought you were just an ideal couple. You seemed so right for each other."

Merle refrained from rolling her eyes. Maybe it had seemed that way to those not in the know. Kay would certainly have projected that aura, and so did she if she was honest with herself. She dragged herself away from her memory. Miley was still talking.

"Well. I'm glad you're sticking around. You got the house, huh?" Miley's expression was speculative.

"Yeah. She wanted to move. Hey, could we change the subject? I'm still sort of raw and it's tough to talk about."

"Uh-huh. Sure, I get it. Say, after we finish you wanna come over for a visit?" Miley looked absurdly hopeful and sweet. Was she asking Merle for a date? She wasn't ready for that. Not with anyone, and certainly not with Miley.

"Um. Can't. Not this time." Not *ever*. "But thanks for asking." She made sure her last sentence was spritely and cheerful. She wanted to sound grateful but wasn't going to promise anything.

"Do you have Kay's number, by the way?"

At this, Merle frowned and shook her head. It was a lie, but she didn't want Miley calling Kay. Miley was a piece of work.

Merle marched forward with Arthur, tugging him away from a sniff of some interesting glop on the road.

As they rounded the top of the hill, Pacific Gas and Electric Company's ugly microwave tower at the summit loomed on their left. It was the only flaw in the Bernal Heights ambience. Merle tried to ignore it and concentrate on the 360-degree panorama of San Francisco. She never tired of the view, and it was a great alternative to having to talk to Miley. She took a good deep breath and looked toward Diamond Heights to the northwest. Being on her hill with her dog and the view and the fresh air was healing.

At least Miley would take care of informing the rest of the 'hood so she wouldn't have to make the announcement over and over. When had she become so antisocial? She needed to get over that eventually. She might not be young but she wasn't dead! Gah, she'd have to start dating sometime. What a miserable prospect. Merle shook her head. She'd have to face it in the future. And she'd have to not see it as miserable but as an adventure. She hadn't had a date in ten years. That was a long time. But she didn't plan to start with Miley. Miley had been babbling the whole time, and Merle hadn't said a word.

Miley stopped mid-sentence. "Something wrong?"

"No. Just thinking. Oh, hey. Here's Abby and Susan."

The couple was way more palatable than Miley. And she wouldn't be asked on a date.

"Hi, Merle! How are you? Hi, Arthur, you sweetheart." Abby bent to pet Arthur. He soaked up the attention. Merle was hoping that Miley and Abby and Susan would start talking and relieve her of the need to participate.

"Hi, you guys. What's up?" Miley asked her question in the manner of someone who doesn't truly want to know but wants instead to tell you something.

"Not a lot. What about you?" Abby was greeting Tucker, while Susan tried to get their overly sensitive corgi, Mig, to settle down. Once she started barking she wouldn't stop. High-pitched, piercing barks.

"Me? *Nada.* But Merle here has some big news." Miley made it sound as though Merle had won the California lottery.

Abby raised an eyebrow while Susan tried to soothe Mig into silence. A treat finally did the trick, thereby ensuring Mig would repeat the behavior. Merle was grateful Arthur was easygoing.

"Oh? What's that?"

Miley looked expectantly at Merle. At least she wasn't going to take it on herself to give the news to Abby and Susan. Merle supposed she was grateful for that.

"I, um, Kay and I, eh, broke up."

"Oh no!" Susan stopped paying attention to the dogs and caught the eye of her partner, who stared back at her, seemingly struck dumb. Maybe they were afraid that whatever had caused Merle and Kay to split was catching. That idea amused Merle.

"Did you hear that, honey? Merle and Kay broke up!"

Abby scrutinized Merle, looking for wounds, apparently.

"How *are* you? When did it happen?" Abby asked like she'd been in a car accident. The breakup had been happening for a long, long time, but she wasn't about to try to explain that.

"About a month ago. I'm fine. No big deal." Merle shrugged. Both Susan and Abby were therapists. Merle *really* didn't want to talk to any more therapists.

"Well. Good. Susan, honey. We better go."

"Right. See you!" And they walked off so fast, Merle was sure they were afraid of catching the breakup disease.

"Ready to head down the hill?" she asked Miley, who was smiling at her with an expression somewhere between avidity and sympathy. Merle didn't want either emotion directed at her.

As they made their way back, Merle stuck to an innocuous subject: dogs. If they weren't gossiping about each other, the Bernal dykes could be relied on to talk dogs. Ad nauseam. Or the price of housing, an obsession they shared with all San Franciscans.

"So, see you around!" Merle told Miley cheerfully when they reached the path back to her house.

Miley squeezed her arm. "Call me if you need to talk. Or whatever."

"I sure will." Merle turned Arthur and hurried away, glad it was over.

Abby and Susan would no doubt tell everyone they knew. So would Miley. What would happen once the news was spread? More date requests from undesirables? The cold shoulder from nervous couples? She just wanted it all to go away.

Back at home, when she walked through the front door, the emptiness of the house washed over her. She stood still, unconsciously expecting Kay to be there. How long would it take to get over that feeling?

❖

The biggest problem with being single other than the monstrous loneliness was that Merle had to do all the household chores herself. This made her miss Kay more. She'd never thought about how well they divided up the necessary tasks like grocery shopping. Kay had done it, although she drove the car every time, no matter how often Merle had pleaded with her to use a shopping cart. Kay hated to walk and loved to drive. Merle had only her own motivation.

She dutifully dragged her metal grocery cart eight blocks up and down the mini hills around Bernal Heights to the Good Life Grocery. They were, correction, *she* now was lucky to be close to a decent grocery store. The first time she'd had to go the week after Kay left, it had been oddly uncrowded and she hadn't run into anyone she knew, which was a great blessing.

This time it was midday on Saturday, and she was sure a ton of people would be there. Hopefully the word had spread so she didn't have to say anything should she encounter anyone she knew. She could just smile bravely in response to the questions of how she was feeling.

She slid her cart behind the handle of the grocery basket so the wheels kept it from falling and started her circuit in the produce section. She zeroed in on the green vegetables. Next to her, an unfamiliar lesbian couple spoke to each other earnestly, their heads together. Merle needed a plastic bag, and the dispenser was directly over the head of the woman nearest her.

"Excuse me." Merle essayed a polite smile. The woman turned to her, blinked, and didn't say a word, though she moved slightly to one side and returned to her conversation with her girlfriend/partner/wife. Neither of them even acknowledged Merle's existence. They were oblivious, as though they were in a bubble, a couple bubble. Merle kept going. She'd worried that she'd have to talk to people, and the opposite was true. The sudden stab of loneliness surprised her. This was ridiculous because she and Kay had rarely shopped together. Merle cruised on to the deli counter and stood before the display of free-range, organic meat and fish in a quandary. What to buy?

She was on her own. She'd been part of a dysfunctional couple, it was true, but still she was with someone. Now she was single. In the Good Life Grocery, that realization truly hit her. Everywhere she looked she saw pairs of women who seemed completely absorbed in each other. This was so unnerving. Why had she never noticed the Good Life Grocery clientele was entirely composed of lesbian couples?

Also, in the long run, food for one was more expensive than food for two. She didn't mind cooking, but cooking for herself really depressed her. Merle slid into a full-blown black, bottomless funk. She wasn't with Kay anymore. At her age, how the hell did you start over, and where the heck would she find women? Merle didn't think she wanted to try dating in AA. One alcoholic in a relationship was enough, even if they were both sober. Clea and Sigrid were the exception that proved the rule.

She walked up the juice aisle. Since she didn't drink alcohol, she indulged in fancy organic juices. They'd moved the Knudsen juices. Again. They were up on the top shelf. Yet another lesbian couple stood next to her. *God.* Was there no end to them? Merle reached up to grab a bottle of the Morning Blend. After their first night together, she and Kay had sat in bed, exhausted and covered in sex juice, and toasted each other with Knudsen Morning Blend. Better choose another flavor. She tried to return the juice to the shelf, but her hand slipped and the bottle of juice crashed to the floor, spraying glass and orange, grapefruit, and mango juice everywhere, including onto half of the couple nearest her.

The un-splashed half of the couple gave her a glare that almost turned her to stone. She'd apparently splashed juice on the wife of Medusa. Merle muttered "Sorry!" and wearily went off to find a staff member and tell her of the accident. She took up her shopping again and tried to calm herself.

In the grocery store, she reminded herself she'd soon have to figure out her housing situation and interview potential roommates. Another one of those single-person things, like dating, she'd thought never to have to do again. She decided on a couple of chicken breasts that were on sale. As the butcher wrapped them up, her thoughts flew ahead. She reckoned craigslist was the way to go. Or maybe use a rental service, although there'd be a fee. Never mind. She could screen people herself.

She hadn't lived with a roommate since the early eighties before she moved in with her first lover, Sara, the one before Kay. That was at the height of her alcoholism, so Merle was hazy about what it had been like to live with roommates. She only remembered that she and Sara had shared a flat with some people but recalled nothing else. Well, she'd have to pull herself together and find a housemate.

❖

Merle heard from an acquaintance how common it was for people to lie about their financial health. It was as common as lying about sex, the woman said. She had to take that into consideration, as well as other potential pitfalls like drug addiction, alcoholism, and failure to do dishes. Not to mention just general weirdness. She'd heard stories from the neighborhood about roommate nightmare scenarios. She decided it would be helpful to make it known to the dykes-with-dogs posse that she was in the market. This entire process seemed as fraught with peril as dating. At least with dating, she could call the whole thing off after a couple of encounters. Could she kick someone out of her house after a couple weeks? She needed legal advice or something.

During her dog-walking forays, whenever she met people she knew, she mentioned she was looking for a housemate. She got more horror stories than referrals or suggestions.

"Skipped out on the rent."

"Said she was a dyke but surprise, she was bi. Found out when the guy who stayed over was peeing in the bathroom with the door open and I stumbled upon him early in the morning. Yech."

"Never washed a single dish. I found out she burned one of my Calphalon skillets and threw it in the trash without telling me."

"Speed freak."

"Slut."

"Psycho."

"Bitch."

"Hoarder."

"Pothead."

"Thief."

"Meat eater." This last one didn't seem quite that big a deal to Merle, but some folks took it *very* seriously.

Merle wanted to call the whole thing off, but she couldn't. In another month, she was going to have to choose between eating Top Ramen for dinner and not paying the mortgage or paying Kay back. She had to start doing that soon. She worded her craigslist ad very carefully and tried to think of every single thing. She even added her approximate age as a disincentive to the young and restless. Some part of her thought just maybe an older woman would be less trouble. More reliable. Easier to live with. Safer.

Clea asked her, "Do you want a friend or just someone to share the space?"

"I don't know. I suppose it would be nice to be friends, but maybe I don't care."

She'd invite the prospective house sharers over for a cup of tea, then try to read their minds. A lot of people were immediately disqualified due to financial instability. Saying no to providing a credit report or references was a non-starter.

The woman who sat at her kitchen table seemed like a good bet. She was the correct age and had proof of income. She worked downtown as an executive assistant. Merle understood that to mean she was a secretary for some bigwig. No matter. She got paid a decent salary.

They exchanged pleasantries about the wonders of the Bernal Heights neighborhood and the difficulties of finding good housing in the City. Pat was her name, and she smiled and cooed over Arthur in a reassuring way and scratched his head.

Merle had interviewed people who had insisted in email they were fine with dogs but then freaked when the met Arthur, who, since he was a male Lab, was a big dog. He was eighty pounds of mush, a big baby, really, but it didn't matter. One woman complained, "I thought you had a Chihuahua!" Merle loathed Chihuahuas on principle, but she smiled and said thank you and dismissed the woman.

Pat smiled vaguely and sipped her tea. There was an uncomfortable pause. Merle waited. She liked to let people free-associate so they could either reveal their good qualities or hang themselves. She was on the verge of making an offer to Pat when Pat said, "There's one little thing. I'm waiting for word from Minnesota, but I may have to leave suddenly when we get notice that Earth's magnetic poles are going to switch. Then the only safe place will be Hibbing, Minnesota. And I'll have to leave without much notice. I hope that wouldn't be a problem?"

Merle was so dumbfounded all she could think of to say was, "Wasn't that where Bob Dylan was from?"

"Oh yes. Odd coincidence, huh?" Pat beamed.

"Well. Thanks for coming, I'll be in touch."

Merle was getting very discouraged.

Chapter Three

Hayley Daniels sat at her kitchen table with the divorce papers in front of her. They'd arrived folded up in thirds in a legal envelope. She smoothed the pages, trying to get them to lie flat. They came with a nice heavy blue paper backing and helpful little sign-here tabs.

It was miraculous that what she'd considered for so long was finally about to happen. She was holding the concrete proof of what she was about to do. These pages with their dense legalistic language would make it official. She was getting a divorce from Howard. She repressed a tiny flicker of indecision. It was the right thing to do, and it was the right time. If there was ever such a thing as a right time for divorce. Not getting married in the first place would have probably been a better idea. But no, she'd done the expected thing. She'd gotten her man and got hitched at twenty-four. That was twenty-eight years ago. Christ, she'd been married for more than half her life. What a horrible thought.

Hayley picked up the first page and stretched it with her fingers. She pushed her hair out of her eyes and behind her ears and tried to focus on the document instead of her regrets. The language didn't intimidate her. She was a paralegal and had read thousands of legal documents. It was really just another document. But it wasn't. This time it was personal.

She looked at the last page and saw Howard's signature. She knew it so well and yet it looked strange. She picked up her pen and tapped it on the table, then turned back to the front page. The dry prose could hardly capture what this really all meant. Most people would see it as evidence of failure, but she refused to think of her divorce in those terms.

They'd tried to make it work for long past the point where it was worth it. Howard knew it and she knew it.

The only problem, if it even could be called a problem, was their son, Robbie. As far as she was concerned, Robbie was one positive aspect in her married life. So far, he'd taken the divorce in stride. When they sat him down to tell him, he looked from one to the other for a moment, then shrugged.

"I could tell you weren't happy."

Hayley and Howard had stared at each other and then back at Robbie.

"How?" Howard asked. They'd never fought or argued. They got along very well, in fact.

"Well, you never spent any time together. You never talked about each other. You never talk *to* each other."

And that was about the size of it, Hayley recalled. They'd been living separate lives since the day Robbie had gone to college eight years before.

So hurting Robbie's feelings wasn't an issue. The only one who had an issue about their divorce was Howard's mother, Ida. She was one of those till-death-do-you-part, do-or-die, stand-by-your-man women. She couldn't believe it when they told her.

"Why now? Whatever will you do, Hayley?" She sounded stricken.

Typical of Ida to form the question with her name in it when what she really meant was whatever would *Howard* do?

As for Hayley, she knew exactly what she was going to do. She intended to be a lesbian. She supposed it was sort of silly to make a statement like that, even to herself. Of course, everyone knew it wasn't a choice. Everyone but the stupid religious fanatics, anyway.

No, it wasn't a choice to be a lesbian, but it was a choice to have ignored it for most of her life. She was done. Ergo, she'd always been a lesbian, but she planned to change the theoretical to the actual, change the thought to action.

When Hayley's mother heard the news of their divorce, she'd been noncommittal. She'd never been especially fond of Howard. But Hayley hadn't told her the real reason for the divorce. She decided to wait for another day to announce that to her mother.

Of course her lesbianism hadn't occurred all of a sudden or out of nowhere. There'd been that time in college with her best friend. They'd been very drunk and started to get intimate but didn't go through with it. Hayley had decided that had been a fluke. So she got married. She had a son, she had Howard, she had a so-called normal life that she was conditioned to believe was happy and secure. Though she had random thoughts and fantasies, she just dismissed them as mind tricks.

Then something else had happened a few years before.

Her law firm had acquired a new client, one Sabine Mills. Sabine was a software engineer who was suing her employer for employment discrimination. Sabine was unmistakably, visually and verbally, a lesbian. And a big flirt. Every meeting they had, every time Sabine came to the office, she flirted with Hayley openly. When they went to court (Sabine won her case, her lawyer was Hayley's boss at the time and was excellent at her job) and then afterward when they went to a fancy downtown restaurant to celebrate, the flirtation turned into making out in the bathroom of the restaurant. But that was that. Hayley didn't want to go further, though she thought Sabine was funny and sexy. But she was clearly an alcoholic, and well, Hayley was still married to Howard and didn't want complications.

But the experience lingered. She spent many nights lying awake thinking about how it had felt when Sabine had kissed her and squeezed her breasts. The point was she felt *something*. She no longer felt anything with Howard. Not that she'd ever felt much to begin with, even when they were first married. Maybe a twinge or two. Hayley had found out about true pleasure when she taught herself to masturbate right after she got married. When Sabine had kissed her, her stomach had turned over and she'd nearly passed out, she was so aroused. She remembered her friend from college and the puzzle pieces clicked into place.

Hayley started looking up lesbian sites on the Web. She very shortly found out that a lot of women figured out their true sexual natures after a long, long time of being ostensibly heterosexual. Women were thought to be more flexible in that way. Go along to get along. Stay with the husband and raise the kids. Well, for Hayley that was over. The kid was an adult and Hayley wasn't getting any younger. It was time to find out what this whole lesbian deal was about.

So here she was. She was getting a divorce, they were selling the house, and she was going to start a whole new life. An entire city full of lesbians was waiting. San Francisco was ground zero for LGBTQ culture; at least that's what Hayley thought. How hard could it be to meet women? It ought to be easy. Like shooting fish in a barrel. Hayley smiled to herself at that old cliché. Then she looked at the divorce decree again. One last time, she tried to get the pages flat, this time with her forearm. She stared at Howard's signature, then added her own on the line below. After she folded the papers and stuffed them into the envelope Howard's lawyer had provided, she went to find the stamp he had *not* provided, the cheapskate. Then she put on a jacket and went outside to find a mailbox.

They lived in the "Avenues," the numbered streets to the south of Golden Gate Park, officially called the Sunset District. Their soon-to-be former home was on Thirty-sixth Avenue and Pacheco. Hayley loved living near the ocean. It made up for having gravel for a front yard and a miniscule backyard, which was more than a lot of San Franciscans had. She walked west on Pacheco Avenue, the blue Pacific straight ahead of her. After she dropped the divorce papers into a mailbox, she continued the eleven blocks to the Great Highway.

It was a sunny, breezy afternoon. The fog had burned off, and the sun brought out the people. She skipped up to the path and walked north, facing the Cliff House and Ocean Beach in the distance. She admired the gray-green Pacific and the long, rolling waves. Setting herself a good pace, she cheerfully dodged between the strollers and the runners and the bicycles. Hayley didn't mind the crowds on the Great Highway.

She'd miss this part of living in the Avenues, taking her walks with the ocean crashing in the background, but so be it. Soon she'd be moving and would be taking a different walk in a different neighborhood. Everything in her life was going to be different. She was done with settling for what she had. She was going to get what she wanted now. No more pretending and no more evading the truth. She was finally ready to really be herself, with no need to hide and no need to be ashamed.

Hayley's knowledge of lesbian culture so far was confined to the Internet and to her conversations with Britt, a law-student intern in their office. Since Britt was a generation younger, Hayley didn't think her experience was especially relevant. Britt was a twenty-something who talked a mile a minute about hooking up and Girl Bar and online dating and sexting and what have you. Hayley doubted that her life would be anything like Britt's. There was a generation gap for everyone, she guessed.

"Oh, dude. That's great," she'd said when Hayley took her out to lunch and confessed what was up with her. "You gotta get out and about. So to speak."

"Um, I don't think it's going to be quite the same for me," Hayley said.

"Nope, guess not. But hey, there's plenty of older dykes around. This is San Francisco, right?"

Hayley winced at the term "older dykes." She felt the opposite of old—entirely too young and naive. Also the word "dyke" grated on her ears. "I may be chronologically older than you, but I have zero experience with women, so that's why I'm talking to you about this."

"You're like a baby dyke, but um…not." Britt grinned to show her that was a joke.

She wondered again why Britt used the word "dyke." Wasn't that derogatory? "What's that mean?"

"Oh you know. Like. Just out, brand-new. Kind of like a virgin." Britt had the grace to blush when she said that.

"That's true."

"It's awesome, dude. You're gonna have a blast."

Hayley hoped that was true but wasn't sure how to get started, so she asked Britt for suggestions.

"OkCupid," Britt said.

"What?"

"It's a dating website. That's how you, like, meet women."

"I want to meet women my age, not women your age."

"No, dude, it's all ages. And how come you don't want to meet women my age? Are you ageist or something?" This time, Britt seemed a little offended.

"Dude. No offense, but a younger woman just wouldn't work for me. I need someone closer in age, and I want to meet her in a more traditional fashion," Hayley said.

Britt frowned. Was it possible Britt wanted her to ask *her* out? Yuck. That would be liking dating one of her son's classmates. This whole thing was sliding into inappropriate territory.

"Yeah, okay. You can meet women at meet-ups."

"Hmm. What are those, exactly?" Then she waved her hand. "Yeah, yeah, online, right?"

"Obvi."

Hayley knew that meant obviously. She liked to think she wasn't hopelessly out of touch. She wasn't discounting the resources on the Web, but she didn't want to limit her options.

❖

One day shortly after Hayley signed her divorce papers she took off work and went to Castro Street to walk around. Do reconnaissance, be gay, whatever that might mean.

A lot of men around but few women. She liked the neighborhood feel of it. Would she end up living in the area? That might be fun. She found a copy of a newspaper, *The Bay Times*, and snagged a table at Starbucks on Eighteenth Street. There, she practiced smiling at the barista, whom she assumed was a lesbian, although it could be hard to tell with younger people. She thought about Britt and grinned. The barista smiled back, but it was a professional smile. Hayley needed a more flirtatious milieu than Starbucks on a Thursday afternoon.

Like maybe a dark, crowded bar on a Saturday night, though that thought scared her. She couldn't picture herself waltzing into a gay bar and picking up a woman. It wasn't as though she had anything against casual sex. Never mind. That wasn't what she wanted to do. It would probably be pointless anyhow.

She doubted many people in any bar would be over thirty-five.

Nope, she wasn't ready for the pick-up scene, so she found out about meet-ups online and decided that was probably worth a try.

But the first thing on her to-do list was to find a place to live. Everyone told her that was going to be tough. San Francisco's rental market was the second tightest in the country after Manhattan. Some people said the dot-commers were to blame, but Hayley thought it was just a simple case of supply and demand. A lot of people wanted to live in San Francisco, but there weren't nearly enough places for them to live in. Therefore, the rents were sky-high. It wasn't anyone's fault; it was basic economics.

When she finished her iced coffee at Starbucks, Hayley strolled around the residential streets of the district. She spotted a few hand-lettered for-rent signs. It wasn't the worst idea in the world to consider living with gay guys. Might be a lot easier than living with women. She'd known a bunch of them in the law practice, and they were sweet and fun to talk to. She also couldn't imagine their housekeeping habits would be problematical.

Back in the old stucco on Thirty-sixth Avenue, she surveyed her belongings. She didn't have much to move. She'd let Howard take some furniture to his new place. The rest they were donating or giving away. If she was starting a new life, she wanted to start with as little baggage as possible, both the physical and the emotional. She could at least get rid of the furniture she'd bought while she was married. Hayley giggled to herself. This was better than going off to college. It was kind of like Christmas. She didn't know what sort of gifts she'd receive. True love would be an excellent gift. Or if not true love at first, perhaps some really great sex.

That part of her new life was especially daunting. Once when Howard was away and after the encounter with Sabine, she'd rented a bunch of DVDs of *The L Word* and watched all of them over the course of one weekend. Her mind was reeling after that. Even allowing for the liberties of cable TV, the drama was way over the top. She didn't know how she'd survive anything resembling what that group of women endured. But the story line with Cybill Shepherd hit a nerve. Also all the sex was fabulous to watch. She had rich fantasies for months afterward where she made love with every single character on the show, more than once. It was fun, but Hayley strongly suspected reality wouldn't be like Showtime.

Hayley logged onto the craigslist site and looked at the housing listings, roommates wanted. One ad leapt off the page.

Bernal Heights. Owner-occupied (50+). Single woman preferred. Charming Craftsman home with garden. Must like dogs. Own bathroom, 2100 per month plus utilities. References and credit check required. Reply ad #93S6.

Hayley quickly wrote an email and waited for the response. It came back in a week with a phone number and invitation to call for a meeting.

What would be the best approach in this situation? She researched Bernal Heights and found out it was a very lesbian neighborhood. That was even better than the Castro District. She wasn't concerned about meeting the financial requirements, but she supposed a lot of people would meet those criteria. Living with a dog would actually be nice. She'd wanted one, but Howard wouldn't hear of it because she would have insisted that he participate in its care. She decided to make friends with the dog, with treats perhaps. She'd heard of people baking cookies to impress prospective landlords. That was a bit too obsequious. Just be yourself, her mother had always said. And that, finally, was what Hayley was prepared to be. She just hoped that being herself would net her a good place to live.

She obsessed over what she should wear to this meeting with Merle Craig, then laughed at her own folly. It was likely that Merle would only be concerned that she could pay the rent and not trash the house. She wanted to stand out from the crowd though, and then she thought of something.

From owning a home for years, she'd become adept at fixing things, such as ordinary plumbing and a little carpentry or simple electrical work. Howard would've called in an expert every time if she hadn't learned such skills, and they would have been paying through the nose. If Merle was a lesbian, and it seemed likely she was, she doubtless knew all this stuff already, didn't she? Wasn't there some sort of stereotype about lesbians and power tools? She didn't know for sure, but it couldn't hurt to mention her skills. She also could help with yard work. Though she loved flowers, she had no feel for gardening, but she was certain that cutting grass didn't require any special skill. Nor did cleaning up the inevitable dog feces. Hayley decided on her approach and was ready to audition for the part of Merle Craig's housemate.

❖

Hayley got off the bus on Cortland Avenue and walked several blocks to the corner of Bonview and Stoneman. It would be easy to get fit walking from the house to Mission Street to catch the bus. Or even walking all the way to the Financial District. The neighborhood was beyond charming. In the sun, the gardens and landscaping were showy and inviting. She spotted a marvelous variety of plants: marigolds, jasmine, roses, ice plants, ferns, and bougainvillea. The multicolored jumble of architectural styles felt just right, and Cortland Avenue had several types of businesses that seemed to cover anything she might possibly want to buy. The passersby were also a pleasant mélange of people of all races, ages, and, she presumed, sexual orientations.

In her old neighborhood in the Sunset, the residents were either Asian or white. And very straight. The houses there were pastel stucco almost exclusively, with little greenery or trees. In Bernal, the color and vibrancy of San Francisco was more evident both in the people and in the ambience.

She liked it immediately and began fantasizing about living there, then chided herself for getting too invested too fast in an outcome that was far from certain. Howard had often chided her for her tendency to plunge into everything headfirst. He hadn't been on board with her enthusiasm for, well, nearly anything. Again, she wondered why she'd married him, never mind the sexuality mismatch. But why ask why now? She'd done it, and from the marriage she'd gained her wonderful son, Robbie.

Hayley had read that San Francisco's unique neighborhoods that gave the City its character were like little villages. She'd never felt that out in the Avenues, though it was true for multigenerational Irish families that had lived there forever. But they complained about the influx of Asians and, more recently, the invasion of the high-tech crowd. That, at least, had allowed Hayley and Howard to get a terrific price for their house. Seller's market.

In Bernal, Hayley saw the village character immediately and was drawn to it.

Then she noticed the hill and saw it loom closer as she walked from Cortland Avenue down Bonview Street. Bernal Hill certainly dominated the area. She started thinking about taking walks up to the top and then back down. She looked at her phone where she'd keyed in the address and arrived at the house all of sudden. It wasn't colorful, like some of the others, nor was it a Victorian, but she liked it. It looked homey; its neat front porch and brown shingles gave it an air of solidity. She walked up the front steps and noted the two Adirondack chairs separated by a wooden telephone-cable spool. It was very seventies.

But would the house's owner be as wonderful as the neighborhood and her house? Hayley rang the bell, and after a moment the door opened and she stood face-to-face with Merle Craig.

"Hi? Merle?" She sounded foolish, but she was nervous. People thought of her as outgoing, and she was, but she had a shy side that showed up sometimes. Like now.

"That's me. Come on in." Merle held the door open, and Hayley stepped through and into the living room. The large, light-yellow dog glued to Merle's side didn't bark at her, but as she stepped into the house, he crowded close and sniffed her in an amiable way. She put her hand out for him and he nosed it, then grinned a dog grin and panted.

She turned and took in Merle more thoroughly. Merle was somewhat taller than her, maybe five-eight or five-nine, with a medium build. She wasn't thin nor was she overweight; she looked solid and strong. She stood erect, with her head up and shoulders back. Her eyes were blue gray, and Hayley suspected her hair was prematurely gray because she didn't seem old enough for completely gray hair. Her face was weathered in a pleasing way, with small wrinkles at the corners of her mouth and eyes that became more pronounced when she smiled. She had the skin color of someone who spent a lot of time out of doors. She wore broken-in chinos and a white T-shirt under a light-blue sweater.

The dog sat at her side, tongue hanging out. They both seemed to be examining Hayley in a curious but friendly manner. It made a beguiling picture: the handsome gray-haired woman with her well-behaved dog. Hayley didn't want to stare too much, but she was transfixed for a moment. She didn't know exactly how she knew it, but she was certain she was the right person at the right time for this pair.

Merle nodded at the dog. "This is Arthur." She looked down at him and he gazed up at her, the epitome of human and canine connection and understanding.

"Hi, Arthur. You're a very handsome boy." Hayley liked his noble profile and his calm demeanor. "What's his breed?"

"He's a yellow Lab."

"How old?"

"About four. Not old, but he's through his puppy phase, thank goodness."

"He seems well trained."

Merle grinned at the compliment. "Thanks. We work on it. And Labs aren't hard to handle."

"I'm not super familiar with dogs, but I like them. He seems easy to like too."

"Hear that, Arthur? You're easy. He actually *is* easy. Give him food and a toy and a nice long walk, and he's fine. So let me show you the house. Did you have a hard time finding it?"

"Oh, no. It was a snap."

Hayley noticed that Merle seemed a bit shy herself, so that relaxed and emboldened her. Her disquiet of a moment before had disappeared. She was deeply curious about Merle though. Hayley was certain she was a lesbian, but she didn't want to stereotype. However, she very much wanted Merle to be a lesbian. She wanted to meet women in her own age range, as friends certainly. If they were roommates then they could probably be friends.

She followed Merle toward the back of the house, past the dining room and into the kitchen, which was large enough for a table. At the back was the door to what looked like a nice-sized yard. They passed through a tiny laundry room off the kitchen that also housed the dog dishes and other odds and ends and down a short flight of stairs into the backyard.

Hayley stood at the top of the stairs while Merle walked on. She wanted to get a feel for the yard. It wasn't large, but it was well maintained between the collection of plants, including a lemon tree and a swath of grass that was well grown, no doubt from May's late-in-the-season rain showers. In the center of the yard stood an old-fashioned sundial and a single chair. Hayley slowly walked the steps as she took in the look of the backyard. She automatically scanned the ground and didn't see a single dog turd. That told Hayley volumes about Merle. She either maintained her living space very well or she walked her dog often or both. So far so good.

Merle turned around and the sun caught her hair, making it look silvery.

"We'll have to put another chair out here." Hayley couldn't quite divine her expression. She looked sad but hopeful. What she said and the way she said it struck Hayley as though Merle had made up her mind already that Hayley was moving in, which was wonderful, but Hayley was taken aback. They hadn't exchanged more than a few words, most of them about Arthur, and here Merle was ready to have her move in. That both terrified and thrilled her, and she knew it couldn't be true. Merle didn't strike her as the impetuous type but quite the opposite. She was likely just thinking aloud.

"It's beautiful. You've put a lot of work into it. I can see that."

"Thanks. Do you garden?"

"Oh, no. I've got a black thumb, but I can mow the grass."

Hayley watched Merle look around, vaguely, hands on her hips.

"Well, it's not required. The backyard's my thing."

They were silent a moment and then Merle said, "Let's go look at the rest of the house, and I'll show you the bedroom and bathroom."

Hayley followed Merle again, and before she could even think about it, the phrase "nice ass" popped into her head. This wouldn't do. She couldn't be thinking of her potential landlady as a sex object. She couldn't go down that road under any circumstances. The resulting drama would probably make *The L Word* look tame. She shook her head to clear it, glad Merle couldn't see the gesture. They moved through the downstairs area with Arthur trailing them. Some things seemed to be missing in the house, and Hayley wondered if that was true, and if so, who had taken them. She'd have fun shopping for new items. My God, she'd already been accepted, had moved in, and was on to the shopping phase. She needed to get a grip.

They climbed the stairs, and at the top was a small hallway with a bathroom and two bedrooms. Hayley presumed the promised bathroom was the one in the hall and Merle had the bedroom with bathroom attached. She didn't mind that.

"This would be your room." Merle gestured in front of a door. The room in question was empty, but it was newly painted, sunny, and a decent size. The view out the back of the house was of Twin Peaks and the Sutro Tower. Nice.

As Hayley stood at the doorway taking it in, behind her, Merle said, "My ex took a lot of stuff so you'd have to get your own furniture."

Hayley turned around, wanting to see Merle's face. She'd spoken in an even tone, and Hayley couldn't read her expression. "That's no problem. I assumed I'd bring in my own furniture."

"Well. Okay then. We can sit and talk for a bit."

"I'd like that." Hayley flashed her best smile and got the response she wanted. Merle grinned back. If the thought behind the word "ex" had been sad, the feeling had come and gone. Hayley wanted to know more, though, and if she moved in, she hoped she would. She was curious about people and their stories and their experiences. She was able to indulge that part of her personality directly in her work with her law firm's clients. In her personal life, she enjoyed eliciting information from people and listening to them talk.

They sat in the kitchen drinking iced tea and chatted easily about their jobs. Hayley mentioned her son Robbie but not her ex-husband. Merle said no more about exes, and Hayley didn't ask. There was likely a world of pain and regret behind Merle's studiedly neutral persona and her dispassionate use of the word "ex."

"Um. I have to confirm something with you. Do you drink?" Hayley again sensed a story behind that question, but she said, honestly, "Sometimes a glass of wine when I'm out to dinner or beer at a baseball game or picnic, but no, I'm not much of a drinker. I'm a lightweight."

She tried a rueful smile and Merle smiled back. "Okay. Well. I'm still interviewing people. I want to make a decision soon though. When could you move in?"

"Right away, as soon as possible. I have to vacate my home because we've sold it. It's in escrow, and I've got about a month until I have to move."

"Oh. Okay. I'll let you know soon."

"Just so you know, I've had a house for years and can do basic house repairs like change electrical switches, grout bathtubs, and stuff. And I'd be happy to do that if I was living here."

"Wow! Yeah. Sure." The offer seemed to surprise and intrigue Merle.

"Thanks for letting me see the house. I'd like living here, I think. It looks like we're similar ages and might be compatible. At least I think so." That was a little risqué, but Merle didn't seem fazed.

"I think you may be right," she said, nodding. She showed Hayley to the front door and waved casually, saying, "Bye. Thanks for coming," as though it had been a purely social occasion for two old friends to chat and drink iced tea.

Hayley made her way back to Cortland Avenue thinking how much she liked the house, the neighborhood, and Merle and dared to hope that her interview had been a success.

❖

The decision seemed too easy, and Merle berated herself mildly for even being ready just to stop the housemate hunt and give it to Hayley. She'd dismissed a goodly number of prospective candidates on monetary issues alone. As for the group who were financially sound, each of them seemed to have some fatal flaw, such as militant vegetarianism or overly strict political views or a belief that the earth's magnetic poles were going to swap places and kill everyone on earth who didn't live in Minnesota.

Merle certainly considered herself a liberal, but she wasn't fanatical about anything. She doubted she could stand a housemate constantly haranguing her about one thing or another. She'd heard more than enough haranguing about all sorts of subjects during her life as a lesbian. Some girls didn't know when to stop.

One of her prospective housemates had quizzed her on everything from where she grocery shopped to where she worked and frowned when Merle said UCSF. Then she made a remark about animal research as though Merle's employment there made her collusive in animal cruelty. Merle had crossed her off the "possible" list. One applicant had claimed to like dogs in her email but exhibited barely disguised disdain for Arthur when she found out Merle hadn't adopted him from a shelter or rescue group. Another woman had displayed incipient obsessive-compulsive disorder when she'd tried to secretly wipe a cloth on top of the mantel over Merle's fake fireplace. An otherwise lovely and financially secure redhead had spent over an hour talking about herself in extensive and intimate detail. Merle couldn't abide that much talking so she disqualified Redhead too. She'd exhausted Merle on the first day and it would only get worse. At least Kay knew when to shut up.

Oh, wait, that was one of the problems with Kay. Merle frowned. She didn't want to think about Kay, but she was sure it was inevitable. Also she didn't want to continually compare everyone she met to Kay. And these were only potential roommates, not potential wives. She needed to stop doing that.

Merle knew no one could be perfect, but Hayley sure appeared to come close. She was clearly right in all the obvious ways, though

Merle wasn't a hundred percent sure she was a lesbian. Merle had made her ad vague because she hadn't wanted to run afoul of fair-housing regulations. She figured the Bernal Heights location would speak for itself. She also had interviewed a fair number of lesbians who were wrong in one way or another. She assumed Hayley knew *she* was a lesbian: chinos, short hair, Bernal Heights?

Hayley was a perfect cipher when it came to any lesbian tells: no piercings, no tattoos, no labyris necklaces or obvious T-shirt, and no wallet in her back pocket. She could be a femme. But that was all useless speculation and should be irrelevant anyhow.

Her personality and demeanor were so pleasant and even-keeled, even if she was straight, it wouldn't be problematical. Like her, Hayley had contrived to not reveal very much. Merle understood that impulse well. The danger was, of course, that Hayley would move in and then some heinous secret vice would surface. But she didn't think that would happen, and significantly, Hayley was simpatico with Arthur. She was also really nice looking, with her shoulder-length blond hair and big brown eyes. She had a serene and ingratiating personality. She could have just been on her good behavior, but Merle had enough people skills to tell when someone was faking.

She didn't think she'd need to apologize to anyone for finding Hayley attractive. It wasn't the only or even the most important reason to have her move in, but if she was going to live with someone, it helped if she was easy on the eye. Kay, of course, had been nice looking, and her personality was lovely too. It hadn't been until much later that Merle had discovered Kay's flaws, and then she'd tried to ignore them. Who's perfect? No one. Whoa, it was time to stop thinking about Kay, or for that matter it was time to stop thinking about how pretty Hayley was.

They were entering into a business arrangement, and that was all. Merle told herself if Hayley and she became friends that would be a nice bonus, but it wasn't required. And also here she was thinking as though Hayley was going to move in and she didn't have any reason to continue the search.

Merle sighed. It was difficult to make a decision with incomplete information. She only knew she didn't get any weird vibe and Hayley hadn't revealed any overt negative characteristic. Merle was sorry she'd made the remark about the chair in the garden as though Hayley moving in was already a done deal. She didn't want Hayley to get the wrong idea. She had no idea where that came from. She was generally cautious about revealing her thoughts to people she didn't know well.

So she did the only thing she could think of and asked Arthur.

"What do you think, bro? Is this the one? She was perfectly nice to you." Arthur wagged his tail, obviously trying to divine what Merle was saying. He knew she was talking to him and that it was positive. That was the extent of his understanding. Merle was impressed by Hayley's approach to her dog, her open smile, *and* her offer of household-repair help. That last thing alone might be enough to make her the top candidate. Merle hadn't inherited the lesbian power-tool gene, and when something broke, she had to call for outside help and pay for it.

"I don't think we're going to do much better than her, guy."

Merle went up to her room and sat down at her desk and emailed Hayley, then the rest of the possible applicants. She indicated Hayley could move in when she was able to and she would pro-rate the rent accordingly and asked her for a security deposit. She'd downloaded a rental agreement for them to sign. And that was that.

Chapter Four

"So, you think she's a lesbian?" Sigrid asked at breakfast the following Saturday.

"I don't know. It doesn't matter."

"Yes, it matters. What if she's not and starts bringing home random guys?"

"I don't get the impression she'd be like that. She's a professional, a paralegal. And she has a twenty-six-year-old son, so she's not young. And if she's straight, she just doesn't strike me as the slutty type. Why are you being negative?" Merle was surprised how defensive *she* felt on Hayley's behalf. Clea and Sigrid were just being protective friends, and she ought to appreciate that. They looked at her quizzically.

"I'm sorry. I'm touchy because I'm so unsure about this and it's new and it's happened so quickly. I know you're just looking out for me."

"You've got good judgment, Merle. We're not worried." Clea was the soother, the diplomatic one. Sigrid, on the other hand, asked questions like a district attorney, but it was because she cared. Merle wasn't sure exactly how good her judgment really was anyhow, considering she'd chosen Kay. But this was a different situation, thank goodness.

"I'm not really worried about Hayley. It just feels right. I'm more worried about *me*. I wasn't apparently that great a lover so I'm not sure how I'll be as a roommate."

"Will you stop? It wasn't all about you. It was a lot about Kay."

"Keep reminding me of that. Some days I'm totally fine with

saying it was all or almost all her fault, and on others I think I just royally screwed up."

"Well." Sigrid looked thoughtful. "We know that we have to always clean up our own side of the street, so it's good for you to examine your part, like the program says. Still, you can't beat yourself up over it. You can't think you're a failure, because you're not." She looked so sincere, Merle had to smile.

"You're right, you're always right." She knew Sigrid would know she was teasing.

Clea said, "Hmph. Yeah. She's always right unless I'm right."

"And you're always right too, darling," Sigrid said smoothly and turned back to Hayley. "Anyway, we were talking about you and a roommate and not you and a new lover."

"Right. I'm not getting entangled with anyone anytime soon. Let's just see how it goes with a roommate. I'm actually pretty optimistic about it during the times when I'm not totally terrified." Merle grinned at her two friends.

This was true. Once she'd made the decision, she was relieved and looked forward to having Hayley move in. The signs continued to be positive. Hayley had mailed a check in a couple days and advised her she would move in three weeks. It was all easy. So far. The true test would come when they were actually sharing the house.

❖

When she received the email from Merle, Hayley read it twice, then saved it. She sat staring into space for a few moments, letting the news sink into and penetrate her consciousness. She hadn't been wrong about their connection. She hugged herself and gave herself a nice virtual pat on the back for succeeding at this step. First step, divorce, second step, new home. Good-bye pastel Sunset and pastel straight life, and hello vibrant multicolored Bernal Heights and the rainbow gay life. That thought made Hayley giggle. She was such a nut sometimes, but that wasn't the worst way to get through life. Her mind started racing with a mental to-do list, but she slowed it down on purpose and hit her son Robbie's number on speed dial. He picked up after a couple rings.

"Ma. What up?"

"Hi, sweetie. I wanted you to be the first to know. I've found a new place to live."

"No shit? Where?"

"Bernal Heights."

"All right. You're gonna live in a hip neighborhood. That's great. Matt Nathanson lives there. You knew that, right?"

"Nope, Rob. That's why I have you to keep me abreast of important things. Who's Matt Nathanson?"

"Ma!" She knew he was rolling his eyes. "Famous local singer songwriter?"

"Play me a tune of his sometime."

"Sure. I bet you want me to help you move, right?"

"How'd you know that?" She liked to tease him.

"I'm psychic. Tell me when and I'll make time. I'll bring someone with me. I think Roger would be okay with helping."

"That's lovely. I'll get beer and pizza for you guys."

"How can I resist that offer?" He laughed.

"I believe that's what you live on, right?"

"Nah. Sometimes I make Kraft mac and cheese if I'm feeling ambitious." They both laughed.

After she hung up on Robbie, Hayley sat down with her legal pad and started to make her list. Her mind drifted, however, back to the day when she got her courage up and informed her son she was really a lesbian. He was the first person she told.

She was still trying to think of how to break the news to her mother. Her dad had passed away several years before, and she thought it unnecessary to tell her ex-husband since she wasn't planning on him being a part of her life. Her son, on the other hand, had always been and always would be very important to her, and he deserved to know the truth. As she'd hoped, he'd been surprised at first but then took the news much the same way he'd responded when hearing about his parents' divorce: in stride. Her mother was a different story, and Hayley planned to wait as long as possible. Her mom was just not the easygoing kind.

When she was growing up, Hayley had heard her folks make comments about gay people when a news story aired on TV. No one really, and especially no one in the Bay Area, could ignore the existence of LGBTQ folks. In the suburb of Concord, however, not many people

• 45 •

had gotten the memo that gay was okay. That number included her mom, Ellie. That part of Hayley's coming-out process would have to wait. She had more important things to think about, like going on dates.

Between bouts of packing, Hayley took time to try one of the meet-ups. She'd chosen one online, and on Friday, she was off to an art-show opening with a bunch of strange women. She tried not to think of it that way but rather to think of them as potential friends. She was usually easy about meeting people, but the lesbian angle threw her for a loop. She felt like an awkward teenager going to her first dance.

She decided to drive since it was held in the Civic Center area in Hayes Valley. She'd looked up both Hayes Valley and the gallery online. She was mildly interested in art, especially contemporary women painters who specialized in naturalism. This was an abstract artist, but she was going mainly for the social aspect. The meet-up description specified cultural events. What did she have to lose?

At the entrance to the Singer Gallery on Hayes Street stood two women with name tags reading Hazel and Andy. They were the organizers. After she walked up to them and announced her name, they beamed and shook hands. Hazel produced a name label, wrote Hayley's name and, before Hayley could say anything, peeled the back off and smoothed it over Hayley's left breast. She would have preferred to do that herself, but hey, maybe lesbians had different sorts of boundaries that she'd have to get used to. Hazel and Andy told her they were a couple, which she'd already figured out.

"But," Andy said, sotto voce, "lots of single women come to these meet-ups."

Hayley gave a noncommittal smile. She didn't want them to get the idea she was overeager even if she was. She just wanted to talk to a single lesbian with whom she might go out on a date.

The three of them stood at the door chatting, and then, out of the dark, another woman appeared, alone. Hayley took that as a good sign.

"Hi, is this the meet-up?" She addressed the question to the three of them collectively.

Hayley kept quiet and let Hazel and Andy take charge. They got the new person duly name-tagged and introduced her to Hayley.

She stood about a head shorter than Hayley, wore a beret, and when she got close she reeked of cigarette smoke. Her name tag read

"Willow." Under her beret she had steel-gray hair that appeared rather badly cut.

"Hi, I'm Hayley," she said by force of habit, even though her name tag said so.

"Yeah, I see that." Willow focused on Hayley's name tag or maybe her breast. Were lesbians like men and prone to ogling women's breasts? Hayley hoped not. It was probably just a coincidence. Willow's scratchy voice went with the odor of cigarettes that hung about her. Hayley hated cigarettes and cigarette smoke.

"You been to one a these before?" Willow growled rather than spoke.

"No. It's my first time. How about you?"

"Oh ho, a virgin." Willow cackled. "Nah. Been to a bunch a them. Tough to meet women in this town. I'm from Chicago. Got transferred last year. I been single awhile. It's not easy after getting this skin condition. I got it covered up with the hat but still..." Willow smirked and raised her eyebrows.

Hayley tried to think of something to say or, better yet, a reason to stop this conversation.

She was saved by another introduction, this time to another couple.

A mini-rush of people joining them distracted her, and then Hazel and Andy announced they would go inside to the reception. Ambling around in their little group made Hayley feel like she was on a school field trip. Once inside the gallery, she grabbed a glass of white wine and a little plate of hors d'oeuvres and broke away on her own to start looking at the paintings. She took a sip of the wine, which tasted like sweetened vinegar, but she should have expected that. The little noshes were better but a bit soggy. She stood before a painting that seemed to have been created by dumping several colors on the canvas and then stirring them together. It looked like vomit. She was cautiously biting into another hors d'oeuvre when she heard a raspy voice at her elbow. She didn't have to look to know who it belonged to.

"I don't get this art crap, really. I thought what the hell, I might as well show up. Free drinks. *Maybe* some interesting people." Hayley turned to make polite eye contact, and Willow grinned. Hayley guessed that *she* counted as "interesting." She shouldn't be surprised that women would view this occasion as a pick-up opportunity. That was what she was looking for, after all. Well, not a pick-up, not exactly anyhow. She and Willow appeared to be the only single women in attendance. That was depressing. She didn't want to spend the evening being breathed on by a smoker with a rash.

"Say, what about you?" Willow asked.

She was being addressed so she had to answer. "Oh, um. Just wanted to sort of get out and about?"

"You new in town?" Willow talked like Humphrey Bogart.

"Oh no. Not exactly. I've lived here a long time." Hayley didn't think it was the time to get into her entire psychosexual history.

"Huh." Willow appeared confused but still wanting to keep the conversation going.

"Oh, excuse me." Hayley had to escape. She nearly trotted over to Andy and Hazel.

"I'm getting a bit of a headache so I think I'll take off. Nice to meet you."

"Sure," Hazel said. "Take care. Come out again some time."

"Thanks. Maybe I will. See you."

Hayley waved at Willow from across the gallery and received a puzzled glare in return. She retrieved her car and drove home in a funk. This hadn't been very worthwhile, though she didn't know what she'd expected. As she got ready for bed, she counseled herself not to get discouraged, that she'd just started and shouldn't expect things to happen quickly.

She picked up the book she'd been reading. On Britt's suggestion, she'd ordered a couple of lesbian romances online. The one she was currently reading concerned an uptight but hot prosecutor and a charmingly disheveled defense attorney squaring away on opposite sides of a criminal case. It was cute. Hayley made herself read through it page by page and not skip ahead to the sex parts. When she was reading, she enjoyed the buildup of sexual tension and then the resolution of it. She liked to fantasize how that would happen one day for her. The books made it extremely plain what women did. Oddly, the prose descriptions of sex aroused her more than the sex scenes in *The L Word* had.

Hayley was both grateful for the lessons and deeply excited by the books. She wanted to do everything she'd read about. Or have it done to her. She shivered and got butterflies thinking about it. She had vivid masturbation fantasies, but she was making no progress toward living her own lesbian romance. She supposed it was too soon to give up on meet-ups, but she wanted to figure out other ways to meet lesbians that didn't have to do with going to clubs.

She told Britt about her evening the next day at work, and Britt grimaced.

"Yeah, you got to watch out for trolls."

"Trolls?"

"Yep. Ugly people." Britt seemed to think this was a perfectly okay thing to say, and Hayley had to bite her tongue. The next thing Britt said was even worse.

"You know, you're pretty good-looking for someone your age." Britt was oblivious to the backhandedness of that compliment.

"Well, thanks. I guess."

"No, really. You ought to be able to meet someone."

"Yes. I ought to but I'm clueless."

"Don't you know anyone your age?"

"Nope, I don't—wait a minute." Hayley stopped herself. She did know someone: Merle.

But she didn't know if Merle was a lesbian; she only assumed she was. She had to confirm it, and then she could ask her how to meet women—of the right age. She surely would have some ideas. One thing at a time, Hayley counseled herself. Step by step.

❖

"She's got good taste in home furnishings, I'll say that much for her," Clea said. They were there to pick Merle up for a rare evening AA meeting. Sigrid had been invited to tell her AA story at a big Friday-night meeting, and Clea and Merle were going along to be supportive. Also they were going out to dinner first.

"We agreed on what to buy and she bought it. I don't see anything wrong with that deal. If she moves out, though, I'll have to think of something else."

"How's it going, anyhow, other than you have nice new furniture?" Sigrid asked.

"Fine."

"So she's a dyke?" Clea asked.

"Honestly, I don't know, and truly I don't care. She's really nice. She's quiet and neat so far."

"Huh," Clea said. At that moment, Hayley came down the stairs wearing tan slacks and a red cotton blouse. She walked into the living room with her hand out first to Sigrid, then to Clea. Merle watched their reaction. Their eyes lit up and Merle could see why. Hayley looked wonderful. Her clothes fit her well, and she was clearly used to being sociable and meeting people. Merle envied her that ability. Merle could make a newcomer in AA feel welcome and comfortable, but her social skills were learned, not natural, and she still felt shy in a lot of situations.

"Hi! I'm Hayley," she said.

"These are my friends Sigrid and Clea. They've come to take me to a meeting. Dinner first, though."

Hayley tilted her head. "Meeting?"

"AA," Merle said.

"Oh, right. Sure. Well, have fun. Nice to meet you. Sorry, but I have to get going." She smiled one more time and walked back toward the kitchen.

Sigrid caught Merle's eye and raised her eyebrows.

"Let's go." She turned toward the kitchen and yelled, "Bye, Hayley." A faint response came back.

In their car, Merle said into the silence, "So?"

"Not a lesbian," Clea said.

"How the hell can you be so sure?" For some reason, this apparent snap judgment incensed Merle.

"I just know."

"Good thing too, Mer. 'Cause if she was, I'd say you better jump on that."

"Sigi!" Clea sounded shocked.

Merle was irritated. "Come on, Sigrid. I told you. I'm not jumping on anything for a long time. Can we change the subject?"

Later, when they were settled in their chairs and the meeting proceeded through its preliminaries, Merle's mind wandered. The suggestion that she ought to have sex with Hayley really discomfited her. That was a preposterous idea on every level. But Sigrid had put it out there, and Merle was likely going to think about it every time she saw Hayley, which would be just about every day.

That was bad. She wasn't lying to her friends when she said she wasn't interested in starting up anything with anyone. Most definitely she was *not* going to start anything with her new housemate, who wasn't even a lesbian for certain. Merle was actually glad she didn't know for sure so she could put Hayley in a specific category labeled Untouchable.

Sigrid was teasing, as she sometimes did, just to get a rise out of Clea or Merle or both. It was harmless fun, and Merle was being oversensitive. Merle's biggest worry about Hayley was making sure they could function as roommates. That was enough to focus on at the moment.

❖

Merle was sitting on the living room couch reading when Hayley came home from work.

"Hi!" Hayley said brightly. "How are you doing?" Before she could answer, Hayley had gone upstairs. She shook her head and went back to her book.

A few minutes later, Hayley flopped next to her on the couch. "Hey, what would you think if we got a TV? I mean, I'd buy it but we could both watch. Maybe we could split the cable? TV's useless without cable. I can see if I can sweet-talk the cable people into giving me a deal and..." She stopped talking suddenly and looked at Merle.

"Oh, sorry, were you reading? Is this a bad time? I'm really sorry. I just get so excited by whatever's in my head, and I start talking and don't pay attention..." She appeared to realize she was still talking and hadn't let Merle say a word. She tilted her head.

Merle liked that gesture though the tumble of words annoyed her. She placed a marker in the book, put it down on the table, and turned to look at Merle. "I'm not much of a TV watcher," she said.

Hayley looked comically deflated. "Oh."

"But if you want a TV, feel free to put one in your bedroom."

"Oh. Okay. Right. Sorry to bother you." Hayley left the room.

Merle felt like a heel. Hayley's question was innocent, normal. She could have been more open-minded. They had to share the common areas of the house. When she thought about it, watching TV alone in one's bedroom didn't sound like all that much fun, even if Hayley liked it. She was also clearly reaching out to Merle, and Merle had rebuffed her.

Hayley was friendly, generous, and open, and Merle was acting like she had a communicable disease. She'd obviously gotten out of practice living with a roommate. Or maybe she was just too old to make a new friend. That was ridiculous. She made new friends in AA all the time, but that was different. She was there to help people. Why did she need that milieu to spur her to get to know someone new?

❖

Hayley was in the law-library conference room, supposedly doing research for a new case. She had several heavy legal books spread out on the table, but in reality, she was thinking about how to get her new housemate to be more friendly. She'd been living with Merle a couple of weeks, yet she knew no more about her than what she'd gleaned the day they first met. Her TV idea had been soundly rejected, and she hadn't made any other attempts at conversation beyond "hello" or "good-bye." Merle gave off a clear "don't bother me" aura, which made Hayley more curious about her than ever.

"Hayley?" Lois, the office manager, was standing somewhere behind her shoulder.

Hayley turned toward her, trying not to look like she'd been daydreaming instead of researching. "Yep?"

"Adam is still at court but Tom Banner is here. They're supposed to meet at three o'clock. Adam texted that he'll be twenty minutes late. Can you talk to them?"

This was a new client. The case concerned alleged age discrimination. The attorney wanted a complete summary of all the case law Hayley could find since he hadn't tried this type of case before. It involved a big, deep-pocketed corporation and one of its longtime employees, an engineer being "laid off," so they claimed.

"Shit. I forgot. Right. Okay. I'm going to the restroom. Bring them in here, and get some coffee and water. Yada, yada." Hayley went to the bathroom and put on just a touch of lipstick.

She wished the attorney were there. The first meeting with clients was sometimes difficult because they were nervous about suing their employers. She wasn't the authority figure they needed to reassure them like Adam was.

"Hello, Tom Banner? I'm Hayley Daniels, the paralegal. Adam will be here soon." She turned to the woman who stood next to him. "Hello—?" Hayley assumed she was Tom's wife.

"I'm Angie. Tom's sister." She shook hands firmly. Hayley motioned for the two of them to have a seat at the conference table, and Lois brought in the tray of coffee and tea. Sister, eh? That was good news.

"Please help yourselves. I can tell you a little bit about how this process works. We'll be taking your deposition and depositions of some of the key members of your company, including human resources and your manager. We'll subpoena all your records. I presume you have good performance evaluations?"

"He's the best," Angie said, enthusiastically. With her short brown hair and tailored clothes, she was quite possibly a lesbian. She had the look Hayley couldn't quite describe but knew when she saw it. She was trim and seemed somewhere over the age of forty, though it was impossible to tell. Hayley saw no ring on her finger. That, she realized, was no proof of anything either way. Many lesbians now wore wedding rings.

"Angie, stop." Tom patted her shoulder. He looked embarrassed and pleased at the same time.

"It's fine," Hayley told them. "We want to present Tom in the best light. Your good opinion counts, even if you can't testify on his behalf." Hayley beamed at Angie almost without thinking and got a winning smile back.

"I'm here for moral support. Whatever he needs me to do."

"That's great. We all need support in this sort of situation. It won't be easy."

"Just so long as Tom gets what he deserves." Hayley hoped Angie's faith in her brother was deserved.

Then the door opened and Adam strode in. In spite of being late for their appointment, he was unruffled. His dark suit, crisp white shirt, and good haircut all broadcast trustworthy lawyer. Which he was. Hayley worked for all three partners, who all had quirks, but Adam was genuinely concerned more about his clients than about winning a huge settlement.

He shook hands and sat down and immediately engaged Tom, leaving Hayley and Angie to smile vaguely at one another. Every so often, when Adam said something, Hayley took notes on her iPad for discussion later.

"How long have you been working as a paralegal?" Angie asked.

"Twenty-five years."

"Wowie. You must be good at it."

"I don't know. You'd have to ask the partners, but they keep me around so I suppose I do my job properly." Angie's blue eyes were sparkling and merry, and Hayley liked her instantly. A little bell went off in her head. They *could* date, but they really couldn't right at that moment. Though Angie wasn't a party in the case, Hayley's firm was conservative when it came to those issues. It wouldn't be professional so she'd have to wait until the case was over, which could take a very long time. No harm in getting to know her in the meantime. The case wouldn't last forever.

Meanwhile, though, she had to keep up with the discussion. Adam would likely invite them to dinner at least once or twice while the case was undergoing preparation. That would be like being out on a date with two, count 'em, two chaperones. Hayley's mood lifted. It could be worse. Tom could have had an interfering wife that Hayley would be expected to help handle. She'd seen that before. No. He came instead with a supportive, loving sister.

Hayley could afford to be patient. She was waiting for the right person. It made more sense to her to meet someone this way than online. She guessed she was just old-fashioned that way. She caught Angie's eye from across the table as Tom listened raptly to Adam. Angie favored her with another huge smile, and Hayley tingled from her head to her feet.

❖

"I've made way too much food. Would you like some?" Hayley grinned in what she hoped was an artless fashion. She'd cobbled together an idea of what Merle liked to eat based on the food in the refrigerator and purposefully made enough to feed at least four people.

Offering food seemed like a sure-fire way to have a talk. They'd sit together and eat dinner.

Merle raised her eyebrows. "Nice of you to offer. Are you sure?"

Hayley waved her hand. "Of course. I'm used to cooking for a family. I can't seem to orient my mind toward feeding just one person, myself."

"You can have leftovers."

"Oh, but it's better fresh." That wasn't strictly true. Hayley had made a vegetarian ziti, and in her experience it was just fine the next day or the day after, but she had an ulterior motive.

"Okay. If you're sure."

Hayley beamed and retrieved some plates and forks and threw together a simple romaine salad. Merle sat down at the kitchen table looking mildly embarrassed, for some reason. Hayley hoped she'd relax when they started eating.

Arthur sat in the doorway, just outside the kitchen, looking at them longingly.

Hayley cocked her head toward him. "He's not allowed in the kitchen?"

"No. Not unless I invite him and then only for his meals."

"He's so good." Hayley meant that. It was marvelous that such a big dog kept out from underfoot. His expression was priceless though. Hayley could see where the term "hangdog" came from. He looked at her hopefully and edged his big paw over the threshold. She started to giggle and Merle noticed and grunted at him. He withdrew it immediately, then looked toward Hayley and wagged his tail as though appealing to her to overrule his mistress. Much like a kid would try to game his parents to get what he wanted.

Hayley served the casserole and salad and seated herself across from Merle.

"This smells great," Merle said, with a tone of genuine appreciation.

"Thanks. You know, I hate cooking for one and eating alone. We could share food, if you want?" Hayley didn't want to be forward, but it seemed silly to not at least ask the question.

Merle looked at her as though such a thing had never occurred to her. "Sure. I mean. Yeah. I don't think our diets are too far apart. I usually go veggie, but I like a little chicken or fish sometimes."

"That sounds perfect to me." Hayley took a bite of her ziti and grinned at Merle while she chewed. She got a nice smile in return. As she hoped, Merle started to relax. It was perhaps a good time to ask her something she'd wondered about.

"So how long have you lived here? I love this house, by the way, and feel very lucky you've accepted me as a housemate."

Merle's eyebrows went up and she looked pleased, but then her face clouded a bit.

"We bought it in 2004. June, as I recall."

"So you've lived here awhile. Who's 'we'? If you don't mind my asking."

"My, uh, ex-lover."

"Oh. Right. You said you had an ex when I first came over to see the house. I'm sorry. I didn't mean to be nosy." Hayley hoped she sounded sincere, because nosy was precisely what she was being.

"It's fine." Merle paused and took another mouthful. She looked as though she was considering what to say next. Or how much to say.

Hayley decided to forge ahead and see if she could keep the conversation going.

"We're kinda in the same boat, I see. I got divorced about six months ago. My ex-husband and I agreed to sell our house. I wanted to start over anyhow. That's why I was looking for a place to live in, and I wanted to live somewhere like Bernal."

"Oh? Of all the neighborhoods in SF, why this one? Not that I blame you. I obviously like it because I've lived here for a long time, but what about you?"

Here was the chance she'd waited for, but she felt shy and suddenly reluctant to tell the truth. However, she was going to get what she wanted only one way, so she better buck up. She served herself some more salad and put salt and pepper and salad dressing on it, and Merle waited, apparently unperturbed.

"I wanted to live here because I heard a lot of lesbians live in Bernal Heights. Also, it's very pretty and quaint." Hayley locked gazes with Merle then. She couldn't quite interpret what she saw. Several emotions seemed to flow across Merle's regular features—surprise, interest, caution, and something that looked like pain.

"Well. All of those things are true. That was what sold my ex, Kay, and me on buying. Also the hill. I wanted to have a dog and a place to walk our dog. It was Sadie back then." She fell silent.

Hayley didn't say anything right away. She watched Merle, attempting to divine what was going on behind those solemn blue-gray eyes. She couldn't tell. Merle's face reverted to its usual pleasant, noncommittal expression. Hayley wasn't certain she wanted to push for more information. She'd let *her* secret slip in hopes it would prompt Merle to be forthcoming, but it still felt weird to say something like that. She supposed she was still getting used to her new role. She'd received a bit of information from Merle but wasn't sure what to do with it.

It looked like Merle really didn't want to talk about her past, and Hayley didn't blame her. They were still strangers, and Hayley could appreciate that Merle didn't want do that instant-bonding thing women did so often. But she was already interested, and her curiosity slipped into overdrive after Merle's revelation. "So how long were you together?"

Merle was quiet for a moment. Then she looked into the middle distance. "Ten years."

Hayley saw the real sadness then and heard it in the little catch in Merle's voice when she spoke. This woman had been hurt, and hurt badly. Hayley wanted to comfort her, make her smile and laugh and feed her some more ziti. Whatever, just to make her feel better, make her happy. Whoa, where had *that* come from?

"That sucks." Hayley meant it, and she said it with such emphasis that it seemed to have jolted Merle out of her despondency.

"It sure as hell does."

Hayley sensed the anger behind that sadness, or maybe it was the other way around. No matter. Merle was looking at her with a rueful but slightly cocky grin, and Hayley was encouraged to keep talking.

"You know. I didn't feel a damn thing when I told Howard I wanted a divorce. He didn't bat an eye either. He knew it was quitting time too. Our son was out of college. We didn't have the slightest reason to stay together. I've done my time as a heterosexual. Done my duty."

"So..." Merle said slowly, "you *are* a lesbian?" She sounded as though she doubted it.

"Yes, ma'am. You couldn't tell?" Hayley was disappointed.

"No. Not really. I mean, of course. Well. What does a lesbian look like? You know. There's no one answer to that. The stereotypes are wrong."

"Oh, I guess I didn't especially make a point of it. I didn't even know if you were."

"Me? Shit. I'd say it's pretty obvious." Merle didn't appear to be aware she'd just contradicted herself.

"Well, you're not exactly wearing a sign. What did you just say about stereotypes?" Hayley gave Merle a mischievous grin and was gratified to see her reflect it. Her earlier sadness was gone, and her eyes sparkled.

"Righto. Well. See, my friends, Sigrid and Clea, from the other night?" She stopped.

"Yep. I remember them."

"Yeah. They don't think you're queer. Sigrid didn't sense any vibes from you."

"What does that mean?" Hayley was truly frustrated now. How in the world would she ever get any women if she didn't give off the right "vibes"? She not only couldn't meet lesbians, if she did meet them she clearly couldn't get them interested in her. Swell.

"Honestly. I didn't either when you first came over to see the house."

"So why did you agree to me moving in?"

Merle rolled her eyes. "You have no idea how tough it was to find someone I thought I could live with. You seemed to be a stable, sane woman. At that point, it didn't matter to me if you were a dyke or not."

Hayley flinched at the word "dyke."

Merle picked up on her distaste. "I don't mean that in a derogatory way. It's just a term we use among ourselves."

"Oh. I see. Well. Still glad you decided to have me move in even if you weren't sure I was a lesbian?" She was an "us." That was encouraging, but Merle hadn't answered her original question yet. "Anyhow. Why didn't you think I was a lesbian when you met me?"

She sounded a bit demanding, but somehow she didn't think Merle would mind.

"Your nails aren't short *and* you're wearing nail polish."

Hayley glanced down at her hands. She filed her nails to a decent length. She didn't have long nails by any means. "My nails? What?"

"Most lesbians keep their nails really short. Some women wear polish, but the nails…"

"Huh?" Hayley knew she was missing something.

"Because of...you know."

Merle was actually blushing, which was cute. Then it dawned on Hayley what she was talking about it, and *she* started to blush too. She ought to have known that. She felt silly.

"Uh. Yeah. Okay. What else?" Hayley wanted to move the conversation forward because she was getting some disquieting but stimulating images having to do with her hands and Merle.

"You need to make eye contact and hold it for a while. I mean like zero in and also smile a little at the same time."

"You mean I should flirt?"

"Yes. That's what I mean. And touch."

"I see. Trim the nails more and make eye contact. This is all helpful, but my real problem is meeting women in the first place." She told Merle the story of the meet-up and the art gallery and all the couples except for Willow, pleased when she elicited a hearty laugh from Merle.

Merle shook her head and wiped tears from her eyes. "Yeah. That sounds normal. Too many couples and one ineligible."

"So what do I do?"

"Shoot. I don't know."

"Don't you have any single friends you could introduce me to?"

"Eh. Not really. If you were an alcoholic, I could take you to meetings that are like bars without the alcohol."

"No? Really?"

"Yes. It's subtle but it's there. Wait a minute, I know. You can go out dog walking with me on the weekend. Or you can go by yourself. Around here, a woman with a dog? You'd be a chick magnet. You're pretty and blond. Oh, and you ought to dress a little more scruffy and yep, I think you might meet some women. Some people might recognize Arthur, but there are a few yellow Labs around so it shouldn't matter. It'll still work. The dog walkers are all a friendly lot no matter what sexual orientation you are. And a ton of dykes around here have dogs."

"That sounds like it could be fun. Thanks for the suggestion." Merle thought she was pretty. *That* made her feel good.

"Hey, Arthur gets his walk. You'd be doing me a favor."

"I'm happy to help out with him. He's such a sweetheart. Since we're done with dinner, can he come in the kitchen now?"

Merle grinned at her, then looked at Arthur and nodded. He

bounded in like he'd just been given a longed-for gift. Hayley supposed that was true. He sat down in front of them and looked from one to the other, panting, thumping his tail on the tile.

"You have her to thank, old boy. Don't look at me."

Arthur duly followed Merle's glance around to Hayley. He looked liked a love-struck teenager finally allowed to worship his love object from up close instead of from afar. His expression made Hayley laugh, and Merle laughed along with her.

Chapter Five

While she got ready for bed, Merle thought about the talk with Hayley. She'd hesitated a microsecond before saying yes to the dinner invitation. In fact, as soon as she'd agreed, she'd wanted to take it back. But then they sat down to eat and Hayley asked her questions and she answered the questions and before too long they were chatting like old friends. The connection felt good.

So the burning question of her sexual orientation was answered: she *was* a lesbian. But it couldn't have been for very long. It seemed like she was just recently divorced. The picture she was slowly forming of Hayley was still incomplete, but the blank spots were filling in. Not only was her new housemate just coming out, but she was on the make for women. Merle was going to send her out on a busy dog-walking weekend with Arthur in tow, and she would certainly be beset by suitors. Well, Hayley was an adult; she could handle it and would likely have a very good time.

No doubt, Miley would be first in line to ask the new girl out. She'd also heard Twyla and Lara had recently split. The list of possible women for Hayley to date was virtually endless. It didn't hurt that the median age of the lesbian population on Bernal skewed a little older. Hayley probably wasn't in the market for someone young. Or maybe she was. It was silly to even speculate about the subject. Merle tugged her quilt irritably and turned her pillow over. From his dog bed on the floor, Arthur looked up with a soft interrogatory bark and thumped his tail a couple times.

Maybe she ought not to send Hayley out on her own for her first time on a walk with Arthur. She could probably use some coaching on how to handle Arthur. Even though he was a good walker, he was still an eighty-pound dog. Also, Hayley could probably use a wingman. Merle decided she would go with her. It seemed like a reasonable idea. As she fell asleep, the notion that her motives might be mixed occurred to her, but she dismissed it.

❖

On Saturday afternoon, they prepared for their dog walk. Following Merle's advice, Hayley chose an old T-shirt that was just a bit too small because it had shrunk in the dryer. She also found an old sweatshirt and put on her oldest, most ragged jeans and added a San Francisco Giants baseball cap.

If she didn't look like a lesbian now, she didn't know what else to do. She drew the line at getting a tattoo and cutting off her hair.

She liked that she looked younger than her age, which couldn't hurt. The jeans fit snugly, which also could only be a plus. She adjusted her cap and squeezed the visor to the correct shape, then smirked at her mirror image.

When she went downstairs to meet Merle and Arthur, she struck a pose and asked, "So? What do you think, boss?"

Merle was putting Arthur's harness and leash on with her back to Hayley. She was crouched on the floor, and her T-shirt had pulled out of her chinos. Hayley could see the outline of her spine. This moved her in some way she didn't quite comprehend. Merle's arms and shoulders were flexed, and Hayley thought that other than the gray hair and the slight crow's feet, she could pass for mid-thirties maybe. Was being a lesbian the key to not aging?

Merle stood up and turned around and took in Hayley, scrutinizing her impassively for a moment and then breaking into a wide grin. "You look terrific. The ball cap is a very good idea. It's windy on the hill."

"Is that the *only* reason I should wear a cap?" Hayley asked.

"Well, no. It's a nice touch. Ditto the sneakers. You're a dream date for practically any lesbian. With Arthur in tow, you'll be a big hit."

Hayley beamed in response. She was ready to conquer the lesbian world. "I'm going to have hat hair!" she quipped.

"That's even better!" Merle started laughing and Hayley laughed with her. She wasn't sure really what they were laughing about, but it felt good.

They walked out into Bonview Street.

"Could we maybe walk around a little before we go up the hill?"

"Oh, sure," Merle said agreeably. "We have lots of little streets around the hill that are pretty and hidden. We don't have to go up the direct way."

Outside on a dog walk, Merle seemed far more relaxed than she had so far. Their dinner together had broken the ice as Hayley had hoped, and Merle was now engaged in helping her meet women.

They reached the corner of Bonview and Coso, walked down Elsie Street, and doubled back to Bonview Street's dead end.

"Holy crap. What's this?"

They stood facing a carport with a giant statue of the Buddha underneath.

Merle stood there, hands on hips, shaking her head, apparently enjoying Hayley's reaction.

"I've no idea, but I've always liked it." The Buddha, at least eight feet tall, was made of some sort of grayish-blue material. The sunlight filtering through the carport's roof onto Buddha enhanced his standard air of serenity.

"I can see why. It's so eccentric. So Bernal."

Merle laughed, then said, "Come on. Here's a path I really love." She jumped up onto a tiny dirt path at the end of the Buddha driveway so fast Hayley had to trot to keep up. The path skirted a fence, then meandered past more backyards. Between the houses, Hayley could glimpse the Sutro Tower and Twin Peaks in the distance. She mentally oriented herself for future reference.

They passed a huge cypress tree with a rope swing attached.

"Look at this," Merle said.

Hayley didn't even think about it. She grabbed the rope and jumped on it, and her momentum caused her to arc over the hill and then back. Merle caught her in mid-swing. She hadn't noticed that Merle was standing so close. Her hands held Hayley's legs, and she was hyperaware of the touch. She looked at Merle's hands on her thighs and then into her face.

After a moment of silence, Merle blinked and cleared her throat. "The neighbor may not like us messing with his rope swing."

"Oh, right." Hayley dropped to the dirt. Merle's hands fell to her sides and she looked a little embarrassed. It was charming.

"Sorry."

"No worries."

Merle stepped back on the path and Hayley followed her, trying to analyze how she felt. She found herself staring at Merle's back and watching her legs move and her arms swing. Arthur trotted ahead of her, stopping every so often to mark. Hayley visualized them in the wilderness somewhere. In the mountains perhaps, hiking through an evergreen forest. Merle would be wearing a backpack, Hayley would be walking behind her, and they'd climb a High Sierra trail together. At the summit, they'd look at the view, then at each other, and kiss. Hayley shook herself. She was venturing into dangerous territory again. This would never do.

She caught up to Merle and asked, "How did you choose Arthur?"

"Friend of a friend's dog had puppies. I wanted a larger-size dog, but I also wanted an easygoing breed."

"I, um, heard Labs aren't the brightest bulbs in the chandelier." Hayley had Googled Labs to learn something about them before she moved in. Somehow she knew her slight of Arthur's intelligence wouldn't offend Merle.

Merle looked at her for a moment, then said, "That's what makes them so great! If I wanted a problem solver, i.e., a problem maker, I would have gotten a border collie or a corgi." She laughed in that open enthusiastic manner Hayley was getting familiar with, and it caused her to laugh too.

"Where did his name come from? It seems a little formal for him."

"I was a sci-fi nut when I was a kid. So he's named for Arthur C. Clarke. Even when he was a pup, he was solemn, so it seemed to fit." On cue, Arthur turned around to stare at them.

"Righto, boy. You understand we're talking about you."

Hayley watched Merle's profile. She liked how her eyes crinkled up at the corners as she looked at her dog. Arthur trotted forward and then turned and looked at them, wagging his tail.

"Oh, okay, a little faster. Roger." Merle strode ahead as Arthur picked up the pace of their walk.

Hayley followed Merle and watched the way her body moved through space. She had a self-assured walk. Not a swagger exactly, but she was confident and at ease in her environment. They emerged on the other side of the trees into an open area and made a right-hand turn on up the hill.

Arthur chose his bathroom spot. While Merle cleaned up, Hayley looked to the north to Twin Peaks and then to the east where the downtown high-rises loomed. Beyond them was the Bay. Then she turned her gaze back at Merle and Arthur. She could see them out in the woods somewhere with no civilization around, no people, no houses. Merle was by all indications a sophisticated urbanite, but Hayley saw that at another time, another place, she would be at home in much less citified surroundings. Hayley could see her standing on a boulder. Then she stopped herself. This fantasy was really getting out of hand.

Again, to get out of her head, she spoke. "This is so cool. It seems like we're in a small town somewhere."

"Yeah. It's a reminder of the Bernal neighborhood's rural past. They used to graze goats around the hill. Most of the southern parts of San Francisco were Mexican ranchos in the early part of the nineteenth century. The City grew outward from the waterfront."

"Where I used to live was nothing but sand dunes for a long time."

"That's for sure. Nothing there but dunes and beach grass except for Sutro's places out on the cliffs, until they built Golden Gate Park."

"You know the City pretty well?"

"Only some parts of it. The ones I like. Land's End, for instance. We could go for a walk there sometime."

"I'd like that." There was a beat of silence, but it wasn't uncomfortable or anxiety producing. Hayley wasn't sure what, if any, significance to assign to it, but she noticed its existence.

"All right. Ready to go meet the multitudes of lesbians?" Merle had drawn herself up to full height and looked as though she was prepared for action. Hayley was beginning to recognize this trait and was charmed by it. Merle wasn't dominating, but she was positive and behaved like a leader. Hayley found herself very much wanting to be led.

"I think so. After the buildup you've given me, I hope I don't get too nervous and act like a doofus."

"You're very undoofus-like." Merle stated this with such certainty, Hayley wanted to hug her.

"Thanks. I'm glad you think so." They walked around to Bernal

Heights Boulevard and to the parking lot. Bernal Hill's red dirt and red rocks glowed in the midday sun, but it was windier than ever. As they marched up the road, Hayley took deep breaths and tried to match her stride to Merle and Arthur's speed. They approached what looked like a huge crowd of people and dogs gathered in the parking area.

Hayley heard Merle mutter under her breath, "Uh-oh." Before she could ask what was wrong, standing before them was a short woman with jet-black hair undisturbed by the breeze. She stood with her hands on her hips and her head tilted, a challenging grin on her face.

"Well, it's about fucking time. I was wondering why I hadn't seen you and why you hadn't called me." The woman was clearly teasing, but the undercurrent to her words sounded a bit bullying. Hayley glanced at Merle and saw her mouth form a perfunctory smile very unlike her usual expression.

"Oh, hi, Miley. Yeah, been pretty wrapped up in stuff. I had to get the house reorganized and find a new roommate."

She stood still, but Arthur, unusually for him, didn't sit down but stood and crowded close to her thigh. Miley threw her arms around Merle, who raised her arms but only lightly grasped Miley's shoulders and gave her a little pat on the back. Her unease was palpable.

"Well, I forgive you this time, but don't be such a stranger, okay?"

"I'll try. Miley, this is Hayley, my roommate."

"Oh well. Then I *really* forgive you." Miley's eyes widened and sparkled. She was attractive—sort of. She was well built, tanned, and fit looking. Up close, Hayley could see her hair was obviously tamed by gel. She exuded sexuality from the top of her shiny black head down to her Nike-shod feet.

"Hi. I'm Miley." She promptly wrapped Hayley up in a tight hug. After a moment, Hayley tried to pull back but she was trapped. She didn't care for hugs from strangers, even nice-looking female ones, and Merle's reaction to this woman had put her on guard.

"Oh, Merle, baby. You scored."

"Miley."

"I'm just kidding. Nice to meet you, Hayley. Where'd you move from?"

"Out in the Sunset, a couple blocks from the ocean."

"Way out in the boonies. Sheesh."

"Well, not that far. Nothing in SF is that far away from anything else."

"Guess so, but here you are now." Miley showed a lot of teeth. *The better to devour you with, my sweet* popped into Hayley's head.

She looked at Merle, who nodded slightly, and said, "So good to meet you, Miley. We're kind of on a schedule here. So we have to get our walk done."

"Well, all right. I gotta let you go." She mimed putting a phone in her ear. "Call me!"

"Sure. Bye."

Hayley said, "Nice to meet you." But she didn't flash the grin she was starting to think of as her flirt grin. They made their way over to the path and continued their hill climb.

"I've got her number. If you want it." Something about the way Merle said the second sentence made Hayley think Merle knew she most definitely *didn't* want Miley's number.

"I'll pass," Hayley said with a slight edge.

"No worries. I'm just making introductions. It's all up to you."

"She seems to be into you."

"That would be a momentary state, I assure you. Miley's into everybody. Sometimes literally."

"Very funny," Hayley said, but she laughed anyhow. She liked Merle's dry, understated humor. She delivered the punch line of her quips in such a deadpan voice, Hayley had to really listen.

"Hey, Merle!" Hayley turned toward a voice behind them and saw a figure of indeterminate gender waving broadly at them.

"Hi, Terry," Merle called back with a tender quality to her voice Hayley hadn't heard before.

Terry held a thick leather leash, at the other end of which was a brindle pit bull who started to pace and leap when it saw Merle.

"Oakley. Hey, dude." She took the dog's head in her hands, and Terry looked on fondly but didn't release the leash.

"Oh, and hello to you too, Ter." They embraced.

"How are you, honey?" Terry was dressed in a leather vest and extremely worn loose black jeans. She/he wore gloves with no fingers and had a chain looped from his/her belt to his/her back pocket. One side of his/her head was shaved, leaving just a thatch of thick brown hair flopped over one ear. She/he had a silver ring in his/her nose and some sort of tattoo beginning on his/her neck and likely extending down his/her arm.

"I'm fine. Better every day."

"Kay's gonna burn in hell," Terry said fiercely. "She's toast as far as I'm concerned."

Hayley watched Merle's face and saw that now-familiar sadness wash over her features.

"Hi, my name's Hayley." She extended her hand, and Terry's mouth widened into a grin. She/he didn't look exactly wolf-like but it was close. With the touch of his/her hand, face-to-face and at arm's length, Hayley concluded she was female.

"Helloooo. I'm Terry. Good to meet you." She didn't release Hayley's hand right away. They stood there, connected, until Hayley grew slightly uncomfortable.

"Hayley's my new housemate. She just moved in last month."

Terry peered at her, eyes narrowed. "You don't say." She tilted her head back and continued to scrutinize Hayley, though she thankfully took her hand away.

"You want to head up the hill with us?" They started walking again.

Merle said, "Terry's a professional dog trainer. I took a puppy training class with her when I first got Arthur."

"Oh, wow. You must be really good at it. Arthur's *such* a nice dog."

"He is, but his training's mostly due to Merle's efforts. I gave her some pointers, got her started."

Oakley barked suddenly. It was unexpectedly loud and ended in sort of a squeal.

Terry turned to him and hissed through her teeth. "Quiet!"

He stopped barking.

She ordered him to sit, and as soon as he sat down, she gave him something from a bag hanging on her belt. His giant jaws worked as he chewed his cookie. They resumed walking.

"Oakley's a special dog," Merle said, smiling at him and then back at Hayley.

"That's one way to put it," Terry said. Hayley sensed something behind both statements.

"So what's the story?" she asked, directing her attention specifically at Terry, though for some reason, she was hyper-aware that Merle's attention was now focused on *her.* She appeared to be studying Hayley's reaction to Terry.

"Oh, man. It was really something. I work down at ACC and—"

"What's ACC?" Hayley asked.

"Animal Care and Control. Basically, the pound, but we don't call it that. 'Cause this is San Francisco, you know? It wouldn't be PC. The animal-control officers brought him in one day and told us he'd been a drug dog."

"Like one who looks for stuff at the airport?"

Terry's expression turned bitter. "Nah. Like as in the dog who protects a dealer's stash."

"Oh."

"Yeah. Fucking assholes. They try to make the dogs vicious by beating them. They ought to be castrated."

Hayley was shocked both by the story and by Terry's vehemence, but she understood the emotion behind it. "So what happened?"

"Yeah. So they didn't think Oakley could make it. I mean as in being rehabbed and put up for adoption. But I thought I could do it. So I did. Mostly he's okay. Just a little nervous and jumpy. Reactive."

"He's a pit bull, right?" Hayley eyed the dog cautiously. They'd stopped once more to let the dogs sniff and explore. As Oakley's large tongue slurped in and out of his mouth, she thought of the news accounts she'd read about pit bulls mauling children.

Terry looked at Oakley fondly and said, "Yeah. Pits get a bad rap. They've got incredibly strong jaws, but if you train them correctly, they're fine. He's not dangerous. Just a little touched in the head." The three of them laughed then. The mood lightened up and Hayley was relieved.

"So. You just moved in with Merle?"

"Yeah. Not long ago. She's helping me get the lay of the land."

Terry raised an eyebrow. "Really? Well, she's darn smart but she don't know everything. What do you want to know? I can probably tell you."

Hayley got it that she was being hit on and she liked it, though she wasn't sure how she felt about the hitter. This would be the stereotypical dyke she'd heard about, that people looked down their noses at. She mentally shook off the dismay she felt at even thinking about Terry in that manner and decided to take the bait.

"You think? Maybe I've got a question or two Merle doesn't know the answer to." And Hayley winked at Merle, who flicked both her eyebrows up and grinned amiably.

"Well. I think I'll run Arthur up to the top of the hill. I can meet up with you two in a little while."

"Don't be in a hurry. That mutt of yours is getting fat. Better watch that," Terry called to Merle as she went off at a half trot with Arthur loping beside her. Hayley watched them go and then turned back to Terry. She tried out a wide, flirtatious grin and asked, "Doesn't *your* dog need to be walked as well?"

Terry's smirk deepened. Hayley really couldn't decide if she liked what she saw or not, but she was talking to a lesbian who appeared interested in her, and she wanted to see where it led.

"I think I like you already. Let's go." Terry pointedly took the opposite direction of Merle and Arthur.

"So do you live in the neighborhood?" Hayley started with an easy question.

"Nah. Glen Park."

"Oh, nice. Do you own or rent?"

Terry emitted an unpleasant grunt. "Huh. Are you kidding? I'm a renter. I've had the same flat for twenty years. I won't move. I *can't* move. Rent control. They'll have to carry me out. If the landlord sells, I'm screwed."

"Uh-huh." Most of what Hayley knew of rent control was from the other side. She'd heard landlords in the Sunset district complain bitterly about it.

"I'm a renter now too. I used to own a house with my ex-husband."

"Husband, eh?" Terry regarded her with distinct suspicion. In her mouth, "husband" sounded a little like "cockroach." Hayley supposed that was to be expected. Some of the stuff she'd read indicated that "real" lesbians had deep reservations about women like her. She wondered how to convince someone she could be trusted. A track record with women might help, but getting one started was the problem.

"That's all done with," Hayley said with as much conviction as she could. "I'm not interested in men anymore, not in the least. Been there, done *that*. I'm looking to date women, seriously, not as a fling. That's partly why I moved here."

"Well, you came to the right place, honey." The "right place" was clearly embodied in Terry.

"I sure hope so. So far, I love it. Merle's a great person. She's got an awesome house. I love living there."

"Merle's the best. She got a raw deal."

"Oh? Why's that?" Aha. At last she could really get the story on what happened.

"No one really knows. Kay was here, then she was gone, and Merle doesn't talk about it though it's obvious she's devastated."

"I don't like to pry. I know they'd been together a long time."

"Yup. Anyhow, this is a depressing subject, so let's move on."

She wasn't going to hear the story.

"Sure. How about telling me more about Oakley? He's a lucky dog, for sure."

"He's a gem, just he's a bit wacko at times. But I can handle him. He's my best friend."

"No girlfriend?"

"Nah. Not for a couple years."

Hayley could do without the "nahs," but she wanted to know more. As Terry talked about Oakley and about dogs and their training, she grew more animated and more articulate. Hayley tried to get past her looks, which she couldn't quite comprehend. Why would a woman make herself purposefully unattractive? She didn't have anything against butch. On Merle, for instance, it looked really good. But Merle was well groomed and neat and had a nice head of artfully cut silvery gray hair.

Hair was important to her, Hayley decided. She couldn't see dating bald or partially bald women. Probably no crew cuts either. Piercings? Meh. But any prospective dates had to wear clean clothes. It looked as though Terry's jeans had been washed in salad oil, then dipped into a vat of dirt.

They walked up the summit of Bernal and stopped to admire the view, then walked back down, and there stood Merle and Arthur at the water fountain.

"Hey, you!" Hayley called out with relief. Merle turned at the sound of her voice, her face radiant. She looked a little windblown and ruddy. She and Arthur must have taken a brisk walk.

Merle turned back to the water fountain, where she stood, pressing the button to give Arthur fresh water, and bent and took a drink herself. When she looked up, she wiped her mouth and their eyes locked. Hayley tried to discern what she was seeing in Merle's face, but she couldn't exactly. It looked like longing, like the way Arthur gazed at them before he was allowed in the kitchen. Then she got self-conscious because she felt like she was staring. Terry's loud voice broke the moment.

"Hey, Craig. Your new roomie's a great gal."

"Yep, I know. You two had a nice chat?"

"We took a hike. Whaddya talking about?"

"Are those two things mutually exclusive?"

"Don't fret. Me and Oakley get enough exercise. Arthur's getting a belly. I can see it from here."

"That's your imagination. He's in perfect condition."

Hayley listened to them banter. Terry was showing off a little by teasing Merle. She thought that Merle might be engaging Terry to divert her attention from Hayley. That was an interesting idea, but she thought it seemed far too juvenile. It was likely her imagination. She wondered about the look she and Merle had exchanged. She didn't know what sort of signal she'd given but was afraid it might have appeared as though she was attracted to Merle. She really needed to watch herself. No more fantasies about Sierra hikes.

"Ready to go home?" she asked Merle.

"I am. I think Arthur needs a nap."

"Maybe it's you who needs a nap. Okay, I'm ready."

She turned back to Terry. "So nice to meet you. Thanks for the walk." This time she turned on her flirt grin full force.

"You bet. Here's my card. Call me *anytime*." And she winked, roguishly.

Hayley accepted it and tucked it into her jeans pocket. "Maybe I'll do that."

As they walked back home, Hayley debated with herself about saying anything to Merle and concluded she needed to talk. She needed Merle to help her understand and correct her misconceptions and generally keep her from making a fool of herself.

"So. I get how lesbians are super different from each other."

"That's putting it mildly. We all like women but that's about it."

"Miley's a player, right?"

"Right."

"I didn't like her too much. I liked Terry though."

Merle didn't say anything but kept walking. The silence made Hayley nervous and she sought to fill it. "Do you think I should go out with her?"

"That's entirely up to you."

"Well…" Hayley was a bit miffed at Merle's lack of engagement and failure to offer any additional information.

"Can I ask you a question?"

Merle turned to her, her expression unreadable. "Of course."

"You won't think I'm silly or homophobic or anything?"

"No, of course not." Now she seemed a little impatient.

"Why does Terry look like that, dress like that?"

"What do you mean?" Oh, great. Merle was surely playing dumb. This was unhelpful.

"I mean the dirty clothes, tattoos, piercings, hair style, or whatever?"

"Haven't you ever seen straight women who look like that?"

"No, honestly, I haven't. Why do you ask?" Hayley was suddenly feeling very defensive.

"Because that look isn't confined to lesbians, and lesbians look and dress in a lot of different ways. So does everyone else. I mean, you may have not run into many hipster-type people in the Sunset—"

"Wait a minute. Are you saying I've lived a sheltered life? I've lived in San Francisco for a really long time and—"

"Take it easy, Hayley. I'm not putting you down." Merle spoke calmly. "But your question leads me to believe you just didn't go to certain parts of the City. You can live in parts of SF where you wouldn't run into too many different kinds of people—"

"I see panhandlers and crazy people all over the Financial District!" Hayley said, feeling put down anyhow.

"Right, but that's not what we're talking about. I'm talking about people you actually *know*. I'd imagine you don't know many people like Terry. She's an outlaw. She's got a job where she doesn't have to look a certain way. She can be herself, whatever and whoever that is."

"Yeah, I see that."

"She's a wonderful person. She's been enormously helpful to me with Arthur. She accomplished something remarkable by rehabbing Oakley. *You* may not be attracted to her. Nothing wrong with that."

And there it was, the truth clearly stated by Merle. It was a little painful, but it was true.

"Am I a bad lesbian?" Hayley needed reassurance. Merle's expression was compassionate. She wasn't trying to embarrass Hayley.

"No. Not at all. Lesbians look all sorts of ways. You'll know what you want when you meet her."

Merle waited a beat, then asked, "Are you going out with her? 'Cause I can pretty much guarantee she wants to go out with you."

"I don't know. I'm going to think about it."

"Yeah. Okay. Good then." They walked down the east path toward their home.

At the bottom of the hill they stopped and Merle said, "This tree has some squirrels, and Arthur likes to stop and see if they're home."

"Look at him," Hayley said.

Sure enough, Arthur stood on the path, his tail wagging a mile a minute as he scrutinized the big cypress tree, but no squirrels showed up. They waited a few more minutes, then walked back toward their home on Stoneman Street.

Chapter Six

Merle bicycled to work the Monday following their first Bernal Heights dog walk and thought about the walk with Hayley. She'd been embarrassed when she grabbed Hayley to stop her from swinging on the rope swing. Invading her personal space like that probably wasn't that big a deal, but Hayley must have thought she was trying to hit on her. Her expression when she jumped off the rope swing had been so odd: her eyes wide and alarmed and she'd blushed. It had been a dumb move. Merle needed to keep her hands to herself.

She'd been on the lookout for Miley and never once thought about Terry. It wasn't a regular spot for Terry to walk Oakley so she'd been surprised to see her. Merle had great affection for Terry, as well as tremendous respect and admiration. She just didn't want Hayley dating her. It infuriated her to think this and not be able to come up with a satisfactory reason for why. It was none of her business.

Her job, if she had one, was helping put women in Hayley's path, and the consequences were irrelevant. She turned the situation over in her mind a few times and then sternly lectured herself to let it go. Next time, Hayley could take Arthur for a walk by herself and get as many phone numbers as she could manage. Merle chastised herself for her cranky attitude. This type of thinking was pointless. Besides, she needed to be focused for work.

She liked to arrive at her lab fairly early in the morning so she had a few hours of quiet before the rest of the group drifted in. Her principal investigator, the faculty member for whom she worked, was an easygoing fellow, and she had mostly free rein when it came to the day-to-day running of the laboratory. Since Collier Thompson was a very senior faculty member and a successful researcher, he could maintain a large research operation.

Ten years previously, they'd moved from their cramped rickety lab space on the UCSF Parnassus campus to the shiny new Quantitative Biology Center on the UCSF Mission Bay campus. It was a vast improvement in many ways, not the least of which was its closeness to Merle's home. She'd never wanted to commute and now she never had to. She had expected to work a few more years; then she could retire and walk twice a day every day. She didn't, however, have anyone to retire *with*. That little detail bothered her and reminded her of Kay's departure.

She'd been managing Thompson's lab for fifteen years, and he depended on her to keep everything non-science-related organized and running smoothly while he oversaw the research. She'd started as a technician and then became a staff research associate or SRA and finally had been promoted to specialist, but she did very little lab work anymore.

Managing the Thompson lab was a full-time position. It was, in fact, more than full-time, and she'd asked him for a year to hire another staff research associate to help her. The graduate students and post-doctoral scholars and visiting scientists and interns who floated through the lab for a year or two or even just a summer had to be wrangled almost 24/7. Collier couldn't be bothered with the details. He directed the research and spent a great deal of time attending conferences and lecturing all over the world. He was said to be in line for a Nobel Prize.

Merle locked her bike and used her ID card to open the door to the building and took the stairs to the third floor. She sometimes missed the funky old lab in the Health Sciences building on the main campus at Parnassus, but not often. The QB3 building was somewhat sterile, but they had more room and everything worked properly and was designed according to modern health and safety codes.

She stopped in the kitchen to make coffee and then took a cup to her office to begin organizing herself for the day. She consciously swept thoughts of Hayley out of her mind so she could focus on work.

❖

Hayley sat at her desk and looked at the time in the corner of her monitor. Close enough. She was going to take a lunch break. She typed "lesbian" and "relationship" into the Google search box, and a list popped up on the screen. She unwrapped her cheese and avocado sandwich and took a bite, then clicked on the first link, Match.com.

She thought about the dog walk the previous weekend with Merle and Arthur. It'd had been instructive, if nothing else. It was always good to know what you *didn't* want. She grinned to herself. For sure, she was staying far away from Miley. But she couldn't decide what to think about Terry. She was put off by her looks, although she didn't want to be. Terry was perfectly pleasant and friendly but…It couldn't hurt to see her. Maybe more time and a little more conversation would help.

In the meantime, there was the Net. Britt had sworn that was the best way to meet people. Hayley supposed it couldn't hurt to try, though she was pretty sure she wanted to meet women face-to-face through introductions or at parties. So far, the results from that effort were definitely mixed.

She opened one site and found the section for women seeking women. The profiles were unbelievable. She supposed people must lie in them, though she didn't know where lying would get you unless you planned to have a relationship purely online. Even photos couldn't tell the whole story. Well, it was a place to start. She set up her profile, paid the fee, and left a few notes on some that looked promising. It was all a matter of statistics, and the more places Hayley looked, the more likely she'd find the right person or, as Britt had said to her once, "You could just settle for Ms. Right Now." That wasn't what she had in mind, but she had to keep her options open.

She took out Terry's business card, which carried a nice abstract-like logo of a dog and contained all manner of ways to get in touch with her. She turned it over, then framed it with her fingers and tapped it. She was about to call and ask someone out on a date, someone she found pleasant and interesting, but she was pretty sure there ought to be a little more *there*, there.

Among the resources Hayley had read, she recalled an admonition that, contrary to some straight people's stereotypes, lesbian relationships weren't like being with your best friend. The attraction was far more intense than uninformed people might imagine. Hayley hoped she'd know it when she saw it. Maybe it would appear over time. She grew irritable at her mental fidgeting and procrastination, so she called and left Terry a message.

A few hours later, Terry called back and they made plans to go out to dinner that Friday evening.

When Hayley keyed off her phone, she stared at it for a long time. She *was* excited. This was her first date, after all. She ought to be *really* excited, but she wasn't. It wasn't quite like contemplating a household chore she had to do or having to finish writing a long brief at work. It gave her more pleasure than that but wasn't quite what she'd thought it would be.

She was looking for *the* feeling: the one she'd read about in romance novels and one she saw enacted by *The L Word* girls. She wanted the dizzy, logic-defying surge of anticipation and arousal, and it wasn't happening. She suspected she might be experiencing the same phenomenon that had occurred with Howard. She'd ended up marrying him because she'd convinced herself she was attracted to him, when all she was attracted to was his wanting her. That was a powerful incentive for an inexperienced twenty-four-year-old girl. She was a lot older now and ought to know the difference. She suspected it might be because she was developing an attraction to Merle, but she was determined to keep *that* tamped down.

Never mind. This was all about experience. She needed practice dating anyhow, and she needed practice with women. So she was going to go out and do just that. Maybe Merle would let her take Arthur out on her own this weekend. She hoped so. She wanted Merle to go with them because she enjoyed her company, but it was probably better if she went by herself. It was up to her to fail or succeed, and Merle's presence, while welcome, wouldn't help her get her sea legs.

She could depend on Merle for support and advice, but there was a limit. She ought to get back to work, but she kept thinking about Merle. Was Merle going to be going out on dates too? It seemed natural. Maybe they could go together. Double dates. That would be fun.

She clicked open the document she'd been working on, the Banner age-discrimination case, and forced herself to get to work. Thank goodness for deadlines.

❖

"I'm really glad you called me," Terry said, her voice and her expression heartfelt and winning. They were seated across from each other at a picnic bench at Foreign Cinema, the Mission District's palace of nouveau cuisine and old black-and-white European films.

Hayley arranged her face in a pleasant if noncommittal smile. She wasn't going to deploy her full 100-watt, all-teeth grin. She didn't want to send the wrong signal to Terry. They were having a friendly dinner, though Terry insisted she would pay. This certainly made it feel like a date. Also, Terry had cleaned up very well. She wore tailored pants and a nice white shirt. Her clothes were fitted properly and showed her muscular physique. The hair, piercings, and tattoo were still there, however. As was the absence of any spark in Hayley's heart or sexual heat in her body.

"I wanted to get to know you better and hear more about the work you do and Oakley's story."

That at least was true. So Terry talked and they sipped their wine and then ate their very good dinner. It was time for the movie to start. *Jules et Jim* was the feature. Hayley loved movies, but this wasn't one of her favorites, which was good. It would be rude if she ignored Terry to watch the movie.

"I've run on way too much. Occupational hazard when you have a passion for your job."

"It's fine. I truly admire that and admire you for doing that kind of work."

"What about you?" Terry cocked her eyebrow, causing Hayley to focus on her eyebrow ring. "How do you feel about what you do?"

"I love it. Mainly because the lawyers at my law office are on the side of justice. They don't defend big businesses who defraud the public or destroy the environment. They help people with employment-discrimination cases."

"Awesome. Any queer clients?"

"For sure. Many." Hayley flashed on Sabine and herself in the restroom.

"The work *you* do is important."

"I like to think so."

Terry reached across the table to take Hayley's hand.

"Trust me, it is." Hayley didn't withdraw her hand, but she felt uneasy and unsure.

Terry squeezed her hand, grinned, and said, "Let's take a walk."

"All right."

They went out to Mission Street, then over to Valencia Street, where the sidewalks were clustered with people. The young and the hip, Hayley thought a little sourly, but she wasn't uncomfortable because of the ambience. She knew she was going to face a kiss sometime soon.

They walked slowly with no special destination and looked in store windows. Valencia Street hosted a number of decorating and furniture stores. Hayley seized upon these as a distraction, and Terry was indulgent.

"I've still got a couple things to buy for the house. You know Merle. Do you think she'd like this lamp?"

"Don't know that side of her, sorry."

Hayley looked over the lamp critically. "What side do you know?"

"The animal-loving, dog-training side," Terry said with a slight edge to her voice.

"Oh?"

"Yep. That's how we relate."

"I see." Hayley sensed the energy shift and knew Terry wasn't interested in discussing Merle.

As if on cue, Terry said, "I'd rather talk about you, if you don't mind. Tell me more about you." And then Hayley knew she was going to have to have the same conversation with every new woman she met. The one where she had to tell her backstory.

She'd have to come up with something that didn't sound lame or reveal too much info. Like how she had exactly zero sexual experience with women. The bathroom grope with Sabine was it. She presumed everyone in her age range had a lot of years and a lot of different women behind them, but she was starting from scratch. She really was like a teenager, which wasn't a welcome feeling.

"There's not much to tell. I was married for years and—"

"Yeah. So you said."

"I've got a twenty-six-year-old son named Robbie."

"Nice. So you haven't been out for very long?"

"Right."

"Am I your first?"

"My first? What?" Hayley was a little alarmed.

"First date."

"Yes. You are."

"That's nice. I mean. I'm glad you decided to go out with me."

"Well. I wanted to." That was true enough.

"Let's go get a drink. I know a place close by. Not a gay bar but it's okay."

"Sure." Hayley didn't especially want a drink, but she didn't want to be rude, and she wanted to see this through to the end.

Once they'd gotten their drinks, beer for Terry and dry white wine for Hayley, they huddled close at the bar. Hayley was aware of the pressure of Terry's arm on her own. It wasn't unpleasant but didn't cause any of her nerves to zing.

"I haven't gone out with anyone for quite a while. Certainly not anyone as fine as you."

Hayley absorbed the compliment, but it didn't make her tingle. It embarrassed her. She could only manage a weak smile in return.

"That's very sweet." They sipped their drinks during a semi-awkward pause.

"This isn't going anywhere, is it?" Terry asked this question in a matter-of-fact way.

"I'm sorry, no." Hayley *was* sorry.

"Don't be. I'm not. I can always tell on the first date what the deal is, and you're not there."

Terry was way more astute than Hayley would have expected, which was refreshing, as was her honesty.

Terry took a big swallow of her drink and said, "We both know it's not good to waste time. Friends?"

"Yes. Of course. Absolutely."

"Good. Let's take you home." That phrase instantly brought Merle to mind. Hayley hoped she'd be there and be in the living room or kitchen. Hayley always left her alone when she was in her bedroom. They weren't college girls who had to talk all the time about every little thing. They gave each other mental and physical space.

The ride back to Bernal was blessedly short. Hayley practically leaped out of the car in her haste to get away from any possible kiss.

"Thanks so much. We'll talk soon. Might see you out dog-walking!"

"Maybe. So long." With that, Terry drove away.

Hayley opened the front door, and to her delight, Merle looked up from her seat on the couch. Arthur was next to her and looked up too, and his tail started to wag. Hayley was irrationally happy to see both of them, although Arthur's greeting was the more animated of the two. Merle smiled, but just barely. This wasn't unusual. Hayley attributed her apparent lack of affect to her being at home alone and missing her ex-lover. Merle never said anything about her feelings. Hayley was just speculating but knew that was how she would feel.

"Hi there," she said brightly.

"Hi yourself. How was your date?"

"Oh, fine. It was Foreign Cinema and the Mission district and Valencia Street corridor and all."

Merle grinned. "Didn't you feel like you were with the in crowd?"

Hayley had learned when she was teasing, though her tone was as dry as the Mojave Desert. "I don't think people call it that now, Merle. That's kind of a sixties phrase."

"Yep. Sure is. But we're sixties-type girls." She put a bookmark in her book and set it on the coffee table. She said, "Arthur, buddy. Down!"

Arthur took a long time to unwind himself and slide to the floor. Merle and Hayley looked at each other and giggled at his comic reluctance to give up his cushy spot on the couch.

Hayley sat down next to Merle and curled her legs under her. She'd preferred to sit that way since she was a little girl. She angled herself to face Merle and propped her elbow on the back of the couch.

"Funny you should say that. I'm a child of the sixties for certain. My mom loved Hayley Mills movies, and that's who I'm named for."

Merle was sitting with her stocking feet propped up on the coffee table and her hands loose at her side. She half turned toward Hayley and stretched her arm out so that her hand nearly touched Hayley's arm. It seemed she was comfortable and willing to talk, and that cheered Hayley.

Merle grinned. "You don't say. Which was your favorite? Which was your mom's fave?"

"Mom loved them all, but her favorite was *Pollyanna*."

Merle chuckled. "Okay. How about yours?"

"I liked *That Darn Cat* best. I think because of the cat mostly."

"Yep. I remember that."

"I love movies. All kinds, but especially the romantic comedies like the ones with Doris Day and Rock Hudson."

"Yeah. Those movies are a lot of fun. What was playing at Foreign Cinema?"

"*Jules and Jim*. Not really my style."

"Not mine either. How was dinner?"

"Dinner was tasty. Really good. I had some fish and kale made some sort of way that made it taste great."

"Sure."

A silence followed, and before she could think about it too much, Hayley said abruptly, "Does it make me a bad person if I don't want to date Terry?"

Merle furrowed her brows. "Not at all. Why would you think that? Haven't we processed this already?"

Hayley turned around and put her head back on the couch and said to the ceiling,

"I don't know. I want to meet women, but when I meet them, I can't get interested."

"Hayley. You're not expected to be attracted to everyone you meet. That's not only not possible, but it could be a very bad idea."

"I guess I know that's true. I just don't want to hurt people's feelings."

"Don't worry about Terry. She's tough."

"I know. That's part of the problem. She's too, I don't know, too hard."

"Well, she's got a total heart of gold, empathy to spare, so some of that's façade. It's hard to explain."

From what little she'd seen of Terry, she was empathetic and self-aware. It was a good combination, but not enough to light Hayley's fire.

"Did you ever go out with her?"

"Nope. That wouldn't work." Merle fell quiet, and Hayley wanted her to keep talking. She wanted to know more about what and who Merle liked and why.

"Why not?" Merle seemed somewhat unsettled.

"I—uh. We don't…"

Her discomfiture almost made Hayley want to drop the subject, but instead, she asked, "Is it because you're both butch?"

"Sort of. She's not my type, I guess."

"Not mine either."

Hayley almost said, "You're more my type. If I have a type." But she didn't want to stir up any trouble, and she wasn't sure what that meant anyhow. She thought Merle was nice looking but in an aesthetic way, not a I-want-to-rip-your-clothes-off kind of way. She'd determined that was the only safe spot her feelings could inhabit. Let out of their cage, they could be truly dangerous and could end up getting her kicked out of her new home.

Her thoughts about Merle were instructive, though, because they informed Hayley of what to look for when it came to women. It couldn't be that tough to find other women like her. But when it came to Merle, she wasn't going to give her thoughts free rein. She wanted someone *like* Merle but *not* Merle. Merle was the model, not the real thing, not the ONE.

Merle was looking at her with a strangely vague expression and nodding. She seemed to be thinking of something else.

"What about your ex?" Hayley asked boldly.

"Yeah. Kay. She had longer hair, brown and wavy. Gray eyes. Pretty."

"She must have been. You loved her very much?"

Merle sighed. "I did. I guess, after a while she didn't love me back so much. She didn't articulate her feelings very well, and she was a go-along-to-get-along sort. Some people call that codependent. Maybe. I call it dishonest."

"What in the world does 'codependent' mean?" Hayley was dumbfounded by the term.

"Well. It can mean someone who enables an alcoholic to keep on drinking, but not always. It can mean someone who takes care of everyone else but herself. For Kay that meant not telling me the truth about her feelings. She fell out of love with me, but she hung on for a really long time trying to get it back so I wouldn't be upset."

"That's terrible."

"Yes, it is." Merle folded her hands in her lap, looking glum and resigned.

She said no more and that seemed to be the end of the conversation.

Hayley yawned. "Well. I think I'm going to bed. I'll see you in the morning. I can walk Arthur by myself tomorrow, right? Look for more dog-loving dykes in the hood?" She was relieved to see Merle laugh lightly. Her despondency had passed.

"Yes. He's all yours. You can have fun seeing who stops to talk to you."

"Great. Sleep well. See you!" Hayley stood up and stretched and went upstairs to her bedroom, leaving Merle behind on the couch.

❖

Arthur wasted no time in hopping back up on the couch and lying down in the warm spot Hayley had left. Merle put her hand on him and patted him, letting the feel of his solid body help her get over her mild discomfort.

She'd been glad to see Hayley come home early. She'd predicted this date would be a one-shot thing and didn't seriously believe it would be extended overnight. Nonetheless, she'd been relieved and gratified when Hayley walked through the front door. Not that there'd be a thing wrong with Hayley going out with Terry, but Merle was still happy to be proven correct. Their conversation had taken an unexpectedly intimate turn, though, which unsettled her. She was always being reminded of how good-looking Hayley was. As time went on, Hayley was becoming even more alluring than she'd been at their initial meeting. She'd widen those big brown eyes and tilt her head. Even her mild confusion and uncertainty about women was endearing. She enticed Merle to talk about Kay even if she didn't want to.

But Merle didn't want to go there, no way, no how.

She was fine as long as they kept a fair amount of distance, but their intimacy was deepening, and she both wanted it and wanted to push it away. Hayley sitting close to her on the couch and talking in her open and artless way and asking questions made her uneasy and happy at the same time. They were straying into very personal territory. Hayley was obviously naturally open and understandably curious about women and sexuality. And she was vulnerable. It was reasonable for her to ask Merle questions.

By temperament, Merle was a helpful person. She responded to other peoples' needs as best she could while establishing good emotional boundaries. She'd put a lot of work into developing those boundaries while she was in recovery and helping new people get sober.

It was vital to be very supportive but to also be very self-protective with newly sober alcoholics, or she could get sucked into their drama. She'd been well schooled by other sober alcoholics and by experience on how to walk that tightrope. She'd heard far too many harrowing stories. A friend of a friend had ended up drinking because she got too close to the woman she was sponsoring, who got drunk. She knew more than one instance of a person with long-term recovery who became sexually involved with a newcomer, and it was a mess for everyone.

She ought to be able to keep good boundaries with her newbie lesbo roommate. It shouldn't be a heavy lift. Hayley wasn't a screwed-up drug addict or alcoholic. She was a pleasant, intelligent woman with very little life experience. Merle voiced an exasperated snort that caused Arthur to look at her with his head tilted. The more she tried to justify her interest in Hayley, the more irritable with herself she became.

"Arthur, your mission tomorrow is to find some women for Hayley to focus on. Eligible women. I can do only so much." How much and what she'd be able to do to help Hayley without getting entwined in her life in an unhealthy way was the real question. As she got ready for sleep she decided she needed to explore this topic with Clea and Sigrid. She needed some good old-fashioned tough love, and they were just the people to deliver it. The proverbial iron-hand-in-the-velvet-glove approach worked every time, on her as well as on anyone else. And she needed to stop talking aloud to Arthur. It was starting to bug her.

Chapter Seven

Hayley thought maybe she ought to give a meet-up another chance. A couple things on the calendar looked good. On impulse, she Googled "lesbian" and "coming out" and "San Francisco." A dozen listings popped up. She investigated them one by one. Most were for younger people, she surmised, just by their wording. But one read "Coming Out Late in Life." That had a certain ring of familiarity to it. Hayley was skeptical of so-called self-help methods. They all sounded hokey to her.

But she really needed someone to talk to. Merle was okay, but she wanted to keep their relationship on a nice, friendly, even keel. Right where it was. Further emotional intimacy between them might inevitably ratchet up Hayley's attraction. She was grateful that though she wasn't mature enough to stop the feelings cold, she was experienced enough to know when to put the brakes on. She had to stick to her plan of getting out and about and meeting women.

She typed a meeting listed for Thursday at six p.m. at the Women's Building into her phone calendar. It was worth a try. It might be good to find other people to talk to because she was feeling lost and unsure. Maybe she needed to try something different. She couldn't rely on Merle for support all the time.

The Women's Building of the Bay Area took up an entire block of Eighteenth Street right on the border of the Mission District and the Castro District. Its outer walls were completely covered with riotously colored murals, all depicting women, naturally.

Hayley took a moment to admire the paintings and to collect herself before going upstairs to attend the Forty Plus Coming Out group. She should have known, if there was an issue, there'd be a group for it. The Bay Area was a hotbed of self-improvement. Well, there was something to be said for talking with other people who had the same problem as you. AA obviously worked for Merle. Hayley had rarely seen anyone so self-confident and together and so genuine… There she went again, thinking about Merle. *Stop it*, she told herself sternly. *Focus.*

Hayley was at least as nervous about this meeting as she'd been about attending the meet-up. For that matter, she was more nervous about going to this group than going on a date. What it would be like to bare your soul in front of a bunch of strangers? It was definitely not her style. She'd never had anyone *to* talk to, at least about anything important. She'd deliberately tamped down her emotions for most of her life. Being in a dead-end marriage didn't help. She'd had friends but couldn't remember saying much of anything that really meant something. Her friendships were superficial at best. She supposed therapy might be a good thing too, but this coming-out group somehow seemed more palatable. It was free, anyhow.

She walked into the room, feeling like the new kid in a school where everyone already knows one another. That feeling went right along with all the other awkward teenage emotions she'd experienced recently. If she was going to have to relive her adolescence, she might as well hit all the stops.

The chairs were set up in a circle, and she had a moment of indecision over which one to pick but finally settled on one that didn't have a person on either side. Hayley smiled vaguely at the few women who were already there and tried to find a comfortable position for her butt. The chairs were just a small cut above cheap folding chairs. The other chairs filled up, and Hayley looked around curiously. She wasn't sure what she'd expected, but most everyone looked pretty normal. The age range of the group members, she guessed, went from fortyish to over seventy. Coming out at seventy. Now that was something. Anything's possible, she guessed. Even finding love at such an advanced age.

Finally, a dark-haired, butch-looking woman spoke up and said, "Let's get started. I'm Amy. Please everyone introduce yourself. If it's your first time, please say so."

Hayley tried to find clues to remembering names, but it wasn't her forte. She gave up.

When it was her turn, Hayley said her name and that it was her first time at the meeting. A lot of people murmured "hello," "welcome," or "nice to meet you." She was embarrassed but in a good way.

Amy said, "This is a coming-out group. The format is modeled after the consciousness-raising groups from second-wave feminism. We focus primarily on issues relating to sexuality and age, although we do discuss other things. There are no rules, but we ask that everyone be respectful of others, not criticize or judge, and speak from her own experience. That's how we help each other. Also please be respectful of time limits." Well, that all sounded good to Hayley, but she wondered if everyone went along.

"Let's hear from Hayley since it's her first time here. Tell us about yourself—where you came from and how you ended up here." Amy gave her a great big encouraging grin.

Hayley was speechless. She'd thought, somehow, she could just listen, at least at first. Not to be.

"Oh, uh. Thanks. Yes, I uh. After, um." Oh, great. She couldn't even form a complete sentence.

She haltingly told an abbreviated version of her history up to the point of moving in with Merle.

"So how do you feel now?" asked Norma, the oldest woman.

"Good, I guess. It's wonderful to not be stuck in a worthless marriage. To be on my own. It's nice." Even to herself, she didn't sound convincing. She could see some skeptical looks around the circle.

"I was terrified," said Amy.

"So was I," said someone else.

"Petrified. Completely lost," said a third woman.

"I had no idea what to do."

"It was half agony, half ecstasy."

"More like ninety percent agony and ten percent ecstasy. And I think you can guess what part was the ecstasy." The woman, whose name was Diane, smirked. A few women laughed, but most of them seemed to ignore the cynicism.

"It was like taking a trip to a foreign country where you don't speak the language and don't even have a phrase book to help you translate."

Hayley absorbed their words and calmed down. This was the core of self-help, she supposed: you identified with each other. She'd thought maybe she was having a harder time than other women. Not the case. It was reassuring to know she was no more scared or inept than anyone else.

"So," Amy said, "we all agree it's a scary thing to become a lesbian at our age?"

There were lots of nods and muttered assents. Hayley joined in.

"That said, what's good about it?"

This question perked everyone up, and this time the round-robin statements were far more positive.

"You get to be yourself."

"You're not faking anything anymore."

"It feels natural."

"It feels right."

"It's like coming home." The "coming home" phrase was arresting. To Hayley, it made sense. In an essential manner, she was coming home to herself, her true self. Up until the year before she'd been enacting some inauthentic version of herself. She was a person who looked like Hayley, talked like Hayley, but wasn't truly real.

Amy said, "Well, let's do check-in, and then I think it's Moira's turn to pick a topic."

She turned to Hayley and said, "Every meeting, we do a drawing, and whoever's picked comes ready to start a discussion at the next meeting."

"Sounds good," Hayley said. "Uh-oh" was what she thought. Then she reminded herself that she'd come for some help and support. If she was going to get any benefit out of this exercise, she'd have to participate and quite likely be honest about what was going on with her.

"Moira, you have the floor," Amy said.

"Right, what I want to talk about is coming out at work." With that she launched into a long description of the various responses of her coworkers at the high-end store where she was an assistant manager. Hayley found it fascinating in a voyeuristic way. But it also made her think about herself.

No one at Flaherty and McQuillen law firm except Britt knew about Hayley's recent changes. Surprisingly, Britt was good at keeping her secret. She hadn't asked herself why she hadn't told anyone else. They all knew she was divorced, but that was it. She figured nothing else was important. Maybe. Maybe not. As she heard the rest of the group members describe their experiences, she realized that without exception, they'd tried to let everyone in their lives know about the radical change that had taken place.

One woman said, "It almost made me pass out when I told my boss I wanted to bring a female date to the annual company dinner. He was fine with it, but it made me nuts. I assumed everyone was going to be like 'Oh no. She's a lesbian. Oh my God.' But it was me who had the problem with it."

Hayley dreaded taking her turn, but when it came around, she took a deep breath and said, "No one but one person at my law office knows. But I don't think it's any of their business who I see outside of work. My son knows. He's fine with it."

"I think," Amy said, "the more people I can tell, the more real it makes it. It's not 1972, and we don't live in the flyover states. This is the fucking Bay Area! No one should have a problem with it. If they do, it really is *their* issue." Many assents from the group.

Hayley said, "Well, I suppose that's true. I'll think about it."

After the meeting was over, Hayley took time to talk to a few women and was struck by their friendliness. Her preconceptions were basically unfounded. No one hit on her. They were actually there to help each other through a big transition. It was as simple as that, apparently. She had no doubt some would date each other. It made sense. But no one there really sparked any interest for her. She wondered why.

Her thoughts jumped all over the place as she drove home. She thought about work, she thought about Merle, she thought about her mom. She hadn't come out to her mother. Yet. Why was she so reluctant? More teenage angst, she guessed, and snorted. When was she going to be a grown-up?

Well, none of this was boring, that was for sure. And she didn't have a time schedule. Where it would all lead, who knew?

❖

Merle invited herself to Clea and Sigrid's for dinner. They lived in the outer Mission, not far from Bernal Heights, in a brightly painted Victorian duplex they'd rented for years. Clea always said they'd missed the window of opportunity to buy and so they'd kept the same rent-controlled flat. They had a reasonably good landlord so it was okay. No pets allowed though. Merle wouldn't be able to abide that, and she'd come to consider renting the equivalent of throwing money down a rat hole, but not everyone looked at home ownership as the ultimate goal.

When the door opened, Merle handed Clea the gardenias she'd picked from her garden.

"Oh, girl, you don't have to do this every time. I told you." They hugged. "But thanks anyhow."

They settled down to eat the roast chicken Sigrid had prepared. She was the cook in the family and was good at it, so Merle loved to eat at their house. Usually, they went out. It was much nicer to be in a home though. Restaurants were fine, but Merle always felt like they had to get up and leave as soon as they finished eating so the restaurant could turn the table. She and Kay had gone to Spain a few years before, and it wasn't like that in Europe. They'd had to practically beg the waiter to bring them the check.

"So, Mer. What's new? You dating anyone yet?" Sigrid asked brightly as she stirred what appeared to be a risotto.

"Nope. I told you I'm not ready to go there."

"I know you've got some healing to do, but in the meantime, what's wrong with dating or having sex with someone? I'm just a little concerned with you getting stuck in a celibacy rut. Better look out. Use it or lose it." Sigrid shook her head. Then she dished up the risotto and some steamed veggies, and they sat down to eat.

This remark aggravated Merle, but she quashed her irritation because Sigrid was only yanking her chain. Besides, it was too close to the truth, and she knew it didn't apply just to her body. If she was too protective of her emotions, the romantic loving ones, that is, they, too, could atrophy. The breakup with Kay had shut her down emotionally. She couldn't spend the rest of her life in a state of high alert in case someone might want to get close.

"Spare me. I think I've still got a few good years of use, as you put it, left."

"Well. Sure, but get going is all I'm saying."

"Sigrid, love, leave Merle alone," Clea said. "She's got to go at her own pace. She don't need you nagging her."

"Okay, then. I surrender. We'll change the subject."

"Good. Because I've got something to ask you about Hayley."

"Oh yes, Hayley. What about her? Are we really changing the subject?" Sigrid speared a piece of asparagus, took a bite, and grinned.

Merle glared at her. "She's looking for women to date. I took her out to the hill with me a couple weeks ago, and well..." Merle described the consequences.

"Sounds like she's doing okay."

"Well. Yeah, kind of, but she wants to widen her net. Not surprisingly, she's a bit old fashioned. She says she's looking online, but I get the impression she'd rather have introductions. Got any suggestions?"

"Yeah. You," Sigrid said flatly.

"*Other* than me. I told you I'm not interested. Besides, she's not the kind of woman I'm looking for. She's just coming out so she's got a lot of living to do, you know? And we're roommates."

"Oh, is this what she told you?" This time the skepticism was coming from Clea.

"Well. No. I just think that's what's going on. She keeps talking to me about stuff. She went out with my friend Terry, though it didn't go anywhere."

"So what's the problem?" Sigrid asked. "Was there blowback from the date with Terry? What are you *really* asking?"

"No, there wasn't any blowback. I just don't want to get into some codependent quagmire with her. I like to get involved with people. I like to help, as you know, but I have to not get pulled into the drama."

"What drama?"

"Well, nothing. So far." Sigrid was making her feel like her attitude was ridiculous. Maybe it was. Maybe she was way off base. She was running for cover when no actual bombs were falling.

"So. She's asking to meet people. That doesn't seem too complicated." Clea was eyeing her critically.

Merle realized she wasn't conveying the real ambivalence of her feelings. She didn't want to get involved with Hayley because she *did* have feelings. Her two friends and their pointed questions were hitting her right where the problem was. She wanted them to tell her to back off, but she wasn't being totally honest. They likely wouldn't say that anyhow. Merle decided to drop the subject. She was going to have to monitor herself. She could be friendly and helpful to Hayley, but she couldn't get involved with her. She was going to have to hang on until the feelings dissipated, which they would, eventually.

"Yep. So if you can think of anyone, let me know."

"We can hardly help her find people to date if we don't know anything about her." Sigrid smiled brightly.

"Uh-oh. What are you thinking about?" Merle asked.

Sigrid glanced at Clea, who merely cocked an eyebrow. She generally went along with whatever scheme Sigrid cooked up.

"We're thinking about a hike in Point Reyes. Why don't you ask her to come along?"

"I love Point Reyes, but I'll have to leave Arthur behind."

"No you don't. Bring him along. If we get stopped by a park ranger, you can just play dumb."

"All right," Merle said begrudgingly. She didn't know why she was being such a dipshit about it. It was a perfectly reasonable suggestion. With Sigrid and Clea, they couldn't get into trouble. It would just be a group of friends on an outing. Sigrid and Clea could get a better idea of what Hayley was like. Maybe they'd have some ideas for women for her to meet. Hayley also ought to see what a functional lesbian couple looked like.

Merle reproved herself again for feeling like she ought to manage Hayley's experience. She was having a very tough time between wanting to help Hayley adjust to her new life and trying to keep her distance emotionally. Furthermore, she'd come over to Sigrid and Clea's to talk to them about how not to get involved, and now she planned to invite Hayley on an outing with them. Somehow, this wasn't going the way she wanted it.

❖

"Thanks very much for asking me along on your hike," Hayley said as they got settled in the car for their drive out to Point Reyes. She caught Merle's eye and grinned. Merle's nod was affable.

Arthur sat upright between them in the backseat of Sigrid's Subaru wagon. He clearly knew they were going on an adventure, and his excitement was palpable.

"Merle told us you've never been. We hope you like it."

"Oh, I'm sure I will."

When Merle had asked her a few days before, she was thrilled. Other than dog walks, they hadn't done anything together besides eat dinner a couple of times. Taking a hike in Point Reyes struck her as a quintessentially lesbian thing to do, though she realized all sorts of people did it all the time. She was going with lesbians, and that made it special to her. When Hayley confessed she'd never been to Point Reyes or done any other kind of outdoor activity, Merle's solemn instructions about what to wear and what to bring were endearing.

"Are you sure it's okay with your friends?"

"Yes. Absolutely. They asked me to ask you along."

"That's so sweet." Merle had smiled vaguely but said nothing more.

So here they were. Hayley felt like a kid being taken on a special trip, kind of like Arthur. She hugged him and he tried to lick her face. She looked up at the towers of the Golden Gate Bridge as they crossed. The movement made her dizzy, but in a good way.

Other than crossing the bridge, the car ride wasn't especially fun. They followed US 101 with all its traffic through the northern suburbs of Marin County, which consisted of nothing more than fast-food places and car dealerships for an interminable amount of time. Once they exited the highway and left San Anselmo behind and got on the back roads, it was far more pleasant.

"Oh, look how cute!" Hayley exclaimed as they passed through the village of Olema with its Victorian B&B, the Olema Inn.

"We can come back here for dinner or go into Point Reyes Station."

"Merle said you like this place in Point Reyes. The Pine Cone Diner?"

From the passenger seat, Clea turned around and fixed her dark eyes on Merle and Hayley. "Merle is very good about matronizing businesses. Keep it in the family."

"What do you mean?" Hayley asked.

Merle had been looking out the window at the passing scenery somewhat dreamily. What was she thinking? Was she remembering another trip at another time with her ex?

"She means the Pine Cone diner is owned by lesbians. A couple."

"How nice. So you've been there?"

"Kay and I used to come up here." Merle looked unhappy.

Hayley was sorry she'd said anything, but how was she supposed to know this was a sensitive subject? "Anywhere's fine with me."

Sigrid asked Clea, "Should we go up Sir Francis Drake a little ways so Hayley can see Tomales Bay?"

"Sure."

"How gorgeous is this?" Hayley said in wonderment. The two-lane road wound along a huge, flat body of water. It was so still, the hills on the other side were reflected perfectly on its surface. It looked like a lake.

"So, Merle," Clea said. "Tell Hayley all about Point Reyes."

Sigrid turned in her seat so she could look at Hayley.

Merle gave her a tiny glare, but then she smiled brightly. "I'm the geek in this group. I always look up everything about everywhere we go. I want to know all about it."

"Oh, tell me. I want to know too."

Merle explained that the Tomales Bay was part of the San Andreas earthquake fault and separated the Point Reyes Peninsula from the mainland. She showed Hayley where Black Mountain was and Mount Vision and the village of Inverness.

"We could drive this road for another hour before reaching the very end," Sigrid said.

"I wish we could go," Merle said, "but it takes too long and not that many places are okay for Arthur. So we're going to Bear Valley."

"It's all wonderful. Why can't we take Arthur some places?" Hayley asked.

"Point Reyes is a national park and they have strict rules about dogs."

They parked and set off on their hike, which took them from the visitors' center through the woods out to the ocean. As they found their pace, Sigrid engaged Hayley while Merle and Clea strode ahead. Hayley watched Merle from behind again. Was this becoming a pattern?

"So Merle said you're divorced and you think you're a lesbian. Is that true?" Sigrid's tone was friendly, but her directness startled Hayley.

"Boy, you don't mince words, do you?" Hayley didn't know if she was relieved or annoyed.

"Try not to. Was that too direct?" Sigrid asked in a manner that told Hayley she didn't particularly care if Hayley thought she was too direct.

"Nope." Hayley gave her a wide and she hoped winning no-sweat grin. It was true, she supposed. She had so much to learn. No sense in pretending.

"Well, I'm curious about what it feels like to you. I've been a dyke since I was thirteen."

"It feels good. A little scary, like I've missed a lot of experience that I suddenly have to get caught up on. How in the world did you know you were gay at such a young age?"

"No idea. I just never had any attraction to anyone but other girls. It wasn't a big hit with my family, 'specially my mom. She was a strict Catholic."

"Ow. That must have been hard."

"It wasn't a piece of cake but she came around. After a while." Sigrid's smile was rueful. "Years. But I want to know about you."

So Hayley gave her the *Reader's Digest* condensed version.

When she finished, Sigrid shook her head. "Geez. That must have been a shock to your family."

"No one knows except my son, Robbie. He's fine with it. He's twenty-six."

"The youngsters are pretty evolved these days. But what about your ex-husband? How about your folks?"

"Howard sort of knows and doesn't care. He's not part of my life. My dad's gone. I haven't told my mom."

"Ooee. Brace yourself, girl. The older generation isn't generally known for open-mindedness about queers, and this is going to be a big surprise to your mom."

"I know. I'm putting it off. I'm going to have to sometime. I might get my son to help. He gets along better with my mom than I do."

"You may have something there. Enlisting your son's help could work. So you met anyone interesting?" That question put Hayley off balance again. She wanted to say, "Yes. I think I like Merle," but she didn't want to cause trouble with Merle and her friends.

"Yes and no. I've met a couple women, but no one that really grabs me. Why? Do you know anyone single?"

Sigrid cocked an eyebrow. "Might. Maybe, maybe not. I'll have to think about it. You okay with a set-up?"

"Oh, my God. I would so rather do that than try to hook up online."

Sigrid laughed. "I wouldn't want to be in your shoes and looking for love at my age. I don't want to deal with all that nonsense ever again." She shook her head.

"I know. It feels weird to have to date and to learn how to date women to boot."

"It's not rocket science. You'll be fine. It's just all the frogs you got to kiss before you find the princess."

"How long have you been with Clea?"

"Twenty years."

"Wow. How many girlfriends did you have before her? Do you mind my asking?"

"Nope. I don't know exactly. What do you consider a girlfriend? Someone I lived with or a one-night stand? Could be real different numbers."

"Live with, I guess."

"Four."

"Four!" Hayley was aghast. She didn't have that kind of time. "How many lovers has Merle had?" Her question was a little brazen, but she didn't think Sigrid would be offended.

Sigrid raised an eyebrow and scrutinized her before answering. "Before Kay? Just one. She was still drinking in those days though."

"But she hasn't had a drink in a long time, right?"

"No, she hasn't." Sigrid looked at her speculatively. Was she showing too much interest in Merle? They caught up with Clea and Merle, who'd stopped to look at some mushrooms.

"Hey, honey," Clea said to Sigrid.

Hayley couldn't get any more answers to her million questions. She caught Merle's eye and Merle smiled, but it seemed like a sad smile. What had Merle and Clea been discussing?

❖

Merle leaned over and checked Arthur's collar. Nothing was wrong with it, but she needed an excuse not to answer Sigrid's question. Clea and Hayley walked on about twenty feet ahead of them. They were deep in conversation, and Merle longed to know what they were talking about. Just as she wanted to know what Hayley and Sigrid had discussed. Neither would tell her, probably, because it was none of her business.

Sigrid stood still, arms folded, head tilted.

"I don't understand why you're so stubborn about this. She's perfectly lovely. Why won't you go out with her?"

Merle stood straight but focused on the dirt road under them. She couldn't be dishonest about her feelings. Not to Sigrid. But they were probably just a reaction to her traumatic breakup with Kay. Rebound was a terrible state to be in to meet someone. She had no idea if she was even capable of love again. She might be, but she wasn't sure when it would happen or even if it ever would again. And Hayley was too new, her emotions too raw. She was fragile even if she didn't seem to be.

"You know why. It wouldn't work. We're fine as roommates."

"I think you've shut down completely. That's not like you. It's not—"

"Sigrid, I love you. I've always trusted your advice, but not this time. I would be doing Hayley a real disservice."

Sigrid shrugged and shook her head. "All right already. I won't say anything else. I spent a lot of time biting my tongue around Kay so I should be good at it."

"Thanks. Now let's catch up to them." They took off at a good clip and pulled up alongside Clea and Hayley.

Sigrid took Clea's arm and led her off to one side and began whispering in her ear.

"They're a great couple." Hayley looked at them with an air of wistful envy.

"They are. They truly love and care for one another."

Hayley sighed. "That's beautiful. And so is this place." She gestured, encompassing their environment and the Point Reyes gestalt.

Merle looked up and then around. "Yes, it is." They walked a wide, smooth path through a canopy of trees. In the distance, they could see the sun shining near the horizon. "We'll be at the beach in a few minutes."

"We can stay until sunset?"

"Close to it."

"Arthur, sweetie? Are you having a good time?"

At the sound of Hayley's voice, Arthur's big head came around and he moved toward her. Merle let go of his leash and he crowded in close to Hayley, who rubbed his ears and knelt to make eye contact with him.

A tremendous sadness washed over Merle. Arthur had fallen in love with Hayley. If only her emotions could be as uncomplicated as his. She watched Hayley lavish attention on him and thought about being the object of Hayley's affection. Hayley looked at her with a tender smile as she petted Arthur. Then she jumped up and cried, "Come on boy, let's go!"

She trotted down the path, and Arthur happily loped after her. The sun flashed in front of her, momentarily looking as though rays of sunlight were emanating from her head. She turned around but Merle was stuck in place, stunned by how beautiful Hayley looked at that moment.

"Come on, Merle. Don't be so lazy. Run with us." She smiled brilliantly and waved, motioning Merle to follow them.

Merle shook her head but picked up her pace, and the three of them caught up with Sigrid and Clea.

Five minutes later, they reached the coastal path. The sun bounced off the surface of the Pacific, and where it hit, the ocean looked gold instead of blue. Only a few people were about. That was one of the many beauties of Point Reyes. It was far enough from civilization and big enough that it wasn't crowded. Merle had come there at times when scarcely anyone else was nearby.

She stood at the trail junction, staring out to the west, not thinking any more of anything but the beauty of a California beach and how wonderful to be able to experience it. She was aware, though, that Hayley stood beside her, looking in the same direction.

She turned and so did Hayley as the exact same time. They stared at each other.

"It's really something, isn't it?" Hayley said, quietly.

"Yep." Merle didn't trust herself to say more than that.

"Come on, you two. We can't stop now. We have a few more miles to go to complete the loop." That was Sigrid in her control mode, as Merle thought of it.

"Right," Merle called. The moment was over.

"Let's go to the beach and let Arthur swim in the ocean," Hayley said.

"Fine. You know he'll smell like rotten seaweed all the way home."

"So? It's worth it."

As they walked on the beach, Sigrid and Clea held hands. Merle was content to watch Hayley play with Arthur. He chased the waves, and Hayley chased him and then made him chase her. They were like kids playing a game. Hayley really was like a teenager in a lot of ways, not just in her newly discovered sexuality. She seemed young and fresh—and very appealing. Merle saw Sigrid watching her with a knowing look and pretended to ignore it.

❖

They were quiet on the ride home. Sigrid said little, as she had to concentrate on navigating the windy coastal highway in the dark. Hayley put her head against the window and daydreamed. She wondered about finding love, finding someone to spend the rest of her life with. She wanted what Sigrid and Clea had. The other side of it, though, was what Merle had experienced. How would she know? She couldn't predict what might happen; she could only try to choose well. But she couldn't conceive of how she was going to choose. She'd been on exactly one date, and here she was thinking about forever.

Well, she was fifty-something and had a duty to think clearly about the future. She glanced at Merle. She was dozing with Arthur cuddled up next to her and looked peaceful. Hayley thought about the two of them living together and in love for the rest of their lives with Arthur and his successors in their house in Bernal Heights. Like Clea and Sigrid. It was a lovely dream, she realized, but it really was only a dream.

She shook her head, trying to clear it of this inappropriate fantasy. She was grateful no one in the car could see her or hear her thoughts.

❖

Hayley had been walking around Bernal Hill for almost an hour and hadn't managed a conversation with a single woman. A guy with a little kid and a black Lab had engaged her in a friendly manner on the habits and temperament of the Labrador breed, to which she'd responded politely but briefly. Otherwise, she'd done nothing but walk and clean up after Arthur. At least she hadn't run into Miley or Terry.

She'd made the circuit and climbed to the summit and was on her way back down the hill toward home. It was about three in the afternoon and the wind wasn't too bad. Hayley clutched Arthur's leash, and he automatically sat down beside her. He certainly wasn't interested in sightseeing, but he didn't mind if she was. He was a good conserver of his energy and took the opportunity to rest.

At one of the benches, she stopped to admire the view. She didn't even have to pretend to enjoy it because it really was spectacular.

Hayley shaded her eyes against the western sun on her left. She could see the Bay Bridge arching over to Treasure Island, most likely crowded with bumper-to-bumper traffic. The Bay was placid. The Transamerica Pyramid's white spire pierced the sky. She heard a voice behind her.

"Nice-looking dog."

Startled, she spun around. She took a closer look at the speaker, and it slowly dawned on her that finally, she'd gotten the attention of someone whose attention she wanted.

"Oh, thanks." She turned on her flirt grin and got a mirroring response.

Before her stood a woman with a chocolate cocker spaniel. That was the first detail she could absorb. The dogs began to sniff one another, and both Hayley and the cocker's owner looked at them for a moment.

"What's your dog's name?"

"Arthur. How about yours?"

"Tulip." The woman's grin turned self-deprecating. It was attractive. *She* was attractive. She had short, curly brown hair and dark-brown eyes. She was a little taller than Hayley and slim.

Her clothes, her shoes, her fanny pack, her whole persona screamed lesbian to Hayley. She could just be friendly, though, and not trying to pick her up. But somehow, Hayley didn't think so. She didn't know why she knew; she just did.

Her adrenaline started to pump. She upped the wattage on her grin and asked,

"Tulip, eh? Why is that?"

"My favorite flower. I could ask you the same question. Why 'Arthur'? It seems rather formal."

"Oh, my friend's a sci-fi fan. It was her favorite writer."

"So he's not your dog?" The curly haired woman tilted her head.

Hayley was embarrassed, as though she'd been caught in a ruse.

"Uh, no. I'm walking him for my roommate."

The woman nodded, seeming intrigued. "I see. So are you walking down or up?"

"Oh. I was going to head back home on this path." She indicated the path down the hill to Stoneman Street and back home. "But I could walk some more. What's your name? I'm Hayley."

"I'm Sherrie. I'm going up the hill. If you want to go, that is?"

"Sure, why not."

They set off back up Bernal Heights Boulevard and started to chat. Sherrie clowned around and played with Arthur. She was funny and irresistibly silly. She bounced up and down, waving her arms, and got both dogs so excited they started to bark. She made faces at them and at Hayley, who couldn't help laughing.

Sherrie resided on the east side of Bernal Hill on Powhattan Street and worked at a South of Market start-up company. They strolled all around the summit, and then Sherrie said, "Well, I've got to go this way. If you want to take another walk sometime, give me a call." She gave Hayley a card, which Hayley accepted, and they said cheerful good-byes and split up.

Hayley practically flew back down the hill. Finally, she'd gotten the connection she wanted, the one Merle had predicted. She couldn't wait to tell her and was disappointed she wasn't at home.

Hayley gave Arthur some fresh water and a cookie, then went upstairs and lay down on her bed to think. Arthur followed her and flopped on the circular rug in her room. It charmed and gratified her that he was so companionable. He clearly adored Merle but had, it seemed, grown to think of her in almost the same way. Merle had told her he was friendly with everyone, unlike some breeds of dogs who were only keyed to one person, their owner.

"Arthur's your basic attention whore," Merle had said, and that had made Hayley laugh, but it was lovely to have him hang around.

She lay down with her arm over her eyes, and Arthur licked her hand as it dangled over the side. She replayed her conversation and walk with Sherrie, thinking about her warm brown eyes and crooked grin. She shivered. She was getting the right signals and finally sending the right ones out. She'd wait a couple days so she didn't seem too eager, then call and ask her out. Sherrie's company wasn't that far from Hayley's law offices in the Financial District, so lunch seemed like a good possibility.

She was startled out of her reverie when Arthur leaped up and ran out of the room. He raced downstairs, his nails chattering on the wood steps. Hayley heard the door close and knew Merle had come home.

She walked down the stairs and saw Merle in the entryway with a very excited Arthur. "Hey."

Merle looked up from greeting Arthur and said, "Hi there. How was the walk?"

"Oh, great. Arthur was a good boy."

"Were you a good boy?" Merle asked him, and he wagged his tail wildly.

"He was a very good boy. Today, he got a nice girl to stop and talk to us." Hayley's grin was triumphant.

"You don't say?" Merle smiled back.

"Absolutely. I'll take him out any time!"

"Of course. And what happened with this girl?"

"I've got her phone number. She invited me to take a dog walk with her."

"What's her name?"

"Sherrie. Sims, I think. I have to look on the card."

"Outstanding. So you're going to call her?" Arthur had rolled over on his back so Merle could rub his belly.

"Yes. I am. She lives over on Powhattan. We met just up at the intersection of our path and Bernal."

"Really? She was on this side of Bernal?"

"Oh, yeah. Why do you ask?"

"It's a hike back around to the other side. Which direction did she come from?"

"I don't know. I was looking at the view, and she said Arthur was a nice dog. She was behind me."

"Oh, okay. Well, sounds good. Hey, I think I might be ready to buy the TV you talked about."

"Hallelujah. She's seen the light." Hayley rolled her eyes

heavenward but beamed at Merle. After a couple of months, Hayley had again broached the subject of maybe, just maybe, they could have a TV. Though Merle wasn't a TV watcher, Hayley had prevailed on her to upgrade to something at least a little bigger and a little better than the old nineteen-inch screen she'd had for years because she watched it so rarely.

"I'll pay for cable," Hayley said. "So what do you think?"

"I'll consider it. You talk so much about movies, you may have changed my mind."

"I hope so." Hayley had even offered to buy the TV, but Merle refused.

"So what's for dinner?"

"I think we have the right stuff for vegetarian marinara and pasta." It was Hayley's turn to cook. They had a system worked out and a grocery budget.

"Can I help you with anything?"

"Nope. Shoo. You can clean up. Though I may let Arthur sit in the kitchen with me."

"Please don't. He'll just get confused."

"Oh, all right. Arthur, you can watch from your spot by the door."

Chapter Eight

Merle went upstairs and sat down at her computer, intending to check the news and read emails until dinner was ready. Instead she wondered about the woman Hayley had met. For someone to be all the way over on the opposite side of Bernal Hill from her house wasn't unheard of, but it was unusual. Who was she, what was her story, and what were her intentions for Hayley?

But she'd encouraged Hayley to take Arthur out for walks specifically so she could meet women, and her suggestion was clearly working. She was hovering and being intrusive and really needed to mind her own business. They *were* becoming closer. They shared dinners a lot of the time, and she planned to let Hayley introduce her to different movies. Well, it was normal roommate stuff, nothing surprising. In addition, after all the horror stories she'd heard, it was a real vindication of her choice. She was blessed by having someone she got along with well and who was pleasant to share space with. Yet this didn't give her permission to get involved in her love life.

Merle counseled herself yet again to remember her boundaries. However, they seemed to be growing weaker little by little, and she felt powerless to stop the process. Well, it was fine. Next week she'd go get the TV and they'd get the cable hooked up as soon as possible. She just needed to stop wondering about Hayley's dates. With that decision made, she was able to get online and stop speculating about Hayley's love life. Hayley would likely tell her about it anyhow.

❖

For their lunch date, Sherrie picked Delancey Street. Sherrie had been late for lunch, which made Hayley anxious, but she'd finally arrived. Once they were seated, all was well.

"What's good here?" Hayley asked as they read their menus.

"Oh, everything. I'm not much for eating out, but I thought this would be nice for us."

"I'm glad you wanted to meet for lunch. Especially glad," Hayley said. She'd wanted to see Sherrie again to see if this was what she thought it was, and so far, it was. Sherrie's dark eyes scrutinized her over the menu, and she kept up her eye contact like Merle had instructed. The effect was mesmerizing. Hayley was growing warm though it wasn't hot in the restaurant. They were seated at a sunny outside table, and the breeze off the Bay kept them cool. The whole scene was perfect. The sun, the glittering San Francisco Bay, lunch with an attractive woman. Nothing was missing. Hayley dared to hope she was finally making some progress.

After their lunch, she and Sherrie walked along the Embarcadero and admired the waterfront, continuing to talk.

"Tell me about your company," Hayley said.

"It's one of those places that sells services online. I do the business-side financial systems."

"That must be fun, to be in a start-up."

"It is. All the kids there are younger than me. I'm the old lady." Sherrie laughed.

"Me too, though the attorneys are all different ages. Some of them are just out of law school. It seems sometimes like they're from another planet." She told Sherrie about Britt.

"Well, getting her perspective is probably good."

"It's eye-opening, I can say that. What's your experience with dating?"

"Up and down. Do you use any of those websites or meet-ups?"

"Oh, sure." Hayley told Sherrie about her meet-up at the art gallery, and Sherrie rolled her eyes.

"You know, in our age range, if someone isn't in a relationship something's most likely wrong with her."

This statement took Hayley aback. Did Sherrie even know how bad that sounded and was she aware that observation could just as easily apply to her? Evidently not. Hayley thought about Merle, which unsettled her. There was nothing at all wrong with Merle. Hayley still didn't know the whole story about Kay, and she might not ever. Merle wasn't into spilling her guts about everything. She must have worked through it all in AA.

But here she was thinking of Merle, again, when she ought to focus on Sherrie, with whom she was on a date and whom, so far, she liked. "Why do you think that? Someone might have lost her lover in an accident or she got sick or whatever."

Sherry waved that possibility away. Whoosh. Gone. "Oh, that. Yeah. I'm not talking about that."

"So what are you talking about?" Hayley liked to get to the bottom of things, which was another reason she wished Merle would tell her more about her and Kay. Her curiosity was at war with her respect for Merle's privacy.

Sherry, on the other hand, had invited the questions by her blanket pronouncement. "You *know.*"

"No, I don't know. That's why I'm asking. People get divorced all the time. Look at me."

"What about you?" Sherrie seized on this info to avoid explaining herself.

"Well, I needed out of the marriage because, well, because I'm a lesbian."

"I figured you're a lesbian. Duh. But you were married? To a guy?"

"Yes, I was. For a long time." At least she was getting this out of the way quickly. Sherry's response would likely predict how their relationship would progress.

"Oh. I see. That's interesting."

"So what do you mean by saying something's wrong with someone who isn't with someone, who's not coupled up after a certain age."

"Oh. I, um. You know. Forget it. It was a stupid generalization." Sherrie was looking at her closely, which was pleasant and flattering. "I'd love to hear more about you."

"Sure. It's not a secret. I got married pretty young and had my son." And Hayley started to tell Sherrie her life story, but they had to get back to work.

Hayley returned to her office feeling good, but something was missing. She still wasn't getting the hit of attraction she got with Merle. She and Sherrie had another date for the weekend. It was finally happening the way she dreamed. She berated herself for being picky. Sherrie had made a silly comment. Who didn't make those on a regular basis? It was nothing to be alarmed about, but she couldn't help wondering if Sherrie's generalization applied to Sherrie herself or not. Well, she'd find out eventually.

When Hayley returned to her office, she Googled the company name Sherrie had given her, but nothing came up. That was odd. She'd likely misheard or misremembered the name. Sherrie's card was a personal one and contained only a phone number and an email address.

❖

"You see how they notice when we're in the room. They're very curious." Merle indicated the white lab rats, who stood with their paws and noses pressed to their plastic cages. They were in the animal room of the Thompson lab, and Merle was training the new postdoc, Anik, on the animal-husbandry routine.

Anik said nothing, He looked around, his face a bored mask.

"I like the rats better than the mice. The mice can be a little cranky and aggressive."

"Is there anything special I need to know about them?"

"Most of the info is in the online class. Their diets and their feeding schedules are all listed here. Change the bedding twice a week. The old stuff goes to biohazard waste. Not because it's harmful. Just because. We can expect a visit soon from the animal regulatory people to check up on us."

Anik shrugged and fingered the corner of one of the cage racks idly. "Isn't the care of the mice the work of the technician?"

"There's no technician. You have to look after your own animals. No one is going to do it for you. That's why I'm explaining all this to you."

The corners of his mouth curved down, but he didn't say anything.

After they de-gowned, they went back to the break room to talk some more. Merle poured a cup of coffee and sat down with Anik at one of the tables. She swept a pile of scientific journals aside. The lab people could be pigs.

"How much progress have you made on the checklist I gave you two weeks ago?" Merle asked. "You need to complete that soon."

"I'm very busy. Collier has given me a list of experiments he expects me to finish."

In her mind, Merle cursed mildly. There it was. The too-busy excuse. The first of many to come, no doubt.

She didn't have a doctorate, that was the problem. Anik was the kind of guy who wouldn't respond unless she had the letters after her name. Well. She couldn't bother Collier with trivial management issues. She always took care of them herself. Anik was just going have to get with the program.

He'd come from Harvard to do two years of postdoctoral work on the way neurons communicate. He'd grown up in India and gone to Oxford for his undergraduate degree. He was smart, handsome, and charming but arrogant. Merle had seen his type and knew what to do, or thought she did. It was a matter of laying the ground rules and letting Anik know she would keep Collier informed of his progress.

❖

Hayley got several hits on her OkCupid profile and figured she might as well go ahead and meet a few of the responders. She winnowed the possibles down to about three and made plans to meet them, trying to resist the temptation to show the profiles to Merle and ask her opinion. It wasn't as though she didn't trust her own instincts, but Merle might be a more astute judge of lesbians than she was. She had to be, right? She'd been at it a lot longer than Hayley.

Hayley shook her head. She'd been sharing the house with Merle for two and a half months. They weren't, in her view, that much closer than when she moved in. It wasn't as though Merle avoided her. She just didn't seem inclined to talk about herself. She was always open to hearing Hayley's questions and concerns. They shared pleasant meals and watched some movies, but she stayed behind an invisible barrier Hayley couldn't seem to penetrate without being too pushy.

She was annoyed with herself that she couldn't just let their relationship be what it was and be happy with it. Well. She couldn't force Merle to be more forthcoming. It was a huge mystery though. She thought about Sherrie's crack about something being wrong with someone who wasn't in a relationship.

That hardly seemed to be the case with Merle. She was obviously sane, intelligent, and kindhearted, and she loved her dog. She was great looking with her silvery hair and eyes that could go from glittering and mischievous to cloudy and sad in an instant. Her strong hands... There went Hayley's overactive libido. God, she really needed to get laid soon. This was ridiculous. But she still needed a second opinion on the OkCupid girls.

She went in search of Merle and found her out in the garden, standing in front of some of the monkey flowers near the back fence. Hayley couldn't see her face, but her body language signaled something was amiss. Her arms were slack at her sides and her shoulders slumped.

"Merle?"

She turned, and her usually smooth features were rumpled. She was flushed and had tears on her cheeks.

"Yeah?" she said, and her voice sounded strangled.

"I'm sorry. I wanted...I thought...What's wrong?" Hayley couldn't quite believe what she was seeing. Her calm, self-contained roommate was a mess.

"Nothing."

Hayley couldn't keep the sarcasm out of her tone. "Yeah. Right. Try again." Merle said no more, and Hayley was dismayed. She didn't want to be unkind.

"Look. Sorry. That came out wrong. You look like you feel terrible. Do you want to talk about it?"

Merle's expression switched to one of surprise, as though she'd only just realized something.

"Put down the rake."

Merle literally dropped her beat-up garden tool she'd been holding loosely.

"Let's go inside and get something to drink. I could use some tea. Then we can talk. Come on."

Hayley held out her hand, and Merle took it and followed her into the house. Arthur had been lying in his corner of the yard and got up and trotted behind them. Hayley didn't let go of Merle's hand, and Merle let herself be drawn into the kitchen. Hayley was curious, but more than that she knew she had to get Merle to talk about what was bothering her. She wanted to understand and be able to comfort her. This suddenly seemed of the utmost importance.

Chapter Nine

Merle was weeding and raking and trimming, not thinking of much of anything beyond vague musings on vegetation she needed to cut back and if she should plant pansies in the fall.

Suddenly out of nowhere, Kay's face popped into her inner eyesight. She was smiling in that soft, dreamy way Merle knew so well, the way she'd looked when she wanted to make love. Merle felt a sweet little rush of longing, and then she remembered and the grief swept in. It was over. It had been over for months, and God damn it, here she was, in the grip of futile memory. Perhaps the memory of something that had never been real. That made her feel worse, made her feel stupid, then regretful.

The tears started. She hadn't cried much since Kay left, a couple of times maybe. This was one of the worst. She stood in her garden, unable to move, pinned in place by despair. *My life is over.* Then she heard Hayley's voice behind her, and it was a powerful jolt of reality. She turned around before she could think about it, and there she was. She was staring at Merle, those brown eyes of hers enormous. When had she gotten such huge, consuming eyes? In a daze, she heard Hayley practically order her to come into the house.

They got some drinks and returned to the backyard to sit by the sundial. Arthur took up a spot close to them, sat down and looked from one to the other, panting, his expression mildly troubled. Hayley sipped her tea and fixed Merle with a stern no-nonsense face.

"So. What's up?"

"Oh, not much. I just got to thinking about my ex."

"Oh?"

"I just got sad is all." Merle was reluctant to talk. It was silly, of course. The only way to get better, to *feel* better was to talk and get out of her head. She'd told many an alcoholic the exact same thing. Why was it so hard to take her own advice? Because it was easier to help someone else. That's why she had people like Sigrid and Clea to talk to. Of course, she wasn't listening to Sigrid's repeated suggestions to get out of herself and at least go out with people. She wasn't yet ready to examine her reluctance too deeply. She could readily attribute it to "just too soon."

"I was feeling sad because of the breakup, and then I was getting angry with myself for feeling sad."

Hayley looked baffled. "You were angry with yourself?"

"For one thing, I'm beating myself up for being such a dope and staying with her when the signs were so clear. And I'm feeling crappy because I miss her."

"You're surely not a dope. You shouldn't feel that way. Why shouldn't you miss her? You were in love with her but she left you. No wonder you're sad."

Merle looked away, then back at Hayley with a tight smile.

"Ah. The 'shoulds,'" Merle said.

Hayley's eyebrows shot up to her hairline. "What does that mean?"

Oops. That wasn't a concept Hayley was familiar with. "All the times we say to ourselves shoulda, woulda, coulda. Regret. Remorse. Shame."

"So? Seems okay to feel that way."

"Yes and no." Merle sighed, pulled her knees up to her chest, then let her legs drop. She turned to face Hayley.

"Look. I've been clean and sober for a lot of years. Although I'm aware that I'm human and make mistakes, I feel like this was one mistake I shouldn't have made. I should have been smarter. I should have realized there was something going on with Kay a lot sooner."

Merle shook her head and grimaced. "There I go, 'shoulding' all over myself."

Hayley laughed. "I think I get it. Not very productive."

"No. And worse, if I stay like this, stewing in the juices of my self-pity, I could start thinking a drink is the answer to my woes."

"I can't see that happening. You're such a strong person."

"Hah. If you only knew." Hayley's conviction was bracing even if she didn't know much about alcoholics.

"She wasn't good for you, was she?"

Boy, was that a tough question to answer. "Yes and no. I thought she was everything I ever wanted, but it seems I was in the grip of delusion, and that's the hardest thing of all to accept."

"Well, it's time to move on." Again, Hayley's assurance was attractive, if naive.

"Acceptance is the key." Merle said that aloud to remind herself, aware that Hayley didn't know the meaning of that phrase either. It was a direct quote from one of AA's most famous stories.

"That sounds like a great idea. I've got another one. Let's make dinner and watch a movie. Can you leave the yard work for now?"

"Sure, no problem." That sounded like such a wonderful idea. Leave the thoughts of Kay and what might have been behind and live in the now. Isn't that what she told every new AA person: "Learn to be in the present"?

"Good. And I want to show you some of the women who've contacted me online and figure out which ones I should email. Okay?"

"Oh, yeah. No problem."

Hayley beamed. "I'll bring my laptop down so we can look at them together." Merle steeled herself to be positive. She owed Hayley her support, and it would be churlish to decline her request for help after how she'd just pulled Merle out of a major funk.

She was unenthusiastic about the idea of looking over the pictures and personal information of a collection of strange lesbians whose goals in life were to get into Hayley's jeans and/or marry her. Like Anik, she needed to get with the program and be helpful. That was what she did; she was helpful and supportive.

Chapter Ten

While they were fixing dinner and looking at OkCupid profiles, Hayley's email pinged. It was from Sherrie. Another one. She frowned and blew out a breath.

Merle was standing at the stove, and she turned around, eyebrow cocked. "Something wrong?"

"Nope. It's just that woman I had lunch with a couple weeks ago."

"And?"

"I don't know. I was debating about what to do, and the next day she emailed me this long, long message. It just went on and on about how much we had in common and how much fun lunch was. I thought lunch was okay. Just okay. Then I couldn't find the name of her company on the net."

Merle was stirring soup and looked at Hayley, seeming concerned. "So you want to see her again?"

"I don't know. She was nice and all but..." Hayley struggled with how to articulate what was bugging her. She wasn't all that into Sherrie. She seemed fine but something seemed off. She was likely just being too picky.

"I think you can exercise your own judgment. If it's not there, it's not there."

Hayley wanted to be that decisive. "I don't want to dismiss someone because she's not perfect."

"And just who, missy, is perfect?" Merle was playful. Her earlier despondence had disappeared. "Besides you and me."

Hayley grinned. "No one, of course. But seriously, I think I might be dismissing her too quickly."

"So email her back and go on another date."

"Right. You're right. I need you to help me. I really do. I don't know how to date women."

"It's confusing sometimes but it's not that hard. At least how I remember. I've been out of circulation for a long time. Dating is more like cooking really." Merle put a lid on the soup pot, lowered the heat, and turned around to lean against the kitchen counter. She flipped her wooden spoon back and forth.

"You have to have the right mixture of ingredients, the right spices. You can't cook it too long or you'll ruin it. You can't make it work if things aren't balanced or the ingredients aren't the correct ones to begin with."

"I'm not sure I follow you." Hayley thought she did follow actually, but she wanted Merle to keep talking because she enjoyed listening to her; she liked the way her mind worked. She was logical and sensible and down-to-earth.

"Hmm. Well, you have to have the flavors that complement each other. Like salty and tangy. You don't want too much salt or too much sugar or too much acid. The other woman's personality has to complement yours."

"Oh, like you and me. I'm more talkative, you're quieter. I'm anxious, you're a go-with-the-flow type."

"Um, yeah, sort of. I guess I wouldn't use the two of us as an example because we're just friends. You can have compatibility but not have that, you know, sexual spark. The romantic attraction."

To Hayley's surprise, Merle blushed.

"So without that…you, eh. Well, the dish might taste okay, but it's not going to last." Merle's voice trailed off. What was she thinking about? Herself and Kay?

"I'm afraid your analogy fell apart there."

"No. It's valid. Lots of women get together and think they've got it, but all they've got is a good friendship. Emotional compatibility but no sex."

"Really? That happens?"

"Oh yeah. A lot. Then the person finds a new woman and cheats on her lover and goes off with the new girl."

"No! Yuck."

"Serial monogamy. It's kind of a game."

"Now I'm truly scared of dating."

"Don't be. It's not always like that. My friends Sigrid and Clea have it all. They're totally compatible. They work."

"Yes, I could see that." But Hayley didn't want to hear about Sigrid and Clea just then. She wanted to know why Merle had suddenly gotten so embarrassed but didn't want to come right out and ask. Instead she said, "Look at this one." She moved the laptop around and pointed to the picture of a vivacious-looking woman who had soft, light-brown hair and was clearly mature.

Hayley read the profile out loud. "I'm a dreamer and thinker. I love nature and travel. I can be serious but I like to laugh."

She looked at Merle, who'd crossed her arms with the wooden spoon still clutched in her hand. She looked as though she was ready to do battle. But with whom?

Merle shrugged. "Why not? What have you got to lose?"

❖

Merle went out with Arthur to let him pee before they went to bed. He wandered his backyard sniffing here and there and took his time about it.

She brooded. It was crazy to react the way she had during her little speech to Hayley about the similarities between love and women and cooking.

The problem was, something *was* going on with her. Every time she saw Hayley, she caught her breath. She didn't have to manufacture excuses to spend time with her because they already spent a great deal of time together. She stared at Hayley when she wasn't looking, focusing on her face or the way her hair swept her collar and how she always unconsciously tucked it behind her ear. She noticed the way Hayley walked, the way she sat. She was graceful and at home in her body, which was just curvaceous enough. Her breasts were a perfect size 36C. Merle had actually looked at one of her bras in the laundry room and then felt terrible but secretly vindicated because that was the size she'd guessed.

She couldn't detect anything like this going on with Hayley. The worst was how grouchy she felt when Hayley was talking about her dates. She took special pains to hide this horribly juvenile reaction, for her own sake as well as Hayley's. No amount of self-talk seemed to make it go away though.

"Arthur. Come *on*." Now she was getting cranky with Arthur because he took too long for his business. Sheesh. She was a head case. Hayley kept coming to her and either asking for help or being helpful. It was wonderful yet insane. She was the opposite of Kay; every emotion was on the surface. So if that was true, it followed that if Hayley was attracted to her, she'd show it, wouldn't she? Merle couldn't answer that question to her satisfaction. And, even if it were true, they were never going anywhere so it was all fruitless speculation. Arthur finally came trotting over, quite pleased with himself because he'd accomplished his mission.

The living room was quiet and empty. Hayley had gone upstairs to bed. After she locked the doors and turned out all the lights, Merle trudged up the stairs, her thoughts about Hayley still swirling.

❖

For her date with the "dreamer/thinker" brunette, Hayley chose a simple, low-impact milieu: a walk in Golden Gate Park. They arranged to meet at the Children's Carousel.

Their profile pictures made it easy to locate one another in the crowd. After they shook hands and introduced themselves, Hayley suggested they sit for just a moment and plan which direction to take for their walk. She'd thought of a couple of questions she could ask to help them overcome their discomfort and start talking.

Mona was her name, and other than the fact that her profile picture was clearly outdated, she was as advertised.

"Did you like merry-go-rounds when you were a kid?" Hayley asked. They were sitting on a bench just outside of the park's vintage nineteenth-century carousel.

Mona's eyes lit up like she was a ten-year-old on Christmas morning. "Oh yes. They were my *all-time* favorites. You know, we lived on the east side of Pittsburgh and there's a great amusement park there, Kennywood Park. Have you heard of it?"

"I—"

"We always went there for our school picnics, every year in May. They gave us the day off and everything. I went on all the rides twice and maybe four times on the merry-go-rounds 'cause they were the best. One year, I got a plantar's wart and it hurt like hell to walk around, but I didn't let that stop me, no way. I was hetero in those days so you know I was always plotting to be with some boy in my class. My senior year I was stuck on Rob Jones. Boy, was he ever the cutest…"

Hayley lost the train of conversation even though she tried hard to follow. She couldn't say a thing and gave up trying until Mona, at last, stopped for breath.

"Let's go this way," Hayley suggested and led them past the bocce ball courts and toward Kennedy Drive. They were in front of a sign that read NATIONAL AIDS MEMORIAL GROVE.

Hayley interrupted Mona mid-sentence to ask, "How about we walk down here?" She indicated the path that led downward to a concave area.

"Oh. All right." Hayley thought she detected a note of negativity, but it was likely just because she'd interrupted the flow of Mona's words.

They walked to a small area lined with stones, names engraved in many of them.

"In the law office where I got my first job," Hayley said, "a lawyer, one of the partners, got AIDS. He would struggle to come to work when I could tell he didn't feel well, and then he stopped showing up. We went to his memorial, which was one of the saddest things I ever experienced. Such a waste. I knew a couple of other people, but they were—"

"I don't like to think about it." Mona's eyes were narrowed and her lips a straight line. "It was their own fault. They ought to have known better. It wasn't something women would have ever gotten. We just got caught up in the anti-gay hysteria. I don't know why lesbians even bothered getting involved. They were so misogynistic, they wouldn't have done a thing if it was us…"

Hayley was too stunned to even try to interrupt that monologue. Mona was pretty, enthusiastic and, it seemed, gainfully employed. However, Hayley wondered how her coworkers in the investment office where she worked coped with her conversational style.

They made an hour's circuit and ended up back at the carousel, where they made their good-byes.

"I'll give you a call," Hayley said.

"Thanks. I really enjoyed myself. I'd love to see you again."

Hayley wondered how Mona had reached that conclusion. She knew more than she wanted to know about her, but what Mona had learned about her was minimal.

When she was home and Merle returned, she said, "I can't wait to tell you about this one."

"I have to do some weeding." Merle looked at Hayley with a question in her eyes.

"Oh sure, yeah. Let me help you." They went to work on the foxtails that threatened to crowd out the flowers.

Hayley told Merle about the date with Mona, and she chuckled. "Must be a nervous reaction."

"Oh, do you think that's it?"

"Might be." Merle stabbed her spade viciously at a stalk of thistle.

"Well. I liked her. She seemed nice, but Lord, the stream-of-consciousness talking."

"So you've had three dates. The walker, Terry, and now the talker, Mona. What about Sherrie?"

"I don't know. She wants to go out with me again, but I can't decide if I want to. She's nice enough but there's just something off. Maybe I'll see her again. What do you think?"

Merle wiped her forehead with the back of her arm. It was warm in the backyard in the late afternoon, and she was flushed. Hayley liked the look of the color in Merle's cheeks. And her slightly tousled hair had sweaty ends. Merle was quieter than usual, though. What was she thinking? She waited, watching Merle closely.

"I think," Merle paused and stuck her hoe in the dirt before answering, "you should do what you believe is right for you."

This wasn't what Hayley wanted to hear. She wanted Merle to tell her positively either not to see Sherrie or to see her. Merle's tone was off. She wasn't super-expressive in normal circumstances, but now she was speaking in a monotone.

"I'm asking *you* for your opinion."

"I generally don't offer opinions or give advice. What if I'm wrong?"

"What if you are?" Hayley was being a pill but she truly wanted to know.

"Look. If you're not sure, why not just go out with her again and see what happens?"

"Right. That wasn't too difficult to say, was it? Thank you. I appreciate your feedback. I really do. Now, what can I do to help?"

"If you'd like, start taking out that bitter cress over there. Here's the hoe."

❖

Hayley was in the kitchen fixing dinner when Merle's cell rang in the living room and Merle picked up.

Merle didn't go up to her bedroom to talk but instead stayed on the couch. Hayley knew she shouldn't listen, but she couldn't help it.

"Oh. Yeah. I'm glad you called. How're you doing?" A pause as she listened to the person on the other end.

"Uh-huh. I know…That is pretty awful. It's a sad truth that when we first get sober we don't necessarily get peace. Instead we get a whole lot more chaos. Is he still drinking?"

She was talking to someone in AA, someone evidently in trouble.

"You are not at fault for this. He's going to do what he's going to do. Your first priority is taking care of yourself. Are you afraid you're going to drink?" Another long pause.

"Do you have a safe place you can go?" Pause. "Good." Pause. "Think through the drink." Merle laughed.

Such levity in the midst of what sounded like a tense situation surprised Hayley.

"Oh. It means that you picture the steps that follow that first drink. You have the second, and then pretty soon you're on the tenth. Then you're online to cruise for sex, and then you get high and then you maybe have unsafe sex. Then the hangover. Yada yada. You get the picture." She laughed again. Hayley surmised she was talking to a gay guy.

"Right. Go into the guest room. Close the door. Read your big book. Do the next right thing." Pause. "Yes. I swear it will pass." Pause. "Oh, already? Good. See? Gone. For now." Pause. "Yes. Of course. Call me whenever. I'll see you at the meeting on Tuesday."

While they ate their dinner, they stuck to innocuous, general subjects. Merle seemed calmer and smiled a few times, but Hayley still wondered. She wanted to ask what was wrong, but that would be intrusive. She'd grown so fond of Merle and her quiet persona that hid so much strength and compassion. The tenderness in her voice and the wisdom of her words to the person on other end of the phone greatly moved her. How could someone so loving lose the love of her partner? How could she live without love now?

Hayley longed to ask her those, along with many other, questions, but she wanted to be sure the questions would be welcome. How wonderful it must be to be loved by Merle. Hayley would never have the answer to that question, and she had to stop thinking about or speculating about Merle or she'd lose her mind.

She booted up her laptop and emailed Sherrie, suggesting a movie and coffee or a drink after the following week. She got an answer almost immediately, which startled her. Sherrie's email was effusive, going on in detail about how happy she was to hear from Hayley and how fun it would be to get together and so forth. Hayley wrote a short note back, asking Sherrie to pick a couple of movies, and then she logged off, again feeling a little uneasy, but she tamped the sensation down.

❖

Merle rinsed and put the dishes in the dishwasher and then turned to the pots, which she always washed by hand. She turned over the conversation with Hayley in her mind. Hayley was far too sensitive not to notice how quiet and unengaged she'd become. She simply didn't want to discuss with Hayley the women she was dating. She couldn't say anything about how she felt. She was veering very close to having a huge crush on Hayley, and that was crazy. She scrubbed savagely at the pan Hayley had used to make fried rice. Crazy was the only word for it, and she'd have to do something soon. She was praying for release and for acceptance, but it wasn't working.

She turned on the water full blast to rinse the soap away and stared out the window over her sink into the backyard. Feeling something cold on her left foot, she looked down and discovered she was standing in a pool of water, so she turned the tap off quickly. She didn't seem to have splashed water out of the sink, but it was all over the floor and dripping from the cabinet. Annoyed and somewhat anxious, she pulled the cabinet doors open and peered under the sink. The water was dripping from the pipe, just above the joint.

Shit. It must have sprung a leak. She'd have to call a plumber, damn it.

It was Sunday night, which would mean overtime. The plumber charged two hundred dollars just to walk through the door. Merle strode into the laundry room and found some old dog towels and started packing them around the items under the sink and spreading them on the floor to soak up the water. Then she remembered that Hayley had told her she could do basic home repairs. Merle hoped this qualified as "basic." She ran upstairs and knocked on her bedroom door.

When Hayley opened it, she looked upset, and Merle wanted to ask her why, but she had a more important issue.

"Hey. Sorry to bother you, but I think the kitchen sink's leaking."

"Uh, sure, I'll be right down." Hayley turned away, muttering something about where she might have stored her tools.

Merle pulled all the junk out from under the sink and located her strongest, brightest flashlight. Hayley appeared a few minutes later with a large metal box in her hand.

"Can I have the flashlight? Go ahead and turn the water on—not too fast."

"Right. How's this?"

Hayley was down on her hands and knees halfway into the cabinet. The flashlight roamed. "Okay. Turn it off!" She backed out and stood up.

"How old's the pipe?"

"Lord. I have no idea."

"Well, these things rust and get fragile over time, especially if you cook with a lot of lemon. The acid eats away the metal. But they just get worn out as well."

"Hmm. Kay went through a long phase of eating fish cooked in lemon a couple years back."

"There you go."

"Can you fix it?"

"Yeah, but I need to go get a new pipe fitting. See this part..." Hayley motioned for Merle to lean into the cabinet. They were side by side, kneeling on the floor, their shoulders touching. Their heads were so close, Merle could smell her shampoo, some sort of lavender-scented thing, and a wisp of Hayley's hair brushed her cheek. She held her breath and tried to concentrate as Hayley pointed out where the pipe was leaking.

"It needs a new U-trap. We can get one at a hardware store if we can find one open. Oh. Home Depot—right? That's open like every day till midnight, right?"

"Yeah, I guess. I don't know for sure."

"I'll call but I'm pretty sure. Let's go."

"You want to go now?"

"Sure. Unless you want to wait until tomorrow? We need the kitchen sink, don't we? You don't want to rinse dishes in the laundry room."

"No. Let's just do it."

"Great. Hold the flashlight while I take this one off so I can make sure I get the exact size." That process took a while and featured a lot of cursing and grunting on Hayley's part until she finally got it loose.

They drove a few minutes south on the freeway to Home Depot, where Hayley located the correct pipe, and were back home in under an hour. Merle found another flashlight while Hayley took off her sweatshirt. Merle gulped. Hayley was wearing a fairly tight T-shirt and had evidently been ready to go to sleep because she wasn't wearing a bra. Merle pictured what her breasts would look like and swallowed.

Hayley lay on her back with a sofa pillow underneath to support her neck and laboriously screwed the new pipe into place. Merle knelt next to her, holding the flashlight. Hayley's T-shirt came untucked, and her smooth stomach was inches away from Merle's nose. She lay with her legs propped up but slightly akimbo.

Merle could hear her breathing hard from the effort of screwing the pipe into place, and she started to perspire herself from watching Hayley. She visualized Hayley in the same position except naked and in bed as Merle bent over her and pushed her legs apart. Her thighs were the same creamy color as her abdomen. Merle kissed the inside of one leg, then the other and—

"I think that's it," Hayley said as her arms dropped to her sides and she exhaled loudly.

"Great." Merle tried to keep her voice from shaking.

Hayley slid out from the cabinet and sat up. The moment was

over. She grinned cockily at Merle and said, "So turn on the water and let's check!"

"Right." Merle obeyed and they both watched the pipe, flashlights in hand.

"Looks okay," Merle said. "You're a genius!"

"Hardly. It's plumbing 101." But she looked pleased with herself, which made Merle want to kiss her.

Instead, she stood up and offered Hayley a helping hand. Hayley hauled herself up from the floor, and their hands stayed clasped for just a moment. Hayley's hand was very warm but only a little damp from her efforts.

"Whew. The contortions you have to go through get harder the older I get."

"You're amazing."

"You're nice to say so." They stared at one another for another moment. Then Hayley said, "Guess I'll go to bed now."

"Yep. Good night and thanks again."

Merle cleared up the mess in the kitchen, replaced the items under the sink, and hung the wet towels on the back-porch railing.

She shivered. She'd been millimeters away from making a pass. She wasn't sure which would bother her more: Hayley rejecting her or the opposite. This was a very bad situation, and she had to figure out what the hell she was going to do about it.

❖

The next day at work, Hayley gave up trying to concentrate on the case research she was trying to perform. She slammed the huge law book shut and put her head in her hands. She pictured Merle's smiling face and replayed the night before. When she'd finished her plumbing task and her gaze had met Merle's, she saw that look again. That longing, yearning, hungry look like Merle was just about to grab her and pull her into a passionate embrace. If she'd done that, Hayley would have been right there with her, never mind the consequences. She didn't know what to do. If she was wrong, she'd likely get shown the door. If she was right and they acted on their feelings, it could all go very wrong. It was making her nuts. She had no stomach, essentially, for dating other women. She knew, as well as she knew the color of her son's hair, she had already met the right woman. She slept across the hall, ate across from Hayley at the kitchen table, and sat next to her on the couch. They walked on Bernal Hill with Arthur and laughed at TV comedies.

Except she was off-limits.

Hayley put her head on the table and bumped it, not too hard. Then she got up and paced around the law library. This was maddening. When she took Merle's hand last night, hers had begun to tingle and she had little frissons of sensation in *that* place. That's what her mother used to call it. She was getting the same feelings just thinking about holding Merle's hand.

Hayley looked at her phone and concluded it was soon enough to take lunch. Back at her desk, she opened her personal email and was confronted with a lengthy missive from Sherrie going on and on about movies and cafés and her anticipation of their next date and their fabulous connection. Hayley decided she wouldn't answer. She was getting more uneasy. It was always bad news when the other person was more invested than you were. She was beginning to regret making this date.

❖

Merle pushed her chair away from her workstation and walked into the lab. There, she moved her shoulders around, trying to get them to relax. She decided to go open some boxes that had been delivered and get off the computer for a while. Health and Safety had directed everyone to sign up for a new program to get issued their lab gear. It had taken forever to get Collier through his part, and then she had to nag and cajole the rest of the group, all fifteen of them, into getting online and watching a video and getting organized. Anik would be the last one. She didn't want to have to remind him again, but she'd probably have to.

She sighed. The job was wearing her down. She'd been through the same thing so many times. The cast of characters changed but the play never did. She was growing more impatient with it, probably because her unsettled thoughts about Hayley had raised her stress level She ought to have a talk with Hayley and ask her to move out, but she'd have to tell her the reason. It would be dishonest and hurtful not to. She couldn't abide the thought of hurting Hayley's feelings even if it was for the good of both of them.

The logical thing would be to discuss the situation with her AA sponsor, but she didn't have one. She didn't really need one since she'd been sober a long time and had worked the steps, as well as still going to meetings. She had Sigrid and Clea and others to talk to. She could write about it and then talk to Sigrid. But if she talked to Sigrid, she'd get Sigrid's point of view, which seemed to boil down to "I told you so," likely followed by "Go for it." She didn't want to hear either nugget of advice, but she didn't have much choice.

Having all this crap in her head was driving her batty. The thought of a drink had even flitted into her consciousness and then rapidly out again, thank God. But this wasn't a good sign. She hadn't considered drinking while she was breaking up with Kay. She had a problem and needed to deal with it. She supposed it would be better if she had a heart-to-heart with Hayley, but that didn't seem to be a good first step. Maybe later. First, she needed to talk to Sigrid.

CHAPTER ELEVEN

Hayley was finally on her way to Concord to visit her mom, and today was the day she'd spill the beans about her new sexual orientation. She didn't think she ought to wait until she'd fallen in love with someone and then take her to meet her mother. *Mom, guess what?* That would be too late. Though, at this rate, it might never happen, anyway, Hayley thought. She navigated the traffic on the Bay Bridge and planned her speech. Her mom would give her a helpful opening because she would want to know how Hayley was faring after her divorce. She thought about Sigrid's warning, which made her uneasy.

The sight of her mom and dad's suburban ranch house reminded her how different her life was now. She opened the front door, calling, "Mom?" Ellie had grown a bit hard of hearing. She was out on the terrace. Hayley walked through the living room and dining room and opened the sliding-glass door. Ellie jumped.

"Mom. It's just me."

"Oh, honey, I must have dozed off." Hayley kissed her on the forehead.

"No worries. I let myself in. Is there any iced tea?"

"Yes, dear. You want anything to eat? I can make you a sandwich."

"Nope. Sit. I just want a glass of tea. I'll get it."

She found the pitcher in the fridge and a glass, then looked around the kitchen critically. It didn't seem to be as pristine as it usually was. Maybe it was time to get Ellie some household help. If she'd accept it, that is.

Back on the terrace, she flopped into one of the deck chairs, dumping her purse on the floor after she retrieved her sunglasses. October's sun was still bright.

"Hayley. It's good to see you, dear. You're looking well. Have you been outdoors?"

"Yeah. Some. I walk my roommate's dog a lot."

"Are you remembering to wear sunscreen?"

Right. She was old enough to be a grandma, and her mom was still asking her about sunscreen. Guess mothers never grew out of mothering, although she really endeavored not to nag Robbie about his personal habits. It was so annoying.

"Yes. Yes, I do. What have you been up to?"

"Oh, this and that." Her mother gestured vaguely.

"Have you been walking a bit every day like the doctor said? To keep your arthritis at bay?"

"Oh, trying to, honey. It's hard."

"I know, Mom, but you have to or you'll get so stiff you won't be able to move." Hayley was stalling, trying to delay the inevitable time when she'd have to say what she'd come to say. She was dreading it. She chatted on about trivia, and finally her mother got to the question.

"So, dear, what have you been up to? You've lived in that house for what? Three months?"

"About that."

"Work okay?"

"Sure, it's fine. We got a new case—age discrimination." This made Hayley think of Angie. She and her brother hadn't come in for a meeting since the first conference. It was almost as though Hayley really needed Angie to distract her from her feelings for Merle. Thinking of any of her other dates didn't seemed to be working. Mona was off the list. She had no idea what was going to happen with Sherrie, and anything with Angie would be far in the future and was mostly a fantasy anyhow. It was sort of funny—she was going to disclose her sexual orientation to her mom but didn't even have anyone in her life. Except Merle, who was just a friend.

Her mind had wandered again. She had to refocus. She'd missed a question from her mom.

"Hayley, dear? I asked if you had any men friends." That was Ellie's way of saying boyfriends. It was more accurate, Hayley supposed. She was a touch old for boyfriends.

"Nope. I don't, Mom. I don't expect I ever will."
Ellie looked shocked. "Oh, dear. Don't say that. It isn't true. You're still young. It's too bad it didn't work out with Howard, but never mind. Can't your friends help you meet someone?"

Yes. She hoped they would, but not the kind of someone her mother was talking about.

"Mom. I need to tell you something." Suddenly, she had so much adrenaline in her system, her head started to pound and her mouth went dry.

"What's wrong, honey? Do you need money?"

"No, no," Hayley said. "I'm fine. Do you know why Howard and I got a divorce?"

Ellie looked clueless. "Not exactly. You told me you just drifted apart. You never talked anymore or did anything together."

"All that's true but there's more to it."

"Certainly, there is. These things are complicated."

"Mom, mainly I divorced Howard because I'm a lesbian."

"What?"

Oh, great, now she was *pretending* to be hard of hearing.

"A lesbian." She let it sink in. Meanwhile, she caught her mom's eye and held it.

"I don't understand," Ellie said, finally. "How could that be true? You're fifty-four!"

As if being a lesbian came with an age requirement.

"Mom. Let me try to explain."

Ellie nodded silently. She looked shell-shocked and confused.

"It was always true. I was always attracted to women but thought it was just a passing thing. An anomaly." That was true. She *had* thought that. "I thought I loved Howard so I said 'yes' when he asked me to marry him and one thing led to another and we had Robbie and I was busy with him and with work…" It sounded pretty silly the way she was describing it. She was going to have to be more convincing. "Something happened to me."

"What happened to you?" Ellie's tone was so alarmed, it sounded as though she thought what happened was "I was hit by a bus" or "I have cancer."

"The details aren't important." She refused to tell her mother about Sabine and the bathroom at Boulevard.

"I realized I was lying to myself and wasn't being fair to Howard. I didn't love him anymore. I truly prefer women. So that makes me a lesbian."

"Huh" was all Ellie said for a few minutes. "So if you are, do you have, uh, someone?"

Ellie was trying to ask her if she had a girlfriend. Again, she was too old for girlfriends. What term should she use? "No. Not at the moment."

"Then how do you know—"

"I just know, Mom. Trust me." Hayley was irritable now. This conversation was, of all things, reminding her just how unlesbian she really was. She hadn't actually done it with anyone. But she wasn't prepared to discuss that point with her mom.

"I can't say as I approve."

"*Mom.* There's nothing to approve or disapprove. It just is."

"But you'll get in trouble at work. People don't accept that sort of thing."

"That's not true anymore. Maybe here in Concord but not in San Francisco. It's fine. I've always worked with gay people. Some of the lawyers at our firm are gay. We do employment law. Our clients are gay." If all that was true, why was she so reluctant to come out at work?

"Well, I know things are different now, a lot different. I never gave it any thought, you know. I'm not prejudiced. I just never expected it in my family."

There it was. She was okay with it in the abstract, but when it came to Hayley, not so much.

"Well, things are way different even from when I was young, Mom. So you don't need to worry about my livelihood or anything like that. It's fine. You should be concerned with my happiness."

"I suppose." She sounded dubious, like she'd still like to be concerned about Hayley's social standing. Or something.

"It's true. I want to be happy. You want me to be happy, right?"

"Of course, dear. But how can you possibly find happiness this way?"

"Well. I think I fall in love with someone and that will make me happy. That's the way it usually works."

"There's no need to be sarcastic."

"Sorry, Mom. And sorry I had to just drop this on you. I didn't know what else to do."

"No. I appreciate you telling me."

"I'm going to let you be with it for a while. Kind of absorb it, and then I'll come back again. Maybe I'll bring Robbie with me." She'd like that. Ellie adored her grandson.

"What does *he* think of all this? About his mother being a—"

"Lesbian, Mom. You can say it."

"I know. Did you think of Robbie when you decided this?" Uh-oh. She was pissed. Time to go. This was predictable. Her mom was old-fashioned and thought of everything in terms of how it affected the men in her life. As far as Ellie was concerned, feminism didn't have the slightest effect on things.

"You know, you and he can talk about that. Why don't you call him?"

"I might do that. Well, this has been quite a visit."

Hayley took her mother's hands and looked her straight in the eye. "It's going to be fine."

Hayley was trying to convince her mother, but she was really trying to convince herself.

❖

She told Merle about the big talk with her mother.

Merle shook her head. "It's still a problem for some people, I guess. Even in 2015. Even with marriage equality and everything else."

"She lives a sheltered life out there in the distant East Bay."

"Give her time. She'll come around. I guess this isn't easy for parents no matter what age you are."

"What was it like when you told your parents?"

"Shock and awe before Rumsfeld invented the concept."

"And after a while?"

"They got over it. They loved Kay. That's another ironic thing. Kay and my folks got along great."

"Well, that's good to know. I'm sending my son to wrangle her. She'll hear stuff easier from him."

"Isn't that the way it always works?" Merle grinned. "So. I think it's time for chili for dinner. It's autumn, and that makes me think of soup and chili."

Hayley felt calmer now that she was home and had talked to Merle about her big announcement to her mother, though she still had the issue of her feelings about Merle. Her mother would get used to her "new" orientation, but she wasn't sure she'd ever get over having to keep her feelings about Merle under wraps.

She toyed with the idea of just talking to Merle about it. They could be adults. They could be honest with each other. Maybe it would be better then. That was an idea, but she had to screw up the courage to say something. And find the right time, whatever time that was going to be.

❖

A few nights later, at dinner, Hayley said, "I'm going out with Sherrie and I'm going to decide for sure if I want to keep seeing her or I'm going to tell her we aren't going forward."

"That sounds good." After a small smile and brief eye contact, Merle directed her gaze at her plate.

"The emails I get from her are so over the top, and I just can't get that interested."

"Yeah. You ought to let her know."

Hayley waited for Merle to say more, but she said nothing.

"Is something wrong?" Hayley asked. Merle wasn't the most voluble person, but this evening she was obviously withdrawn again and it bugged Hayley.

There was the tiniest pause and Merle made eye contact. Hayley tried to discern what she was thinking, but it was impossible. Merle's blue-gray irises were impenetrable. Her body language was giving off stay-back signals.

"No. There's nothing wrong. Really." She put her fork down. "I'm fine."

"You'd tell me, wouldn't you? If it had something to do with me?"

"Of course."

"Well. Okay. I don't want you to ever feel like you can't be honest. I want us to be okay." Hayley reached out and put her hand over Merle's. Merle's hand and arm went rigid.

"Yeah. Sure. I know. Don't worry." She looked as though she wanted to leap out of the chair and run from the room. She jerked her hand back. Hayley didn't know how she could do anything but worry. But in the meantime, she had her date with Sherrie.

❖

"There's a place in Bernal Heights we could go for coffee," Hayley said.

"I'd prefer a drink right now, if it's okay with you." Sherrie's eyes shone in the dark. At their first meeting on Bernal Hill, they'd been sparkling and merry but now looked sinister, maybe a little crazy. They were walking toward Sherrie's car in the Stonestown United Artists movie-theater parking lot. Despite her misgivings, Hayley had given in and let Sherrie drive. If she got stuck somehow, she could get a cab. She was likely being overanxious.

"Sure. That's fine." Hayley got the sinking feeling Sherrie wanted to get a few drinks in her so she'd be more amenable for whatever Sherrie had planned. They drove to the Castro District and then spent an agonizing fifteen minutes finding a parking space.

Sherrie got very impatient. "This makes me so crazy. Why can't they put in more parking?"

Hayley wondered just precisely where those new parking spaces would go. "Well. You know, it's Friday night and a lot of people are out."

"Yeah. Guys picking up guys."

Hayley didn't know what she meant by that other than the obvious.

When they walked from their car over to Twin Peaks, Sherrie took Hayley's hand. She wanted to snatch it away but counseled herself to be patient.

The Twin Peaks Tavern certainly wasn't a cruisy bar since the median age of the clientele was at least fifty. They had to sit close together in the crowd, and Sherrie took full advantage of their proximity, touching Hayley's leg and pushing her breasts against her arm.

"I'd like to leave now," Hayley said when she saw Sherrie was on her third drink.

"Sure, can I finish?" Sherrie held up her glass and pointed.

Hayley nodded and sighed. She should have driven herself

because she was going to be trapped in a small car with a half-drunk woman who was trying to seduce her. This was definitely *not* how she'd expected things to go. The sophisticated romantic scenes in *The L Word* she'd imagined for herself seemed in another universe.

She supposed she should be happy that Sherrie wasn't falling-down drunk. They walked the several blocks between the bar and where they'd parked. It was up a pretty big hill, but Hayley walked as quickly as she could manage. She just wanted to go home, but she still had to break that news to Sherrie and doubted it would be well received.

As they drove from the Castro District to Bernal Heights, Hayley picked Sherrie's hand up from her thigh and replaced it on the steering wheel.

"You're pretty safety conscious, aren't ya?" Sherrie asked with a little bit of an edge.

"Yep," Hayley said, keeping her eyes forward.

"Come on. Live a little. It's Friday night in San Francisco. We just saw a great movie." Sherrie's car, a Mini Cooper, careened around the corners and up and down the various hilly streets between the Castro and Bernal Heights.

Hayley looked out the window over at the lights twinkling and in the distance the dark shadow of San Bruno Mountain as they drove down Cortland Avenue.

"Turn here."

All too swiftly, they were in front of the homey Craftsman house. Hayley wondered if Merle was home. It was likely she was.

"So?" Sherrie said, her arm draped over the seat back behind Hayley's head.

"So." Hayley gathered her wits and attempted to form sentences that would be clear without being cruel.

"Are you going to ask me in?" Sherrie asked, her tone arch and seductive.

"No. I'm not. Look. I've had a good time, but I don't think we quite have the chemistry."

"Aw, sure we do. I can feel it…" Sherrie leaned toward her, and Hayley put a hand on her chest, at her collarbone to fend off the assault.

"I'm sorry, Sherrie. We can be friends but that's it."

Sherrie slumped back in her seat. Even in the dark, Hayley could see the pout. It was unattractive, especially for a woman of their age.

"Huh. I could have sworn. Well, fine." She turned the key in the ignition.

"Thanks for a nice evening. I really enjoyed your company. Good night."

"Yeah. Good night." She sounded depressed. Hayley felt a little bad but not enough to change her mind.

Hayley said to herself as she walked up to the front porch, "Phew. Dodged a bullet there." She went inside, hoping Merle was awake and felt like talking. But when she climbed the stairs to the porch, the house was dark. Hayley let herself in and, after getting a glass of water, walked past Merle's closed bedroom door to her own room and got ready for bed, disappointed.

❖

"Thanks for coming out to coffee with me," Merle said as she watched Sigrid stir soymilk into her cup. Sigrid nodded and smiled vaguely but said nothing. Merle knew she was waiting for her to start talking about what was bothering her. Sigrid never tried to drag confessions out of her.

"Promise you won't tease me, please. I'm serious this time." Merle flicked her eyebrows, and Sigrid nodded with a straight face. Merle sighed deeply and stirred her own coffee, attempting to frame what she wanted to say so it would be truthful but not too incriminating.

She wanted help but didn't want to look silly. Typical. She wanted Sigrid to hear about what she'd been obsessing about for the last month. She wanted to confess, more or less, and get the truth out there, just to get it out of her head. But she also needed Sigrid's insight. For all her teasing, she was the one person who could help her sort out her dilemma.

"First off, you were right. I've got a thing for Hayley."

"A *thing*?" Sigrid's lips moved just a smidge, as though she was trying not to burst out laughing. Her ice-blue eyes sparkled. "What kind of a *thing*? A love *thing* or a sex *thing*?"

"I don't know. Maybe both." Merle took a gulp of coffee. She thought about and quickly dismissed the idea of a scone. Caffeine was good enough. She didn't need a hit of sugar though she desperately wanted one. An orange scone would be just right, though.

"Huh. Have you said anything?"

"No!"

"Why not? Are you afraid she'll run screaming from the room and then move out?"

"I doubt she'd scream. She may move out. If I were her, I wouldn't want to share a house with someone who had the hots for me."

"Isn't that what Kay did for years?"

"*Sigrid.* You promised."

"All right, that's true. Sorry. I won't say anything else like that."

"Thanks. I'm serious here. I think she knows something's up, but I don't want to tell her."

"Why not?"

Merle couldn't help it; she rolled her eyes. "Oh, please. Number one, she doesn't feel the same. Number two, she's just coming out, and I don't want anything to do with that. Number three, we've got a great relationship. We get along. I don't want to have to find someone else if she moves."

Sigrid narrowed her eyes, scrutinizing Merle. "Let me ask you something. Are you over Kay?"

Merle was dumbfounded. She'd thought about Kay less the past couple months, but she still thought about her. "I believe so."

"But you don't know for sure?"

"No, I guess not. I don't want to date anyone, I know that. Never mind about Kay. What about Hayley?"

"What about her? You don't know what she's thinking unless you tell her how you feel. She might be holding back for the same reasons you are. She thinks you're not interested."

"She just might be. But still I can't get involved with her."

"Why not?"

"Jesus Christ, Sigrid. I just told you." Merle was losing patience. Sigrid often used the Socratic method to get Merle to figure out for herself what she was really feeling, but she wasn't in the mood.

"Simmer down. I'm not trying to yank your chain. That's a real question. What if she *does* like you? What if she is ready to settle down? You seem to be assuming, without any evidence, that neither of those things is true."

"Oh. Yeah."

"'Oh, yeah' is right."

"But even if she's ready like you say…"

"Careful, love. I didn't say she was. I just said you don't know if she is or if she isn't."

"Right. Well, whether or not she is, I'm not."

"Why not? Is it Kay?"

"No, absolutely not. You said I can't afford to make any more Kay-like mistakes. Remember saying that?" Merle stared at Sigrid, challenging her.

Sigrid met her challenging gaze straight on and mirrored it right back at her. "Yes. I do. Now we're getting somewhere."

"Oh, really? Are we?" Merle was getting grouchy because she knew Sigrid had backed her into a corner even if it was for the best possible reasons. She was trying to get Merle to see her path forward.

"Yes. I believe you know what to do."

"I've got to be honest with her."

"Righto. She can make up her own mind about what she wants to do with the information, and you'll get some useful information back. You don't know what's going to happen, remember? Stop speculating. Get more information. Then decide what to do next. Besides, once you're honest with her, you'll feel better. You must be about to explode, trying to hold in all that energy."

"It's not easy. Maybe if I tell her, I can start getting over it."

"Maybe you will or maybe you won't." Sigrid grinned at her evilly.

Merle chuckled and shook her head. It was time to talk to Hayley and clear the air. If she could be honest, she'd feel better. If it caused Hayley to want to move, that was that and she'd have to find another roommate. But she didn't know *what* would happen, she reminded herself.

First, though, she'd have another cup of coffee and an orange scone. It wouldn't kill her.

❖

Sherrie emailed her again and left two voice mails. Hayley was concerned. Her polite brush-off hadn't worked. She felt like she was being stalked. This was so peculiar. Hayley thought of stalkers as creepy straight guys who couldn't take no for an answer, but this obviously wasn't the case. Here was a lesbian stalking her. She asked one of the attorneys at work what to do, but he shrugged.

"Unless she makes threats to your safety, nothing."

"Nothing?"

"Nope. This area of the law is a big mess."

That was putting it mildly. Hayley supposed she could have her arrested for trespassing if she showed up at the house. But she hoped it wouldn't come to that. She ought to warn Merle about the possibility of Sherrie showing up to Bonview Street out of the blue. During the past couple of weeks, she and Merle hadn't crossed paths much. If she were the paranoid type, she would have thought Merle was avoiding her. This evening, she'd try to catch her at home and tell her about Sherrie.

Hayley was depressed about her lack of luck with dating. She'd met the walker, the talker, and then the stalker. That made her giggle a little. There was also Merle, but she still didn't know how to approach her, and it was likely futile anyhow.

She'd become afraid to open her email. This was no way to live so she changed her email address. That was helpful: no more emails from Sherrie. She didn't want to change her phone number because she'd have to inform everyone she knew. That would be a hassle. She could delete voice mails and not answer Sherrie's calls. She'd have to give up eventually, wouldn't she?

Hayley opened her front door, and Arthur warmly greeted her. She went to the kitchen with him at her heels. If she got home first, she would feed him, and he'd gotten used to that. She gave him a bowl of kibble, and after he'd inhaled it, she sat at the kitchen table petting him and telling him, "Arthur, honey, I really want your mom to like me. But if I tell her I think she's amazing and wonderful and I want to sleep with her in the worst kind of way, she'll boot me out. Then I'll be back to square one with nowhere to live."

Arthur wagged his tail and pricked his ears up. He was so endearing, she hugged him. Then he bolted back to the living room. Merle was coming in the front door. Hayley stayed put and let them have their greeting. It seemed to take forever, but Merle came into the kitchen and said, "Hi there," just like normal. Hayley's conviction that something was wrong seemed ridiculous. Merle put a couple of grocery items in the refrigerator, closed the door, and said, "That cheese you like was on sale at Rainbow. How about enchiladas for dinner?"

"That sounds good. So you'll be able to have dinner?" Hayley thought she sounded a bit forlorn and didn't like it, but what could she do?

"Oh, yeah. I'll even cook." She looked at the clock on the stove. "I'm going to take a walk with Arthur first. So how's six thirty?"

"Fine. Sure. No problem. Do you want me to start anything?"

"Nope. I got it covered."

Hayley wanted to be asked along on the walk but didn't think she ought to invite herself. Their talk could wait until dinner. She turned on the TV and watched the talking heads on MSNBC for forty-five minutes until Merle and Arthur came back.

When Merle went to the kitchen and began cooking, Hayley decided to just keep watching TV until she was summoned. She tried to relax, but her mind kept veering toward what to tell Merle about Sherrie and what she wanted Merle to do or say if she did tell her. Again she returned to thinking it wasn't a big deal and that she was overreacting. The emails had been awful though. They veered between pleading and vaguely threatening, and they were tense and repetitive. Something really bad was going on with Sherrie, and Hayley wanted to stay away from her.

She looked back toward the kitchen. Arthur sat at the door, his tail thumping on the floor as he watched Merle cook. He was right at the threshold, Hayley noted, but not a bit of his body was over it. All of a sudden, he ran to the front door, barking furiously. This startled Hayley, and she sat up and said, "Arthur?"

The doorbell rang. That was so odd. Their street was such a backwater, no one had come to the door during the entire time Hayley had lived there. In the Sunset, Hayley had had to regularly turn away Jehovah's Witnesses and neighborhood kids soliciting babysitting and yard-work jobs.

"I got it!" she yelled.

She opened the front door and there stood Sherrie, a bouquet of flowers in hand, her eyes shining.

"Arthur. Sit." He obeyed her but made a sound like a growl low in his throat.

"What's going on?" Hayley heard Merle's voice behind her.

"Are you going to let me in? Can we talk?" Sherrie's tone was plaintive and pleading.

"I—Yeah. Okay. You can come in for just a moment. We're getting ready to eat dinner." That was true, and it might help hurry this intruder out.

"We?" Sherrie asked, her tone suspicious.

"Merle's my housemate. I told you about her. Now tell me why you're here and what exactly you want. I thought I was clear in my email—"

"Can't we speak privately?" Sherrie was back to pleading.

From behind her, Hayley heard Merle say, "I can stay if you want. Or not. Arthur, sit." Arthur was whining. Hayley had never heard him do that.

Still facing Sherrie, Hayley said, "You weren't invited but still you're here. We'll sit and you can tell me what you've come here to say. Then you can go. Merle, I don't think you need to stay." Hayley hoped her tone conveyed the right message, even if her words didn't penetrate.

"I'll be in the kitchen if you need me."

Hayley turned to face Merle. Their eyes met, and Hayley saw that Merle was ready to do battle if necessary. Hayley was shaken by Sherrie's sudden appearance, but Merle's words and her clear resolve calmed her. Merle nodded and closed the kitchen door.

"Please have a seat," she said, coldly. She took the armchair that sat at right angles to the couch. Sherrie perched on the edge of the sofa with her hands clasped. She was flushed and her eyes were watery. Hayley got a whiff of alcohol. That was only going to make things worse.

"I'm sorry I had to come to your house without an invitation. I didn't see any other way because you didn't answer my emails or voice mails or texts, and I needed to talk to you."

Hayley told herself to keep calm, let this woman have her say, then quietly and firmly ask her to leave. She nodded to Sherrie, indicating she should continue.

"So. So. I want to know why we can't see each other again. I thought we were great. I really like you and I really think we could—"

"Sherrie." Hayley interrupted her because it wasn't clear she was going to stop talking. The stalker and talker all in one. "I don't want to hurt your feelings, but I told you we can't date anymore. I don't think I can be any clearer. You need to leave."

Hayley stood up but Sherrie didn't. She stayed on the couch and wrung her hands.

"Please, Hayley. I'm sure you and I could get to know each other better and then you'd feel differently. I know you would. Let's go somewhere and talk."

Hayley balled her fists. "Sherrie. Please go. Now."

To her dismay, Sherrie began to cry loudly as she continued to speak. She was barely making sense. "Oh my God. This is so awful. I don't know what I'm going to do. I thought you were different. I thought you were nice, not like the other ones. But you're just like all the rest. You're awful. You're such a bitch." She leaped up and threw herself on Hayley and began to slap her haphazardly. Hayley caught her arms and yelled, "Stop it. Stop!"

"What's going on?" Merle said, loud enough to stop Sherrie and cause them both to turn toward her. She stood in the door to the kitchen with Arthur at her side. He was wagging his tail, but he was growling and would have lunged had Merle not had a firm grip on his collar.

Despite her fear and confusion, Hayley loved the way Merle looked. She was standing very straight, her lips set in straight line. Her body language exuded strength, and she was obviously angry. The picture was only improved by Arthur at her side, coiled and prepared to leap into the fray if Merle let him loose.

"Is this your girlfriend? Or what?" Sherrie was nearly shouting, but her voice broke.

Merle said, "Leave. Now." She cocked her head toward the front door for emphasis. Sherrie had stopped trying to pummel Hayley and looked frightened.

"If you do anything to me, I'll call the police."

Sherrie attempted to sound threatening, but it was useless. With Merle there, Hayley wasn't frightened anymore.

"Go ahead. This is my house and you're trespassing. So? I repeat. Please leave. For your own good." Merle took a step forward, and Hayley took a few steps back until she stood next to Merle.

She looked at her. She appeared even fiercer from a side view. Arthur growled again, then barked so loud it made them all jump. The fur on his back was standing up. Hayley's fear receded, her resolve bolstered by Merle and Arthur.

Sherrie backed away, her eyes darting from one to the other.

"Don't ever come around here again," Merle said in a voice quiet but deadly serious. "If you do, *I'll* call the police and have you arrested."

Hayley said, "If I need to get a temporary restraining order, I will. Believe it."

Sherrie looked at them for another moment, then sidled out the front door, slamming it behind her.

"Shit." Hayley collapsed on the couch. Her knees were weak and her stomach upset.

Merle sat down next to her, and Arthur propped his front paws on her knees. She automatically petted him, which calmed her. She closed her eyes and felt Merle's arm around her shoulders. It felt so good.

"Are you okay?"

Hayley struggled to bring her breathing under control and ratchet her adrenaline-charged emotions down. She rubbed her hand over Arthur's ears and head. His cold nose in her palm and Merle's presence settled her a bit. "I think so. Oh, my God."

"Shh. She's gone. It's over." Merle put both arms around Hayley, and Hayley turned into her embrace. Arthur was pushed to the floor but he stayed close. Hayley began to cry as the reaction took her over and her adrenaline drained away. She was swamped by a tsunami of emotions. Fear and anger competed with gratitude and relief. Merle's arms around her called up another host of feelings. Hayley sniffled into her shirt and rubbed her cheek on Merle's warm, solid shoulder. Merle patted her back gently, trying to reassure her, and it worked. Then the comfort began to morph into sexual arousal, which frightened Hayley so much she swiftly disengaged and bent down to hug Arthur to hide her dismay.

"Oh, Arthur, you were magnificent. So were you." She smiled at Merle through her tears.

Merle looked at her uncertainly. Had she sensed that wave of sexual energy that Hayley had felt? She'd let her arms fall the instant Hayley began to pull away.

"I think I should make some tea. If we had any booze in the house, I'd give you some." She smiled ruefully.

"Oh, don't worry about that. Tea would be great. I'll just sit with Arthur and catch my breath."

Merle leaped up and hurried toward the kitchen. "Be right back. I have to finish up dinner too. Are you hungry?"

"Yes. Oddly enough, I am." Hayley motioned for Arthur to climb on the couch, which he did in a second and wanted to lick her face. She had him sit down next to her. Getting comfort from Arthur was a lot safer than getting it from Merle. Physical contact with Merle was more dangerous than Sherrie the stalker. That overwhelming urge to have Merle's arms around her frightened Hayley all over again.

She leaned close to Arthur and whispered into his ear, "Your mom is really something. I'm sort of crazy about her, but don't tell her." He raised his nose to look into her face. Her words might not mean anything to him, but he could surely sense her emotions. She hugged him again and waited for Merle to bring her the promised cup of tea.

Chapter Twelve

Merle set the teakettle to boil and finished seasoning the enchilada mixture. She laid out several tortillas and added shredded cheese, guacamole, and sour cream. After she put the enchiladas in the oven to cook through, she sat trying to gather her wits.

Her thoughts skittered in all directions. The scene with Sherrie and Hayley's distress had been traumatic for both of them. But, as she'd hugged Hayley, empathy had turned into arousal. She was certain Hayley felt it too. Her swift disengagement from their embrace proved that. Merle shook her head at her indiscretion and poured boiling water into two cups, each holding a double bag of chamomile. Confronting Sherrie hadn't frightened her. Her only thought had been to protect Hayley, then comfort her.

It was ridiculous that she couldn't keep her libido under control long enough to properly soothe the poor woman. She really had to have a talk with Hayley, come clean and probably apologize as well. Hayley would surely appreciate honesty. They could reset, recover, and move forward. But this horrible incident had upset both of them, and it wasn't the time for *that* conversation. It would have to wait.

Merle took a cup to Hayley and said, "We can eat in about ten minutes."

Not surprisingly, Hayley looked a little undone. She smiled wanly and nodded as she sipped the chamomile tea, then looked away. She had her arm around Arthur. His canine ESP had made him cuddle close to her. To Merle, he had a concerned expression. She was probably imagining that, but it seemed possible. Dogs were deeply attuned to their human's moods and emotions. That Arthur was so keyed in to Hayley and her feelings was both wonderful and a little unsettling.

Merle returned to the kitchen and made a salad, and then Hayley walked into the kitchen and slowly sat down at the table. Arthur stayed at the threshold, eyeing them hopefully until Merle finally relented and motioned for him to enter. She took her chair, at right angles to Hayley's seat, and Arthur sat between them.

Merle watched Hayley closely, praying she'd be all right. They were silent as they served themselves enchiladas and salad. Out of the corner of her eye, Merle watched Hayley, her emotions mixed. Her wish to be supportive warred with sexual attraction so intense it made her weak.

Her gaze on the enchilada she was munching, Hayley asked, "Why is this dating thing so hard," and turned to meet Merle's eye.

She looked so vulnerable and sad that her expression tugged at Merle's heart all over again. She kept quiet, though, because she didn't have an answer to Hayley's question, or rather, she did have the answer: you could have me. But wasn't the right answer, for either of them.

"I don't know," Merle said. "I haven't dated in so long that honestly I'm not sure what the protocol is any more. I'm pretty certain stalking still isn't acceptable."

Hayley smiled and took another bite and chewed it before she spoke again. Merle was proud she could cheer Hayley up. "How did you meet Kay?"

The mention of Kay threw her. She was thinking so much about Hayley that she was jarred to be reminded of Kay, and she really didn't want to talk about her.

"Through some friends."

"Was it a set-up?"

"Yes."

"So what happened? Was it Clea and Sigrid? Who introduced you, I mean?"

"Oh, no. Someone else."

"Really? So tell me."

For whatever reason, Hayley wanted to talk about her and Kay, and Merle thought she should indulge her, considering what had happened, so she sketched her first introduction to Kay.

"I fell for her right away. Hard. We were living together after two months. That ought to have been a clue because it was way too soon. I wasn't thinking clearly though."

"But it didn't last." Hayley looked even sadder.

"Nope. It didn't last, not forever like I thought it would. Considering what I know now, I think Kay always just tried to do what I wanted."

"Do you know what happened? Do you mind my asking?"

"I don't mind." Unnerved, Merle fiddled with her silverware. She didn't want to think about Kay, yet Hayley seemed fixated on her.

"She fell out of love with me, I guess."

"How? How could that happen? You're so..." Hayley shut her mouth abruptly.

"I'm so...what?" Merle asked quietly.

"Nice."

"Nice," Merle said. "Yeah, I suppose."

"That sounds lame, doesn't it?"

Merle didn't want to make Hayley feel bad, but she couldn't help grinning. Hayley's mortified expression was priceless.

"I meant, how could someone fall out of love with you?"

Merle wanted to kiss her. Her big brown eyes were wide, and she looked so innocent and bewildered. Merle covered up her own confusion by saying lightly, "Yeah. Crazy, huh?"

Hayley looked down and then back at Merle. "So what I really want to know is this. I know it'll sound stupid, but I thought it'd be different with women. I thought I could find someone and then fall in love and then..."

"Live happily ever after?" Merle didn't want to sound too snarky. She didn't want to hurt Hayley's feelings.

"Well. Yeah." Hayley looked adorably abashed.

"Hayley. Lesbians are just imperfect human beings."

"I know. But I still thought...oh, never mind." She crossed her arms, clearly dissatisfied with both Merle's answer and her own naïveté.

"Don't worry. This thing with Sherrie's very unusual. It's been very tough on you, but you'll be fine. You'll meet someone and you'll be very happy. I'm sure of it." Merle patted Hayley's arm. It was an automatic gesture of reassurance she'd used a million times, but Hayley's arm tensed instead of becoming relaxed.

Hayley put her hand over Merle's and they stared at each other. Merle tried a gentle, encouraging smile, but it probably looked forced.

• 153 •

Their physical connection was again arousing her and making her uneasy. Hayley started to smile back, but then her smile faded and a look of profound sadness and longing replaced it. Merle's mind went blank as she stared into Hayley's face.

They both leaned forward at the same time, and their mouths met. Hayley's lips were marvelous—soft, pliant, and lightly flavored with turkey enchilada. Merle slowly worked her lips around and under Hayley's, trying a hint of tongue. Hayley's lips parted to let her in. They stood up suddenly. Merle felt as though she was watching them in a movie. They came together in a rush, kissing and grabbing hair and necks and shoulders. Hayley's chair fell and poor Arthur started.

Five percent of Merle's mind screamed, "Wrong, bad idea, stop." But the other ninety-five percent of her mind and all of her body had a radically different idea.

Merle broke their contact to catch her breath but resumed kissing after one inhale.

"Hayley?" she said. A tiny, almost inaudible voice was telling her they ought to stop. But the realization that Hayley wanted her shut that voice up resoundingly.

"Hmm?" Hayley was kissing her as though she'd discovered a new skill and wanted to perfect it immediately. It was more intoxicating than any sort of alcohol, and Merle was giddy with lust.

"Nothing, never mind." Everything else was irrelevant; she only wanted to feel.

"Can we…? Should we, um, go upstairs?" Hayley whispered.

In a dream, Merle took her hand and they climbed the stairs, Arthur trotting behind them. Very few of Merle's synapses that were unrelated to sexual arousal were firing. On autopilot she chose her bedroom and pointed to Arthur's bed, and he obediently climbed into it. She pulled Hayley back into her arms and they resumed kissing.

Merle couldn't wait any longer. She began to remove Hayley's clothes, starting with pulling her T-shirt over her head. Merle kissed her neck from her shoulder to her ear, while Hayley restlessly played with her hair. Merle unclasped her bra, glad she was able to accomplish that simple act without fumbling. She stopped, inhaled, and looked at her. Hayley stood, letting herself be scrutinized. Merle could barely breathe because she was so moved by Hayley's beauty.

When Merle touched Hayley's breasts, she moaned and nearly fell forward, bracing her arms on Merle's shoulders. Merle fondled them gently, then with more pressure, rubbing her thumbs on her nipples. Hayley's breathing was speeding up. She wasn't passive, but Merle sensed that she wanted to be taken, to be led. That suited Merle fine. She couldn't recall ever wanting to make love to a woman quite so much.

She pulled Hayley toward the bed and threw pillows aside and pulled the covers down as fast as she could, then lowered Hayley onto her back and eased herself on top of her. Hayley tugged at her shirt so Merle tore it off and undid her own bra as Hayley watched, her eyes dark and huge. Merle couldn't help it—she grinned cockily.

When Hayley reached for her breasts, she grabbed her hands and whispered, "Wait for your turn."

Hayley dropped her hands, then stretched her arms over her head. "Okay," she said, making eye contact. "I can't wait long, though."

For a reply, Merle bent and, as in her fantasy of a few weeks ago, kissed Hayley's pale smooth body over and over. It was better than her fantasy, especially since they didn't have a leaky pipe to fix. She giggled into Hayley's body, and Hayley jumped.

She pulled Merle's hair gently and asked, "What's so funny?"

Merle raised her head and looked past Hayley's lovely breasts, their nipples rosy with arousal. "When you were fixing the pipe in the sink, I was thinking about well, doing this."

"You were?" Hayley seemed genuinely surprised.

"I was, but real life's much better than the fantasy, believe me."

"Whatever you were thinking, I want you to do it, and please do it quickly because I'm about to detonate."

"Okay. And I hope that's true, that you're about to detonate, I mean."

Hayley tasted musky but sweet, and Merle took her time, starting with gentle, light touches and then licking faster and harder, following Hayley's sounds and movements. She felt like a desert traveler who had arrived at an oasis just in time. Hayley had an impressively long orgasm, groaning and thrashing and finally choking out the word "stop" in a scarcely audible voice. Merle kept them connected as the contractions subsided. She scooted up to embrace Hayley, who sighed and moved into her arms languorously. Merle kissed her mouth and cheeks and forehead and hair and breasts.

"No," Hayley said weakly, trying to turn them over. Merle shamelessly used her larger size to keep her on her back and then fucked her and stroked her clit until she came again.

"Oh, my word. That was…I don't have any words to describe it." Hayley spoke barely above a whisper.

"You want more? I bet you could go again." Merle tweaked her right nipple. "Yep. You look ready to me." She made as if to get on top of Hayley.

Hayley put a hand on her chest. "No. You promised I'd get my turn."

"Roger." Merle lay on her side, propping her head up with her hand. "What would you like me to do?"

"Nothing." Hayley threw herself on Merle and kissed her ardently. Merle relaxed and gave herself over to the experience. It was Hayley's first time, so let the girl have at it and have her fun. It was marvelous to be wanted so much, and it had been such a long time. Hayley abruptly stopped her kissing and touching.

Hayley made a sound of frustration and dipped her head so that her blond hair brushed Merle's nipples. That was quite a feeling. She was terrifically sensitive after making love to Hayley.

She patted Hayley's shoulder and lifted her chin so they could make eye contact.

"What's the matter?"

"I've thought about this so many times, and finally it's here, and I can't believe how nervous I am. I wasn't nervous with you at all. It was wonderful. But now…"

Merle stroked her hair and patted her cheek. "Don't worry. It'll be fine. As a matter of fact, if you don't do something soon, I may have a coronary from frustration."

"What do you want me to do?" Hayley's voice was charged with desire but somehow plaintive, and she was so sweet.

Merle wrapped her up in a big hug. "Relax, love. We have time to figure out what we both like. There's no right way or wrong way. There's only pleasure and joy."

Hayley sagged against her. "God, I feel so stupid."

"Want to see how I feel?" Merle asked.

Hayley nodded, though she seemed confused. Merle took her hand

and put it between her legs. She was swollen and slick, and Hayley's light touch wound her up.

"Wow." Hayley moved her fingers tentatively, then with more authority.

Merle lay back and closed her eyes. She felt Hayley's lips on her breasts and nipples, and her fingers moved faster and harder. She tensed her thigh muscles and the orgasm built from deep in her pelvis. It hit all of a sudden and she moaned. Hayley rode her back down to the mattress, and Merle finally had to grip her wrist when the touch became unbearable.

"That was amazing," Hayley whispered.

"Yes, it was. You've got the idea. Don't worry about that. If you'll just give me a sec—"

"I don't want to stop now."

Before Merle could say another word, Hayley was between her legs and licking her. Merle relaxed into it, signaling her needs with body movements.

"There," she said, "right there."

Hayley obliged with steady, firm strokes, and Merle had another orgasm, stronger than the first.

❖

Hayley had no idea that she'd fallen asleep or when she'd fallen asleep. She woke up thinking she was in the middle of making love to Merle again. She saw only a little light in the room and no clock. Merle was sound asleep on her side. Hayley admired the shape of her back and remembered how she'd first thought how nice her vertebrae looked. They felt nice to touch too. All of her was nice to touch, more than nice—phenomenally wonderful.

Hayley snuck out of bed to run to the bathroom. She was pleasantly sore in some spots, and she was euphoric. This was actually real. When Merle had made love to her, she'd never experienced that kind of touch; it was tender but firm, gentle but assertive too. She hated to compare it to sex with Howard, but that was the point. There was no comparison; it was completely different. Hayley supposed that had more to do with her psyche than with anything else. It helped that she was genuinely and profoundly aroused. She replayed their lovemaking in her mind, and her heart and her ego swelled as she thought about making Merle come.

She slipped back into bed as quietly as she could, wide-awake and craving that touch again. Merle's magic touch. She smiled in the dark and ran her finger down Merle's spine, probing between her butt cheeks gently. Merle stirred in her sleep, and Arthur snuffled from somewhere on the floor.

Oh, God, Arthur. They'd made a headlong dash for bed, and it had barely been seven in the evening. She ought to get up and let him out, poor guy. She swung her legs over the side of the bed and began to pull her jeans on, then felt a warm hand on the small of her back.

Merle whispered, "What's the matter?"

"Arthur. I'm going to let him out."

"You don't have to. I did a couple hours ago."

"You did? Was I asleep?"

Merle moved over and wrapped an arm around her waist. "You were. Three or four orgasms will do that to a woman." She dipped her hand mischievously into Hayley's crotch, tugging on her pubic hair.

Hayley was getting turned on again. She dropped her jeans on the floor, flung her legs back up into bed, and grabbed the covers to pull up over them. It was so warm and comfortable in Merle's arms yet so arousing.

"I'm awake now. I could go again." Hayley spoke into the hollow of Merle's throat.

"Is that right?" Merle asked, her hands moving over her body.

"Yes. It is." Hayley moved sensuously, her body anticipating what was to come.

Merle rolled over and pulled Hayley on top of her, stroking from her neck to her thighs. "I have an idea," she said, continuing to stroke her. "Sit up."

Hayley obeyed. Her wet pussy rubbed over Merle's body.

Merle gripped her butt and said, "Now scoot up and get your legs on either side of my head."

"Okay." Hayley did as she was told.

"Now hold on to the headboard and just, well, sit on my face."

Hayley laughed but she did as ordered. When Merle's hands gripped her ass and Hayley felt her tongue on her sensitive flesh, she stopped laughing. Her legs jittered and flexed as Merle's mouth and tongue worked on her, first hard and fast, then light and slow, over and over.

"Oh. God!" The pleasure was nearly unbearable. She came, the contractions of her orgasm reverberating down her legs all the way to her feet. She let go of the headboard and collapsed into Merle's arms.

"Like that?" Merle asked, her voice tender and amused.

"I can't even describe how that feels."

"Don't try. That's why they're called feelings."

Hayley shoved her a little but ended up kissing her instead.

❖

The next day, they walked up Bernal Heights Boulevard, hand in hand with Arthur trotting alongside, his leash in Hayley's other hand. They didn't say very much. Merle's head hummed with fatigue. It was a major undertaking just to go out for a walk with Arthur. She desperately wanted to just be horizontal for the rest of the day. Horizontal with Hayley, of course, but that was the problem. In the bright midday sun, things looked much different.

It's always nice when your fantasies come true and reality exceeds imagination, but reality is something far more complicated. Also, be careful what you ask for, because you may get it. Even if the voice asking is unconscious.

Merle squeezed Hayley's hand and smiled at her every so often. Hayley beamed back at her, her eyes sleepy and her smile lazy and relaxed. One of Merle's college buddies had christened that the well-laid look. Hayley surely had it. She supposed she did too. They'd gotten very little sleep, but somehow, substituting sex for sleep worked out okay.

In between the sexy little smiles and the warm hand squeezes and the tingling in her crotch, Merle thought about regret. Along with its cousin, guilt, it was her least favorite emotion.

Now what? This wasn't a question Merle was prepared to ask or to answer. It was her experience that the first time for *anything* made a huge impression on a person. Make that the first time of sex with a woman, and the scale of the impact was upped exponentially. Merle hoped Hayley wasn't in love with her but merely in lust. For the younger version of the newly minted lesbian, lust would easily equate to love. For the more mature woman, who the hell knew for sure, but Merle hoped it wouldn't be the same.

The old phrase "the heat of the moment" floated through Merle's mind. They had certainly shared a moment, as well as heat, and it traveled from Hayley's hand to hers, up her arm to her brain and through the rest of her.

But was either of them truly ready to jump into a relationship? Merle thought for herself, anyhow, the answer was no. Kay hadn't been gone that long. She'd barely processed their breaking up. It had to be the height of stupidity to start another relationship before the old one was truly done. True, Kay was gone, for good, it seemed, but Merle still felt her presence like the toxic cloud left over from a chemical spill. It wasn't really over for her, and she didn't know when it would be or when she would be ready to dive into the dating pool again.

There was also this sticky little detail of Hayley and her living together. It was like they were in a relationship already. That staggered Merle. They'd already begun behaving almost exactly like they were a pair of cohabiting lovers. And then they'd stirred sex into the mix. *Voilà.* They were a couple walking their dog on Bernal Hill on a sunny September Saturday afternoon.

Except…this wasn't right. It was completely wrong. It was a huge minefield. Merle's barely functioning brain struggled to process her feelings.

"What are you thinking?" Hayley's playfully voiced question jolted Merle out of her reverie.

"Ah, um. Nothing. Just that it's a beautiful day and you're a beautiful woman. It's lovely to be in San Francisco."

Hayley grinned and squeezed her arm.

All true enough, but Merle hoped that her lack of complete honesty wouldn't show on her face.

"Really? I was thinking about last night."

"Were you then? What do you think?" Merle asked the question automatically but was terrified to hear the answer.

Hayley grabbed Merle's arm and turned her so they were face-to-face rather than side by side. She kissed her, then held her head between her hands.

"I am never ever, as long as I live, going to forget it. There aren't enough superlatives to describe how I feel. How it felt. That was the single most phenomenal, miraculous, amazing, ecstatic experience of my life. That's what I think."

"Ah." Merle tried to calibrate her smile to appropriately sunny because she feared her face would mirror what she felt inside, which was "Uh-oh." She said, "Me too."

Hayley squeezed her arm and they continued their trudge up the hill.

Merle liked being wanted. She'd missed the feeling for a long, long time. It was as gratifying as the actual sex they'd experienced. But that was the problem. She'd been seduced simply by a woman wanting her. And she wanted to be wanted. God, it had all felt so good.

But the woman in question shared her home. Her bedroom was right across the hall from hers. It gave a whole new meaning to the question "Your place or mine?"

If she gave in to her desire and spent another night with Hayley, she had no idea what would happen next. If she rejected her, it would surely hurt her feelings and cause discord between them. It was the old rock-and-hard-place scenario. Damned if you do and damned if you don't. Scylla and Charybdis. It was hopeless.

When they returned home, Merle said, "Look. I need to go to a meeting. Haven't been to one in a while. Please don't wait on me to eat dinner."

They'd awakened to the congealed remains of their enchiladas. Merle hated to waste food, but they were truly unappetizing.

Hayley looked a little disappointed, but all she said was, "No problem. I'll make something and you can eat when you get back."

"Okay. Great. Thanks." She slunk out of the house feeling like a coward.

❖

Merle slouched in her chair and fought to concentrate on what people were saying at the meeting. What was the topic? Fear. Right. Well, *that* was a good topic for her today. She didn't feel like speaking up though. Her thoughts were way too personal. She'd save them for

Sigrid and Clea. She'd come to the meeting to get a little perspective. In the past, when she was upset about something, attending a meeting had always worked. Not so much this time.

She sat up straight and rolled her head to stretch her neck. It didn't help that she was so tired, and sore. She ought to be happy, but she wasn't. Yes, she was scared. Too scared to keep going forward with Hayley and too chicken to tell her the truth: they couldn't be lovers. That was it. She could tell Hayley it was a fluke, a mistake, and they could go back to doing what they'd been doing before. That was the answer. Hayley could handle it. They weren't sensitive young things anymore. They were mature women, adults with rational perspectives and life experience.

The meeting was over and Merle had her plan. She remembered that she had wanted to talk to Hayley about the attraction she'd sensed between them. Okay, *her* attraction to Hayley. Well, guess they didn't need to have *that* talk now. They were going to have to have a whole other talk. She drove home, her head spinning with dread.

❖

Hayley assembled a few vegetables and some ground turkey into a casserole and looked at her email while it cooked. She couldn't concentrate because she was so tired that she was wacky. But overriding her fatigue was the thought of Merle coming home and going to bed with her again. She didn't know if that would happen though. After a quick kiss when they woke up, Merle had withdrawn. She'd acted as though nothing momentous at all had occurred between them. Her feelings about it obviously weren't as strong as Hayley's. She had to pull her socks up and get over it. Her damn inexperience with women was to blame. Sometimes adults fell into bed with each other without deep emotional attachment. No big deal.

But it had been a very big deal to her.

Hayley slammed her laptop shut and went back downstairs and turned the TV on. She needed something to take her mind off Merle. Once the casserole was done, she carried her plate to the living room and turned on a movie. She didn't really care what it was about. As she watched it, she ate her dinner mechanically.

She must have fallen asleep because the next thing she knew, someone was shaking her shoulder. She opened her eyes and saw Merle leaning over her.

Hayley sat up, yawned, and shook herself awake. The sight of Merle woke her up quickly. Merle looked so good.

She favored Hayley with a small, tired smile and said, "Hi. Sorry to wake you up. Your plate is about to slide off your lap. Arthur may have cleaned it for you."

Hayley looked down and, sure enough, her plate was as shiny as it would be after the dishwasher got through with it. Oops. Arthur wasn't allowed human food. But Merle didn't seem to care. She looked distracted.

Hayley followed her into the kitchen and put her plate in the sink, while Merle served herself some casserole and sat down at the kitchen table. Uninvited, Hayley sat across from her.

"How was your meeting?" she asked, studying Merle for clues about her emotional state.

Merle took a little time to stir her plate of casserole, tasted it, then said, "Needs microwaved."

Hayley watched her perform her little cooking task, then resume her seat at the table. She took a bite and said, "Mmm. Good. Thanks for cooking."

Hayley was about to explode with frustration and leap across the table on top of Merle and ravish her. But she waited, as patiently as she could, for her to reply.

"The meeting was good. I always get something out of a meeting when I go."

"That's nice," Hayley said, faintly, praying for Merle to kiss her or to at least start talking, preferably the former. But Merle stolidly ate the turkey casserole, and Hayley struggled to keep her cool.

"Look, Hayley—" Merle put her fork down, dropped her chin to her chest and stretched her arms on the table on either side of her plate, and sighed deeply. At last she met Hayley's gaze. "Let's go sit in the living room."

They sat facing one another on the couch. "I don't want to hurt you but…"

Oh, boy, here it came, the "I don't want to hurt you" speech.

Hayley was so on edge, her head had started to pound. The next thing to come out of Merle's mouth would be, "It's not you, it's me." She so didn't want to hear that.

She narrowed her eyes and folded her arms. "I know what you're going to say next."

"Would you at least hear me out?" Merle looked very tired and very unhappy, and Hayley had a smidgen of compassion for her, but just a tiny bit.

"Sure. That's fair."

"We shared something wonderful last night. I don't remember ever having an experience quite like the one I had with you."

"Me too. I really like you. I think you already knew that but..." Hayley spoke in a small voice, about to start crying.

"And that's sort of the problem. As lovely as our encounter was, I can't be in a relationship with you. In other circumstances, maybe..." Merle had ignored her confession and just kept talking.

"*What* other circumstances?" Hayley was afraid she sounded whiny, but she truly wanted to know.

"That didn't come out right."

Merle took a deep breath. "Neither of us is in a space in our personal lives that can really accommodate a serious relationship. You're just coming out, you've got a long way to go, and I don't want to tie you down. I'm just out of the breakup with Kay, and I just can't get involved with anyone right now." She stopped talking and stared at Hayley, her eyes wide and sincere.

"How do you know what I need to do?" Hayley asked, gritting her teeth.

"Oops, that didn't come out right either."

Hayley was swiftly losing any sense of feeling sorry for Merle. Instead she was getting really pissed off. All she saw was someone who regretted her encounter and was trying to weasel out of further involvement. This wasn't turning out right at all. She inhaled and mentally crossed her fingers.

"I've been agonizing for weeks about what to say to you. I've met a few women, sure. But none of them are anything like I want. They're not even close. None except you."

"Me?" Merle looked stunned.

"You. I didn't want you to know how I was really attracted to you because I didn't think you felt the same way. But I think I was wrong." She paused to let her words sink in. "I really do like you. Very much." Hayley tilted her head and looked at her like Arthur when he was trying to comprehend his human companion's words.

"Oh, gosh."

"Oh, gosh? Is that all you can say? I've never in my whole life had sex like we had last night. What about *you,* Miss 'Oh gosh'? Are you going to tell me it wasn't supposed to happen or that you didn't feel anything?"

"Er. No. What I mean is...What I want to say is I'm not emotionally available. I'm not sorry we slept together and..." Silent, she looked away, then said, "But you may decide you're not even a lesbian."

Obviously their lovemaking hadn't affected Merle nearly as dramatically as it had her. "That's just great. You've made up your mind I may decide I'm not a lesbian. Boy, wouldn't that be inconvenient since I've already gotten a divorce, uprooted myself, and changed my entire life. You have no idea what you're talking about. You decided how you'd respond *and* how I would, but you forgot to ask me."

She leapt up from the chair and ran upstairs so Merle wouldn't see her tears. She could hear Arthur whining and Merle's murmured reassurances to him. Swell. She'd scared the poor dog.

She flopped on her bed and cried. She couldn't remember the last time she'd cried so hard. Certainly nothing Howard had ever done or said had made her that emotional. She was a mess. She didn't know which was worse: Merle's infuriating emotional remoteness or her own wildly emotional response.

This lesbian thing wasn't working out at all.

She sat on the side of her bed, attempting to pull herself together. "Talk about acting like a teenager," she said aloud. "I'm like an over-indulged fourteen-year-old who hasn't gotten her way."

It helped a little to say it aloud, though her mind was still screaming, "No, no, no," and her body still craved Merle's touch. How could Merle be so cool about it? She hadn't been cool last night—far from it. She'd called her "love" with such tenderness. Guess that was just part of the sex. The contrast between the Merle of the night before and the Merle of today stupefied and disoriented Hayley.

She went to the bathroom and blew her nose and washed her face. She looked like crap, but that wasn't a surprise. After she combed her hair and straightened her clothes, she took several deep breaths. She knew what she had to do. Her reaction was her own problem, not Merle's.

When she walked down the stairs, she could see the back of Merle's head, neatly trimmed, shiny gray hair in place. The TV was off and she was staring at a distant corner of the room. Arthur was surely curled up next to her on the couch and her arm was around him.

Hayley took a breath. "Hi."

Merle turned. She looked a bit fearful, as well she might after Hayley's outburst, but she responded. "Hey."

Hayley walked into the living room and sat down on one of the armchairs at right angles to the couch, then folded her hands. "I owe you an apology."

"No, you don't. It's my fault."

"Yes. I do. Don't interrupt me."

"Sure." Merle fell silent but scratched Arthur's neck. Hayley felt worse because Arthur was staring at her, panting in his usual way. She was sorry she'd scared him.

"I had a bit of a meltdown. I guess I thought after last night, things would turn out differently." Hayley inhaled and gathered her courage. "Do you want me to move out?"

Merle looked shocked. "No. Not unless you want to."

"I don't, but I don't want to make you uncomfortable or cause any problems for you."

"Look, Hayley. I need to apologize to you too. I'm not handling this very well at all. I don't want to hurt you I just can't…Last night was a fluke, a lovely fluke but—"

"I know. You can't be in a relationship right now. I get it. You're actually right about me too, even if I don't want to accept it. I'm not good relationship material myself." Hayley didn't actually believe that, but it sounded good.

"It's not that. You'd be a wonderful lover."

"Just not for you." Hayley couldn't help injecting a little bit of a dig. She was still smarting from the rejection.

"That's on me. Not you."

"Sure. I understand. So we can go back to what we were before. I can be a grown-up."

"I honestly want you to stay, Hayley. I really do. I like you, a lot. Arthur," she looked down at him, "he loves you. You're good for us."

"Nice to hear. Well, I guess that's that. You okay?"

"Yeah, I am. I hope you are too."

"Yep. Just fine. I'm glad you want me to stay." Hayley manufactured a decent smile. "So we're clear?"

"Absolutely."

"Okay then. Good night." With that, Hayley went upstairs again, leaving Merle and Arthur sitting on the couch. She lay down on her bed with her elbow over her eyes and cried some more. In spite of her brave speech, she was far from fine.

Chapter Thirteen

Hayley carried on a conversation with herself as she drove over to the Women's Building for the coming-out group meeting. She was debating about whether to come clean with the group about what had happened with Merle.

She'd been to a few meetings and was relatively comfortable with the women there, though this process was still new to her. She'd never talked about anything intimate with anyone, let alone with a group. But she didn't have any one else to talk to.

They settled in and Inga opened the discussion. When her turn came, Hayley said in a rush, "I slept with Merle, but we talked about it and it's okay. It was all because of the stalker."

Okay, so *some* of that was for dramatic effect. It worked. A chorus of questions erupted around the room.

"Wowie, zowie. What the heck happened?" Moira looked alarmed.

"What was it like?"

"Were you nervous?"

"Are you in love with her now?" Diana asked.

"Are you going to be together?"

"How do you *feel*? Over the moon?" Diane asked. Hayley wanted to be irritable at her sarcasm, but she felt that Diane's insight was actually pretty good if uncomfortably close to the truth.

Amy said, "Whoa, time out, women! Let's give Hayley some space to tell us what she wants to tell us, at her own pace."

The group stared at Hayley expectantly. They already knew about Sherrie and her peculiar behavior and Hayley's ambivalence about dating her. Hayley described her sudden arrival at Merle's home and what had happened. But she left out the details of their sex. She wasn't ready to reveal quite that much.

At last, she said, "We talked the next day and agreed that it just wasn't the right time for either of us to start a relationship." As she said it out loud, she sounded calm and together, but the painful truth lurked under her straightforward declaration. She'd wanted to continue but Merle hadn't. They hadn't agreed. She had only acquiesced to reality.

"Your first time! With your roommate, of all people." This was Sheila, the most romantic and dreamy one in the group. "The way you talked about her, I knew something was going on there."

That startled Hayley. She'd mentioned Merle, naturally, but she hadn't said anything about her feelings because she considered them juvenile. Had something about the way she talked about Merle given her away? Or was Sheila making it up?

Betty said, "I want my first time to be romantic, and, I'm sorry, but that didn't sound romantic at all with the stalker." This sent them all off on a huge tangent arguing about the meaning of "romantic." Amy let it go on for a while until she brought the focus back.

"Hayley? What do *you* think?" That was precisely the question, wasn't it? Hayley thought she and Merle had handled the whole thing gracefully, aside from her little fit of temper. They were cool. But Amy's question caused her doubt to resurface.

"I don't know." Her talk with Merle had made it seem final, but she wasn't sure she could let her feelings go.

Diana said, flatly, "I'd move out. If I really liked someone and it wasn't going anywhere, I couldn't stay. That would be awful."

"But what if she changes her mind?"

"Yeah, that's not happening. Time to cut your losses."

"There's no way to tell the future."

"What about finding another place to live that's as good? You don't find places to live in SF that easily." Hayley had boasted, in a mild way, about the house and location and Merle's fine qualities as a roommate and their compatibility, and so forth. That all seemed cruelly ironic.

But it would surely be a hassle if she had to look for another place to live. She didn't want to go through the process again.

After the meeting, Amy pulled Hayley aside and said, "You're the only one who knows what's best for you."

Hayley nodded.

"Are you in love with her?"

"I don't know if it's love or just hormones. Can women our age have trouble telling the difference?" The evidence said yes.

Amy grinned ruefully. "Unfortunately, I don't think our advanced age gives us any special insight when it comes to love. We can exercise better judgment, but we're not immune to heartache."

"That's what I was afraid of." Amy hugged her, and Hayley felt better, if only a little bit.

❖

Merle updated her inventory spreadsheet with some new items, then saved and closed it. She sat in her office at her desk, staring at her computer monitor. She had a bunch of things to do but no motivation for any of them. It was the week after she'd slept with Hayley, and in spite of their "clear the air talk," she felt no better. She was mired in guilt, an emotion she considered one of the most useless feelings of all. And it was right up there with resentment in likelihood of making an alcoholic drink. She didn't really think she would drink, but she felt like shit in spite of her assurances to Hayley that all was well. All was clearly *not* well.

She'd tried to self-talk her way out of it. Hayley, after all, had seemed to recover, and that should have made it all right. Except *she* wasn't okay, not even close. She wasn't worried about drinking, but she certainly was on an emotional bender.

She sighed, shaking her head. This was so ridiculous. It was bad enough that she'd succumbed to blind lust and ended up in bed with Hayley. Now she couldn't get over herself and move on. She needed to talk this out with somebody. She usually discussed her problems with Sigrid only, but maybe this time, if she brought Clea into the conversation, it would be more helpful. Three heads or maybe two and a half. *Her* ability to think clearly had been severely compromised, that was obvious. She'd slept with her roommate. That was pretty good evidence she was screwed up.

"Merle?" She jumped. One of the grad students, Jacques, was standing at the door.

"Uh-huh?" She supposed it was time to focus on work.

"I think Anik's got a problem." He'd turned out to be one of those types who had a hard time recognizing her authority or listening to her because she was female and didn't have a PhD.

"What sort of problem?" She didn't want to hear about problems right now.

"The PCR is acting up." The PCR, an instrument that measured DNA, was a vital tool for the researchers.

"Okay. Be right there."

She put on her lab coat and went to the equipment room where Jacques and Anik stood staring at the offending instrument as though their mind control would make it work. "What's the trouble?"

Anik rolled his eyes, and Merle wanted to slap him.

"The sample compartment lid won't close."

"Did you try resetting it?"

"Yes. It still doesn't—"

"Here, let me in there." She moved past them quickly. She was being unusually abrupt and saw the confused looks on both men's faces. Jacques was generally quite deferential to her, which she appreciated. After too many ego-ridden post-docs to deal with, grad students were usually like amiable children.

Anik, however, looked irritable and disdainful. "Don't you think we should call for service?" he asked.

"No," Merle said. "Not yet."

She stood in front of the instrument and stared at the digital display. It was designed to measure DNA in tissue samples labeled with a fluorescent marker. It wasn't a complicated piece of equipment. Most of the time, Merle prided herself on fixing things without having to resort to expensive service calls. She'd never bothered to reconcile her ability to fix things at work with her reluctance to do home repairs.

She switched the machine off, then back on again. She tapped on the sample chamber cover and jiggled it. She frowned. Nothing was wrong that she could discern.

"How long has this been broken?" She glared at Jacques and Anik, who glanced at each other. She instantly knew Anik had mucked with the PCR and likely had caused the failure.

"Just this morning I tried it," Anik said, "and it wouldn't work."

"What did you do?"

"No-nothing. I warmed it up for a few minutes. Then when I tried to lift the lid, it..."

To Merle, he looked guilty, but she had no way to know. In any case, the damage was done and it was her job to deal with it. This was a serious problem since not being able to use the PCR could stop their research.

"Did you hit it with something?" Merle was being a total jerk, but she was powerless to stop, it seemed.

The two young men shook their heads as one.

"I'll get the tools and try to repair it. I'll let you know when it's fixed." They drifted off, unwilling to argue with her, which was A-okay with her.

She leveraged a screwdriver under the metal lid and pushed it gently. No movement. She tried the other side. Still nothing. It was stuck. She shoved the screwdriver farther under the lid and slammed her hand down on the handle. The lid popped off and clattered to the floor.

She picked it up. The hinge was broken. She looked at the sample chamber. Broken there too. She'd *have* to call the service technician. The PCR was out of commission until further notice, and she put a sign on it.

After she made the necessary phone call she slumped in her chair and put her head into hands. She felt like she was losing her mind. Hayley's face drifted into her inner view. She looked exactly like she looked when they were making love and she was about to come. Merle shook her head so hard she made herself dizzy. *Stop. I have to stop thinking about her.*

❖

Hayley called Robbie to ask him if he'd talked to his grandmother.

"Yeah. She's not sure why you had to change your life right now. She thinks the divorce has left you with a few screws loose."

Maybe that was true, but not in the way her mother thought. It wasn't the divorce, which was a long overdue event and very good idea. It was her so-called new life that had her emotional screws jiggling, but she didn't want to admit that to her son *or* to her mother.

"Did you tell her that being a lesbian is okay now?"

"Sure did. She doesn't care if other people are gay. It's okay for everyone else. She just doesn't see why *you* have to be this way. She doesn't see it in a very positive way. I think, Ma, you ought to sell it a little more."

Robbie was right, but Hayley wondered how to sell something she wasn't actually feeling that good about. So far she'd experienced the walker, the talker, the stalker, and then Merle. So far, this new life had turned out pretty crappy. But she wasn't going to share any of this with Ellie. That would surely further convince her mom that being a lesbian was a terrible idea. She sighed. The only other option was Angie, but that was a black box. She decided to wait until she was in positive place to talk to her mother again.

"I'll have to go and see her again."

"Righto. So, how are you, Ma? What's up?"

"Oh, not much."

"No? I thought you'd be a social butterfly. A million dates. You know. Hook-up time?"

"Robbie!"

"Easy. I'm just teasing. Seriously, are you okay?"

"Yes, sweetie. I'm fine." She asked him about his work and his friends so she wouldn't have to talk about herself. Good thing he could be easily diverted. She wasn't doing all that well, but she wasn't about to reveal that to her son, no matter how close they were. She felt like a failure and didn't want to admit that to anyone.

She and Merle were polite but distant with one another. It wasn't excruciatingly uncomfortable, but Hayley missed the old times, pre-sex. What, if anything, could she do? Probably she ought to date someone. That would surely help her get over Merle, but she'd have to find someone first. That was the issue. She needed some distraction, though, because coming home every day and seeing Merle, remembering their night together and knowing it wouldn't be repeated, was way too painful.

She went back to scanning the OkCupid profiles, but none sparked her interest. Her calendar pinged. It was time for another meeting with Angie and Tom.

That was something to be happy about. She could exchange warm glances with Angie while Adam and Tom talked. They had a settlement conference with Tom's employer in a couple days. Adam sometimes recommended settling cases in this manner. It saved a lot of time and money to not have to go to a jury trial. The success of a settlement conference depended on so many factors, though: how intransigent the employer was, how good their client's case was, and more.

Hayley had already made copies of all the letters and other documentation. She went to the conference room and set out the documents. Adam was a bit old-fashioned in that he liked paper copies. Some of the other attorneys simply emailed documents.

Angie and Tom entered, and everyone made their greetings and sat down. As always, Adam opened the discussion with some small talk to relax the clients. On this occasion, he talked about the San Francisco Giants, who'd made the National League play-offs and were looking for another World Series chance. This topic got Tom and Angie animated and chatty since they were both huge baseball fans. Hayley was neutral about baseball, but she didn't mind looking at Angie while they all talked.

"So. Here's the deal." Adam opened his folder and scanned something. It was an offer letter from Tom's engineering firm, which Hayley had already read. "We've got an offer from Kallman, but it's not an especially good one. That's normal."

Adam grinned. "The good news is they came with an offer first, because they know you have a good case and their position is weak."

Adam had told Hayley that Tom was an exceptionally good client. He'd saved every single piece of paper he'd ever gotten that related to his employment. During the depositions, he was clear and concise. Even better was that, the HR reps from his company weren't especially good at justifying his abrupt layoff. Adam was confident that the Kallman Company knew it had a weak case, and the powers that be were scared.

"Sometimes, these guys just don't believe a loyal employee would ever sue them," Adam told Tom and Angie. "Then you do and they get rattled."

Adam schooled Tom on the settlement process, and Hayley and Angie made eyes at each other in a most pleasant fashion while Hayley listened to her boss and prompted him with facts where necessary. Tom would be called for the settlement conference when it was scheduled with Kallman Engineering's attorneys. Adam discussed the terms for their response to the offer and got agreement from Tom on what he proposed.

On their way out, Angie went to the ladies' room, and on impulse, Hayley followed her. She waited until they were washing their hands to speak.

As they stood at neighboring sinks, smiling at each other's images in the mirror, she said, "So this may all be over sooner than we think."

"Do you think? Is Tom going to get his job back?"

"I'm sure he will. I'd be very surprised if he didn't, along with some money for the hassles he had to endure."

"That would be so wonderful."

"Well, it's not over till it's over, as they say. Adam likes to be cautious, but things look good."

Hayley shook water off her hands and then reached for some paper towels. Angie was next to her so she made eye contact directly as she palmed the dispenser's electric eye.

"And when we settle, and I mean when and not if, I'd hope I could see you. Outside of the office, I mean." She moved aside to give Angie some room.

Angie didn't answer immediately, but she grinned as she tossed her paper towels into the compost bin. She opened the door for Hayley and said, "I hope so. I would *really* like that."

Everyone shook hands in the lobby, and Hayley's heart was lighter when she went back to her office. Maybe there was hope for her love life after all.

❖

Sigrid seemed suspicious when Merle invited her and Clea out to dinner. "I just know you like to come over here and have us cook for you. Or we go to your house. This is out of the ordinary."

"Exactly. This time, I want to take you out."

"Why not eat at your house? Is something wrong? Are you keeping us away from Hayley?"

"Nothing's wrong!" Merle was getting irritable because Sigrid was like a goddamn psychic.

"I just want us to go out. How's Little Nepal, Friday at seven?" She referred to a popular Bernal neighborhood restaurant.

"That's fine. Don't be upset, Mer. We'll see you in a couple days."

Merle walked Arthur as usual every day after work and on Saturday, but she didn't invite Hayley. Hayley seemed distant and preoccupied anyhow. That was all to the good. They'd just gotten too close and then they had sex and now they were both getting perspective, disengaging. They could reengage at a later time, after a suitable interval.

It was time to come clean with Sigrid and Clea, if for no other reason than to just get it out in the open and out of her mind, where it had been festering for weeks. Merle was sick and tired of her own obsessive thinking. Clea and Sigrid would understand. It was never good to keep things to herself. Her problems roiled around in her mind and made her nuts.

After she'd slept with Hayley and their argument-slash-talk, she figured she could start moving forward. Instead, her thoughts were so tangled and fraught with fear and regret, she felt like she'd been staggering around in the mental equivalent of the Tenderloin on a Saturday night. She was lost and drunk, and menacing people stood on every corner with no police officer or shelter in sight. *My mind's like a bad neighborhood*, she thought. *You don't want to be there alone.*

It wasn't supposed to be this way. She should be able to solve her problems by using the methods she'd learned in AA. Mainly she needed to talk to someone. Instead she was keeping everything to herself. Why was she so reluctant to talk to Sigrid?

She figured Sigrid would again bring up the fact that her long sobriety didn't prevent her from having bad thoughts or bad experiences. It was true, but she disliked being reminded of it. It was all probably just because of Kay and the weird and inexplicable circumstances of their breakup and the breakup itself. Seriously, ten years and then kaput? Who wouldn't be slightly disoriented, even her? And then the thing or whatever it was with Hayley. No wonder she was so messed up. She needed to give herself a break.

She recalled her first sponsor telling her that an alcoholic is like a child; her reactions are outsized. "A flat tire makes us want to commit suicide," Evelyn had said. Remembering Evelyn's advice comforted her a little, but only a little. Her reactions to her breakup with Kay seemed pretty right on the money. She just wanted to get past them.

At Little Nepal, she and her two friends kissed each other hello and settled in their chairs and looked over their menus.

As they waited for the waiter, Merle asked them about themselves and their lives. Clea was an accountant and Sigrid an office manager for an investment firm. They chattered about various things, leaving Merle's mind space to formulate what she would say as she listened to them.

Once they got their food, Sigrid asked, "So, Merle. You've been quiet. What's new? What's up with Hayley?" She bit into her eggplant curry and grinned, her eyebrows dancing.

"I slept with her a couple weeks ago."

"You what?" Sigrid rarely lost her cool, but she stopped chewing and stared at Merle, speechless. It was very unusual for Sigrid to be at a loss for words.

All Clea said was "Hmph" and kept right on eating.

Sigrid put her fork down and fixed Merle with an intense stare. "Okay. Talk."

So Merle told them all about Sherrie and the stalking and the aftermath. "It just kind of happened," she said, somewhat lamely.

"Right. It was waiting to happen. It didn't 'kind of happen.'"

Sigrid was not actually making light of this event. This was reassuring because it meant she was taking it seriously. But it was also scary, because if Sigrid was shocked and treating it seriously instead of teasing her, Merle had certainly made a bad move.

"So what are you going to do now?" Sigrid asked.

"Nothing. We talked about it and agreed that it was better to just be roommates."

"Is that right? Is that what Hayley says or what you say?" Sigrid sounded acerbic.

"As a matter of fact, we agreed. She was pretty upset at first, but she calmed down."

"I'll be darned. That's surprising." And that irritated Merle because Sigrid said it in a deeply sarcastic tone.

"So what about you?" This was a question from Clea, who'd said nothing the whole time Merle was talking.

"I ought to be fine but I'm not. I feel guilty, even though it was something we obviously did together."

"Obviously. And what was it like?" As usual, Sigrid was the one who wanted details.

"What do you think?" Merle said, throwing sarcasm right back at Sigrid.

Sigrid shrugged so Merle said, "Sure. It was unbelievable. Out of this world. Amazing."

"I thought so. Merle, why are you resisting involvement so much? The woman's in love with you."

"She is *not*. She's in lust, not love. Me too. Or I was. In lust, that is."

"She *is* in love with you." Sigrid was insistent. "I saw her look at you when we were hiking in Point Reyes. As for you, it's hard for me to believe you'd just casually sleep with her and then callously dismiss her."

"Hey, it wasn't like that." That remark hurt because it was too close to the truth, no matter how much logic Merle tried to dress it up in. If she'd been a more together person, she would have just stopped it right in its tracks when they kissed in the kitchen. She was clearly not a better person.

"She's not in love with me. She hasn't said anything like that."

"If I were her," Clea said, "I wouldn't say nothing about love to the likes of you."

That was uncharacteristically harsh of Clea and stung Merle. "What do you mean?"

"Merle, honey. Even if Hayley is in love with you, you've got 'stay away from me' vibes leaking out of you all over the place."

"Need I remind you the Point Reyes trip occurred *before* you guys had sex?" Sigrid said. "It was obvious to me what was going on."

"Uh, why didn't you say something at the time?" Merle was suffering from a serious case of sour grapes if she was blaming her friends for her actions.

Sigrid favored her with a sardonic smirk. "As if that would have made any difference. You kept saying you weren't going to date *anyone*."

Clea said, "And I suspect you must have mentioned *that* to Hayley once or twice."

"Um. I suppose so. I'm simply not ready to jump into anything. It was a total mistake to do what I did. I apologized to her, and she accepted. We're back to normal."

"Something tells me you're protesting just a bit too strongly," Sigrid said. "If you were that closed down, how did you end up in bed with her?"

Merle thought for a few moments. "I don't know. She was upset because of the thing with Sherrie. I was trying to be supportive, and it just turned into something else."

"Huh." Sigrid sounded totally unconvinced.

"You know what happens to people when they get scared. Fear can activate all kinds of other feelings. It was just situational."

Sigrid stared at her, seeming skeptical. Merle stopped talking because it all sounded like a huge rationalization.

"You know?" Clea said, and picked up another piece of bread. Sigrid and Merle waited for her to continue. "Breakups are like death. They have to be grieved."

"Oh, come on. What the heck are you talking about?" Merle said, confused at the change of subject.

"No, it's true. You go through Kübler-Ross's five stages of grief just like when someone you love dies: denial, anger, bargaining, depression, and ultimately acceptance. You're in grief about your split with Kay."

Sigrid turned to regard her lover with respect and wonderment. "You know, darling, that's brilliant. It's true. Breakups *are* like death. You've lost someone and it's really hard."

"So, Doctor, what stage am I in now?" Merle asked with just a slight edge, but she suspected Clea was right.

"Depends, could be more than one. But I'll go for anger and depression."

"I'm over Kay. I swear I am."

Clea shrugged. "So you say. You may think you are, but you're not. Not yet."

Sigrid was looking at Clea with interest. "She's not ready to move on. She doesn't have acceptance."

"Bingo," Clea said. "Yet, maybe, unconsciously, you do want connection. You do want love. Ergo, you had sex with Hayley."

They both looked back at Merle, smiling slightly. Merle set her jaw. She didn't want any of it to be true, but she supposed it could be. She couldn't say specifically if she was over Kay. She wanted to be, but she probably wasn't. She wasn't ready to let go of her emotional involvement with Kay even if she'd had to let go of Kay in the physical sense. And aside from all that, the idea of emotional involvement with Hayley scared the bejesus out of her. Hayley was the epitome of the unknown. She couldn't be in love with Hayley.

"Well, okay, I'll give you that. I'm not over Kay. But Hayley's not ready either."

"Maybe and maybe not. She's got to tell you that. Not you telling her. It doesn't work that way." Clea threw her a tight smile and made Merle feel guiltier than ever. She had in fact tried to tell Hayley what she ought to feel and think, which was one of the worse sins of human interaction. She should have just stuck to talking about herself. But instead she'd engaged in a little projecting. Not the brightest thing to do.

"I think she knows what her own best interest is. She's not stupid," Merle said.

"Hey. Then it's all good, right?" Sigrid beamed and Clea nodded.

"I just wanted to tell you about it, you know. Get out of my head about it," Merle said.

"So true, love. It's not good to carry that stuff around in your head."

"Well, I feel better." She did feel better, a little. She'd done the right thing, had been honest with her friends and with Hayley, who was okay or would be in the future, even if she was currently faking it a little. Their relationship would reset itself to where it should be: friendly roommates.

It was time for everyone to move forward.

❖

Adam engineered it so the settlement conference occurred in their office. Hayley asked Angie if she'd like to sit in her office while they waited for the settlement conference meeting to be over. No one but the principals and their attorneys were attending.

Hayley was more than happy to entertain Angie. She wished all her client work were as pleasant. Hanging out and drinking coffee with the client's sister whom she couldn't yet formally date but could certainly talk to wasn't an unpleasant or difficult task.

"So you're from the Bay Area originally?" Angie asked her.

"Yes. I grew up in Concord. My dad's gone but Mom still lives there. You?"

"Watsonville. Artichoke farm." Angie wrinkled her nose and grimaced. She made "artichoke farm" sound like "nuclear waste site."

"Not the life for you, eh?"

"Not me. I went to UC Davis and studied agriculture but ended up being a consultant for agribusiness. My oldest brother runs the farm, and you know what Tom does. You're not opposed to agribusiness, are you?" Angie eyed her cautiously.

"Nope. Never thought about it."

"Good. 'Cause sometimes it raises the ire of some of the more lefty types."

"I guess that makes sense." Hayley wondered if Angie meant she'd gotten some flack from other lesbians.

"What do you like outside of work?" Angie asked.

"Movies," Hayley said promptly.

"What kind?"

"All kinds, but I'm fondest of the romantic screwball comedies from the forties and forward."

Angie grinned. "It'd be fun to see a movie with you."

"Sure." Hayley grinned back. She really did like Angie. She was sweet and good-humored, kind of cute. She didn't feel any jolt of electricity though. Her stomach didn't drop when she saw Angie like it did when she ran into Merle. Although recently, that pleasurable feeling had changed into something more like mild nausea combined with aching regret.

Lois knocked and opened the door. "They're done."

Angie and Hayley looked at each other hopefully.

Hayley held the door for Angie and they went to the lobby. The Kallman people were shaking hands with Tom and Adam, and there were big smiles all around.

Adam said, "Thank you for coming. And we all deserve credit

for reaching a satisfactory conclusion. I'll have the filing ready for signature next week," he said to Hayley and Angie.

"All right, you two. Come on in and we'll tell you all about it." Hayley noted that Adam had worn his lucky red satin tie. He was superstitious about some things.

Angie gave her brother a hug, and they all sat at the conference table as Adam described the settlement conference.

"Just like I expected, they wanted to settle because they know we've got a solid case. Age discrimination. It would be a long and ugly trial and bad publicity for Kallman. I told them the initial offer was way too small and came back with four hundred fifty thousand and Tom's job restored."

He leaned back and put his hands behind his head and closed his eyes. "There's always that moment when you state your figure and there's a big pause as you wait for what they'll say."

Adam opened his eyes. "This time I didn't detect any hesitation. They came back with four hundred and legal fees and Tom back at work. We said 'yup,' and that was that."

Angie hugged Adam and then Hayley. "Thank you, thank you, so much. Both of you. I wasn't sure at all this would work, but this is beyond my highest expectation."

"You're welcome, Angela, and now it's time to celebrate. Lois has made reservations at Boulevard and you'll be our guests. Hayley—you'll come?"

Hayley caught Angie's eye and said, "I wouldn't miss it."

Back in her office, Hayley changed into a green sheer blouse and dress shoes in preparation for their meal at the fancy restaurant. She was buttoning up the blouse when she heard a knock.

"Who is it?"

"It's Angie."

"Just a second."

Hayley's face got warm and she hastily arranged her clothes. She tucked in her blouse, made sure her trousers were zipped, and smoothed her hair. Then she inhaled and said, "Come in."

Angie entered and closed the door behind her and leaned against it, beaming rakishly. "I know I said thanks to you and to Adam, but I wanted to speak to you privately before we go out tonight."

Hayley nodded silently, not knowing what to expect.

Angie crossed the room and gave her a light but warm kiss on the lips. "That's my private thanks to you. See you in a little while."

Hayley touched her lips and smiled. "You bet. Can't wait."

The kiss gave her a little thrill, which reassured her. It looked like things were going to turn out the way she wanted. She'd wanted a date with Angie and was going to have one. Certainly the spark would come.

Chapter Fourteen

Occasionally, Merle attended a Sunday-afternoon meeting on the subject of AA's third step, which said, "Became willing to turn our wills and lives over to the care of God as *we understand him.*" As an agnostic, Merle had a pretty nonspecific view of God. She just knew she wasn't God, and that had worked well enough to keep her sober for seventeen years. Willingness, however, was to Merle one of the most mysterious concepts of AA. She readily embraced acceptance, gratitude, honesty, and faith. Faith in AA, at least, if not in God. She struggled with willingness, as did almost everyone she knew. She figured it was her innate stubbornness coupled with alcoholic bravado. Even though she was years away from her last drink and had no trouble accepting the fact that she couldn't drink, she still resisted letting go of control in the rest of her life.

The sobriety tests for people in AA were not, of course, highway-patrol holiday checkpoints but what normal people would consider unwelcome but hardly unusual life events, such as a divorce or death in the family or loss of employment. Merle thought she'd met *the* test of her sobriety when Kay left her and she didn't drink. Apparently that hadn't been the real test; it was just the warm-up. She was smack up against her lingering unwillingness to let her relationship with Kay go.

The dinner conversation with Sigrid and Clea hung in her memory, causing her to ask herself, *What is really going on with me?*

When faced with a dilemma for which she had no solution, which thank goodness didn't happen often, Merle followed the standard AA prescription. She went to meetings, and she talked (as in to Sigrid and Clea). She stated out loud her willingness to give up trying to control the outcome of whatever her dilemma was and just accept.

This Sunday-night third-step meeting would yield a bumper crop of folks talking about dilemmas. Some would be newly sober, and many, like her, would have years of not drinking behind them. She could learn from both types of people.

She sat at the long table, blinking under the garish light. How many times in how many church basements had she sat, hoping that somewhere, somehow, and from someone, she'd hear something helpful? She'd lost count, but hopefully she'd get what she needed. That's what kept her going to meetings.

This was a mixed, i.e., LGBTQ and straight meeting. Merle had long ago ceased worrying about anything like different sexual orientations. None of that mattered in AA.

Often, she got wisdom and help from people who were radically different from her.

"My name is Alec and I'm an alcoholic." He was a youngish man, with a shaved head, nose rings, and a Megadeth T-shirt. He told a story about how he'd been sober for six months and his girlfriend had stood by him; he was doing fine and talking to his sponsor and working the steps. He was doing all the suggestions in AA. Merle knew from experience that something else was coming.

"So like, yeah. Here I am Mr. AA. I'm the Man. I even got my old job back at the record store. The owner had booted me out and told me never to come back. You know, I took some advice from one of our fellows and just asked him for my job back, and he could see I was sober and I told him I was in AA and he said, 'Yeah. Okay. I'll give you another chance.'" He stopped and sniffed, trying to contain his tears.

"Three days ago, my girlfriend left me. Out of the blue. She said, 'It's nothing I can say for sure. You're different. It's different. I can't hang. Sorry.' That was it."

He paused, to command his emotions. Merle sympathized with him, both because of his story and because of his tears. One of the effects of sobriety is to bring your emotional pain very close to the surface. No longer anaesthetized by alcohol or drugs, you are a very large and very raw nerve.

At the end of the meeting, Merle went over to Alec and told him her name. "My girlfriend left me too," she said. "After ten years."

"Holy fuck, man. That sucks." Alec embraced her and they both cried a little.

"It really sucks. And the not knowing why is the worst," Merle said.

"Maybe we don't have to know," Alec said. "Maybe we're not meant to know. I mean it would be nice to, but who says it all has to make sense?"

"True. That's my problem. I want it all to make sense. I want everyone to do what I want them to do. And above all, they have to behave logically."

"Right, man. That would be a big fucking help, wouldn't it?" Alec laughed. Merle was happy she'd cheered him up. She felt better. She wasn't the only virtuous human whose lover had dumped her for no good reason. It was always good to be reminded she wasn't unique.

She drove home thinking of the inexplicability of human behavior, her own included. She'd slept with Hayley because she wanted to, and it wasn't just mindless lust. She was certainly not completely over Kay, but she was a little further along after hearing Alec's experience and talking to him. She probably needed to talk to Hayley again to try to explain herself better, though how that would cheer Hayley up, she had no clue. God, she despised guilt; it was such a useless emotion. Well, she wasn't going to rid herself of it until she talked to Hayley.

❖

Merle sat on the front porch with a glass of iced tea. It was Friday after work, and since it was October, it was still seventy-five degrees and clear. San Francisco's summer occurred in September and October. The western wind didn't blow so hard, and the fog didn't roll in every afternoon. Merle gazed over the edge of Bernal Hill toward the downtown skyline. She ought to be happy, sitting on her own porch with her beloved dog looking at a striking view of one the most beautiful cities in the world. But she wasn't.

She knew what contentment and serenity were like. She'd felt it before but didn't feel it now. To get it back, she had to start with having a heart-to-heart with Hayley. She expected her home any moment and hoped she'd agree to join her on the porch.

Arthur jumped up from the floor and wagged his tail, his gaze riveted to the sidewalk. Sure enough, Hayley was striding toward the house. She turned up the walkway and waved at Merle, who waved back, mesmerized. She was so good-looking. She'd likely walked from Cortland Avenue so she was slightly disheveled, but it only made her more attractive. Merle flashed on how she'd looked when they were making love, weeks before, then sternly banished the image from her mind.

"Hi there. Would you like some iced tea? I just made some."

Hayley had dropped her bag and was petting a very enthusiastic Arthur. She looked up and grinned. "Sure."

Hayley went into the house and returned with her glass, then plopped into the other Adirondack chair and set her glass on the old telephone cable spool that served as the table. She sighed. "Wow. Is this nice or what?"

"Yep. It sure is. We've got to enjoy summer while we can."

"I know. I guess the only thing missing is the ocean." Hayley took a sip of her tea and looked over Bernal Hill dreamily. "I only miss my old house for that reason. I could see the ocean out the bedroom window and could walk to it in ten minutes. I used to love to do that after work at this time of year. It was lovely with the afternoon sun shining."

Merle looked over at Hayley, who had her head back, her eyes closed, and was slightly smiling, no doubt picturing the Pacific Ocean off the Great Highway on a sunny October afternoon. She looked peaceful and very beautiful.

"I can imagine. Look, Hayley, could we talk for a few minutes?"

Hayley's eyes flew open and she turned to meet Merle's gaze. "Sure."

At the intense eye contact, Merle immediately forgot what she wanted to say. Hayley was looking at her so closely she was starting to weaken again, much as she had on that Friday-night post-Sherrie invasion.

"Again, I regret things have turned out the way they have, and I'm sorrier than ever about the way I acted."

"Are you sorry we slept together?" Hayley's tone wasn't angry but it was crisp.

"Oh, no. Not that. Not at all. I feel bad I did such a poor job explaining myself that I tried to tell you what you should do and how you should feel."

"Hmm. Okay. I'm listening. Go ahead."

She looked so stern that Merle wasn't sure if she wanted to laugh or to kiss her. Neither action would be a good idea.

"I wasn't clear about what kind of mental state I was in, and my own feelings were sort of mysterious to me. I've had some time to think and also to talk to a couple of friends and—" Merle stopped talking and looked at Hayley to gauge her reaction. She couldn't read her, and their eye contact made her lose her train of thought.

"Right. Go on." Merle couldn't tell if she was angry or not.

"My relationship with Kay ended a few months ago, and I haven't truly processed it. My friend Clea said I'm grieving the death of the relationship."

"I see." Again her tone wasn't angry, but it wasn't sympathetic either.

"Yes. So. I can't move on to anyone or anything new until I get over that."

"Got it."

"So, Hayley. I want you to know that I like you very much and I respect you and obviously some part of me is really attracted to you, but it's just not the time, for me. I want to be clear about that."

"You were clear enough the other week. Don't worry. And I'm fine, so you needn't worry about my feelings. I'm over it."

Merle thought Hayley might be overdoing the hard-ass routine just a touch but didn't mention it. She honestly was glad that Hayley seemed all right. "Okay. Well, I want us to be friends and enjoy each other's company as we used to. I miss that."

"I do too."

"Good. So would you like to make dinner together tonight?"

"Sure."

They went to the kitchen and started preparing some fish and some rice and sautéed vegetables. Arthur took up his post in the kitchen door and panted as he watched them.

As they ate their dinner, the silence stretched out longer than usual.

Hayley chewed on some rice and vegetables and stared into space, then said, casually, "I'm going on a date tomorrow. Someone I met at work. A client's sister, actually. The case is over."

"That's nice," Merle said automatically. She was annoyed that, again, the prospect of Hayley going on a date called up all sorts of inappropriate jealous feelings in her. God, she was so unevolved, it was ridiculous. When was she going to get over this shit?

"Yeah. I really like her. She's very nice and very good-looking. Smart, funny. The whole nine yards."

"Good. I'm happy to hear that. Good luck."

Hayley chewed another mouthful of food, then and looked at Merle, expressionless. "Thanks. I feel good about it so far."

They finished eating, tidied up, and went to their separate corners of the house.

❖

Hayley dressed with special care for her date with Angie. She'd gotten a whole new outfit, including shoes, and made sure the fit was perfect. She even had the pants tailored. She felt good in the clothes, good in her body, and fine about the whole idea: Angie, the date, herself. The whole thing was good.

"Not bad for an old broad," she told her reflection. At the same time, she cautioned herself to not get her hopes up. All her other dating experiences had been so, well, so disappointing, it was hard to think this was any different. But it felt different. She'd had a chance to spend time with Angie before even reaching the date stage, and everything pointed to a good outcome, maybe even a sleep-over. Hayley shivered at that idea. She pictured Angie's trim little body nude.

Angie picked her up right on time. When Hayley opened the front door, Arthur at her side, Angie held out a bouquet of autumn flowers to her. It was just right.

"Come in while I put these in water, and then we can go."

"Who's this?" Angie asked, indicating Arthur, who was watching them with his usual mix of benign curiosity and attention-begging.

"My roommate's dog, Arthur."

"He's sweet. Where's your roommate?"

"Out. I don't know. We don't keep tabs on each other." Just talking about Merle in such a casual way made Hayley's heart ache. Would her longing ever go away? She hoped Angie would banish it for good. She didn't want to expect too much from poor Angie, but still, maybe a few orgasms with another woman and her feelings for Merle would vanish into the ether. Poof. Gone.

They went to a romantic movie at the Embarcadero Cinema downtown. Afterward, they strolled through the complex, and it seemed perfectly natural to hold hands. The mild weather was holding so it was pleasant to be out at night. The Financial District skyscrapers were twinkly with light. They walked all the way to Justin Hermann Plaza. Behind it was the San Francisco Bay, featuring the newly rebuilt Bay Bridge's towers and cables outlined with white lights. The black water of the Bay reflected them, along with all the lights along the East Bay shore where Oakland and Berkeley cast their own reflections.

"Look up there." Angie pointed. "You know what that is, right?"

Hayley followed the direction of Angie's finger and squinted. It looked like a castle outlined in gold.

"What the heck is that? I've seen it before. I should know, but I don't."

"Mormon Temple."

"Oh, jeez, really? They're here? In the Bay Area?"

"They sure are, right up there in the Oakland Hills."

"Oh, my word."

"We're safe. They can't get us." Her voice was tinged with humor. Hayley laughed. They became very quiet.

Hayley could see Angie's eyes reflecting the lights. It was a lovely visual. Angie turned to toward her. This was it. Their lips met and molded, exploring. To Hayley it was dreamlike, unreal. She tasted vestiges of the cocktail, a mai tai, that Angie had drunk a short while before, but it wasn't unpleasant.

Angie's fingers entwined her hair and gently massaged her scalp, and that felt good as well.

All elements were present: night-time, the romantic city of San Francisco, a little bit of alcohol, a lovely, sexy woman with whom she shared an easy rapport.

So why wasn't she massively turned on and ready to jump into the car, rush back to Angie's flat, and dive into bed?

Hayley suspected she knew the answer, but she didn't want to bring it into her consciousness. She wanted this evening to be what she wanted it to be. "Mmm. This is nice but I'm getting cold. I should have brought a sweater."

Angie was wearing a nice gray blazer. She immediately took it off and held it up.

"Here you go."

"Are you sure you're okay?"

"Never better. Would you like to head back now or—?"

"Yes, please. Let's get inside."

Angie looked at her tentatively. "Where to?"

"How about you show me your flat?"

"Of course. Be glad to."

During the drive uptown to the Inner Sunset, Hayley went back and forth in her head. *Yes or No?*

The moment of truth would be presenting itself shortly, and she had to decide what she wanted to do. If she went to bed with Angie, it would likely be just fine, but wouldn't she be a fraud if she went ahead and slept with someone she wasn't truly, deeply, profoundly sexually attracted to? She didn't know. She didn't want to be a jerk.

She really wanted to have some more sex, but as nice as Angie was, she couldn't summon forth that headlong, no-holds-barred, deep lust she'd experienced with Merle. It didn't seem right to say to someone who wanted you, "Gee, I don't know. You just don't do it for me." Especially since up to this point she'd exuded come-hitherness. This was a sticky situation; how in the hell had she ever let herself get caught up in it?

Chapter Fifteen

Merle came home after the movie she'd gone to alone and took Arthur out for his last bathroom break. Because it was a nice night, she decided to go for a walk instead of letting him into the backyard. She stuck to the streets because Bernal Hill could be a bit spooky in the dark. She strolled up Bonview, in spite of her best intentions wondering where Hayley was and what she was doing. It was ten o'clock and she wasn't home yet. Merle scolded herself for even thinking about it.

Back home, she thought about how to structure her day. She needed way more meetings to help her get past this obsession, which was threatening to take over her life. She looked online and found a couple of meetings she'd never been to before. Maybe they would help her get a different perspective.

It took her a long time to fall asleep.

❖

"Nice place. Have you got anything to drink?" Hayley asked. If she was going through with this she needed some lubricant—of the alcoholic variety. She'd fluctuated the whole way over to Angie's flat but couldn't reach a conclusion. If she were in Angie's shoes and her date backed out now, she would be royally pissed. Then again, if she went through with it and then kissed her off, that would be worse, or would it? She decided to just see what happened and how she felt.

Angie handed Hayley a large glass of wine, the twin of the one in her hand. Oh ho, someone else was a little nervous. That helped.

They sat on the couch and clinked glasses.

"How long have you lived here?"

"About five years. I used to live over in the Excelsior. Out in the boonies."

"No shit? Why'd you live out there?"

"We wanted to buy a house, and that was the only place we could afford. Outside of Visitacion Valley or Hunter's Point."

"We?"

"My partner and I."

"Oh. Wow."

"She's dead, passed away from breast cancer three years ago."

"I'm sorry."

"Don't be. I'm okay. I'm over it. I don't want to talk about it especially. Not now."

Angie took a healthy gulp of wine and smiled at Hayley over her glass. She ran her wet finger over the rim, and the glass made a ringing sound.

Hayley was stunned, though she didn't know why she should be. Women died from breast cancer with depressing frequency. She took a big mouthful of her drink, and it rushed right to her head. She smiled vaguely at Angie, completely at a loss as to what to say.

Angie saved her from further anxiety about making small talk by moving closer, putting her arm around her shoulder, and playing with her hair. They were close enough to kiss, so Hayley took the lead and brought her head near Angie's, and they met in the middle. The kiss was longer this time and more sensual. Angie was a superior kisser. She was tender and just assertive enough but not overwhelming. Hayley's breathing speeded up, and she grew warm and tingly in the right places. Maybe it would be all right, after all. They got closer and more active with their hands. Hayley ran hers down Angie's sides. She could feel her ribs and the firm muscles in her shoulders and back. It reminded her of Merle.

She firmly shut her mind off and concentrated on pure sensory input. Angie squeezed her breast, which felt really good. They kissed with more ardor but stopped and looked at each other panting.

"Shall we go on?" Angie asked, and it touched Hayley that she would be willing to let Hayley make that decision.

"Oh yes. I want to very much."

Angie's sexy smile, which lit up her face, was enough to propel Hayley to a higher level of arousal. This was going to work out. Her misgivings seemed silly.

Angie stood up, took her hand, and led her down the hallway to a small, cozy bedroom. They took their time undressing each other, kissing and touching. Hayley unclasped Angie's bra to reveal small breasts with large nipples, engorged with blood. Hayley kissed and licked each one, rewarded with a couple of deep moans from Angie. Angie tugged her hair and massaged her scalp more forcefully, but it felt good.

They finally got totally naked and edged toward the bed. Angie drew down the covers and had Hayley sit, and then, with a hand on her chest, she pushed her gently backward. Again, to Hayley, it felt right that she let Angie carry the momentum. Her body was responding in all the right ways, and she welcomed the touch. She relaxed into the pillows and let Angie have her.

Closing her eyes, she imagined Merle was touching her, making her warm and wet and craving an orgasm. Angie kissed her way down Hayley's body from her cheeks to her neck to breasts, belly, and hips. The bed shifted as Angie moved down to her feet, then gently spread her legs. At the first touch of her tongue, Hayley gasped and moaned. Angie was as good at oral sex as she was at kissing. Her tongue was wet and her strokes were slow and steady and felt very good, but Hayley knew she wasn't going to come. She almost got a leg cramp from tightening her muscles, but to no avail. She didn't know how she knew it, but she was sure she wouldn't come. After a while, Hayley tapped the top of Angie's head.

"Is something wrong? Am I doing something wrong?" Angie asked, obviously worried.

"No, not at all. Come up here."

Angie obeyed and they embraced. "It's a problem with me. Don't worry. You're great."

Her words seemed to reassure Angie and they started over again. This time Hayley took over. If nothing else, she'd get to sharpen her oral technique, and Angie's massive orgasm rewarded her. She was proud of herself. It was enormously gratifying to make a woman come, even if that woman wasn't Merle.

Angie fell asleep right away, leaving Hayley to stare at the ceiling and brood. If she couldn't get past this thing with Merle, she'd never have a fulfilling relationship with anyone. What a monumentally depressing thought.

The next morning, as they had coffee and toast, Hayley said, "I want to thank you for a really wonderful time last night."

"But…?" Angie looked sad.

"Huh?" Hayley was mystified.

"I can hear the 'but' at the end of your sentence, even if you didn't say it aloud."

"You're right. I really mean to say, 'It's been swell but I can't see you again.'"

"Righto." Angie looked away then, over to the stove, then refocused on Hayley.

"I admit I don't have a huge amount of experience, but before I met Jane, I dated quite a few women and slept with a lot, including some in the last couple of years. So I can tell when someone's not that into it or into me."

"No, not at all. It's just—"

Angie held up her hand. "Don't worry. I'm not taking this personally. I'm old enough to know better."

"I had a good time, and I don't want you to feel bad."

"As I said, I don't, not in the least."

They were quiet for a few moments, sipping their coffee. Hayley decided to take a risk. "There's someone else."

Angie's smile was wry. "Oh? Is that a fact? Want to tell me about her?"

So they made more coffee and some eggs, and Hayley told Angie all about Merle.

Angie listened without comment until Hayley finished her tale.

"What do you think I should do?" Hayley asked.

"Boy. That's a tough one. I don't know what to say other than you need to wait until she gets to a different place. Are you in love with her?"

That question shocked Hayley. She didn't know how to describe her feelings. It seemed a monstrous faux pas to admit to love for someone to a woman you'd just slept with, but Angie was friendly and nonjudgmental, so she decided to take another chance.

"Yes. I think I am."

"Does she know that?"

"No. I never told her. I never said those words."

"Well, you might want to let her know."

"She thinks I need more experience dating, that I don't want to settle down with just one person right now."

"Sometimes when lesbians get involved with straight women and it doesn't work out, we blame them because they're straight."

"That's not me. Not now. I'm over that."

"I believe you, but that may be what Merle's thinking, even if she didn't say so."

"Oh, she said it all right, and I probably just agreed with her because it was easier and made me feel better about the rejection, kind of. But I don't think I need more so-called experience." She made a face, thinking of sex with Angie the night before and not managing to reach orgasm.

"I had a bunch of dates with all sorts of women, one of whom turned into that stalker that sort of pushed Merle and me into bed, though it was waiting to happen anyhow. So I guess some good came out of those crazy dates."

Angie laughed, and then she said, "You know, when we get to our age—"

"How old *are* you, anyhow? I can't even guess."

"Fifty-four. I was going to say, at our age, I don't feel like I have a whole lot of time to waste. If it's right, it's right. I don't have to do a lot of screwing around or have my heart broken multiple times."

"That's probably true. It's not like I want to keep looking. I just think I ought to."

Angie touched her hand. "Hayley, I think you know the real reason. If Merle really doesn't care about you, except as a friend, you need to find out, but otherwise, I say go for broke. Tell her the truth and see what she says. If it's going to happen, it will happen."

"Thanks so much for everything. I mean it. You're a fabulous woman. If things were different—"

"Don't think about that. Count me as a friend, okay?"

"I'd like that very much."

After Angie dropped her off at home, she stood on the sidewalk looking at the house and thinking about what Angie had said. Did Merle truly care for her? It was impossible to say, but she thought not. It just didn't make sense any other way.

She sighed and squared her shoulders. She might as well accept reality. She could stay in the house and they could be friends and roommates. Merle had made her feelings pretty clear. That was what they were going to be. It was, after all, just sex.

But Hayley couldn't hang around and wait forever for her to change her mind. That would drive her nuts and would be a nutty thing to do. She made her decision right then and there.

❖

The next morning when Merle woke up, she could tell right away that the house was empty. Hayley hadn't returned home the night before. Oh, well. That was going to happen eventually. No big deal. She dragged herself out of bed and downstairs to let Arthur out and make coffee. She'd give him a good walk later and then go to a meeting. She didn't have anything else to look forward to, nothing fun to do. She could watch TV, she supposed, but that sounded pretty blah.

Arthur bolted from his spot by the kitchen threshold, and she heard the front door open. She listened to Hayley's soft greeting to Arthur. She had such a mellow voice, either alto or contralto, but whatever, she loved the sound of it. Some women could be shrill or squeaky. Hayley's voice settled easily in her ears. When she spoke to Arthur, she was tender and loving. Merle would have loved to hear Hayley speak to her as she spoke to Arthur, but it wasn't to be. She arranged her face in a smile just in time as Hayley walked into the kitchen.

"Hi there," she said, much more enthusiastically than she felt.

"Hello. Arthur!" Hayley pointed to the door. Arthur had followed her right into the kitchen. With a regretful look, he went back to the doorway and sat down.

"You've got that part of obedience down really good."

"Thanks. Is there any more coffee?"

"Yup." Hayley looked pensive. Merle was absurdly glad she didn't have the dreamy post-orgasmic smile she'd sported the morning after their night of lovemaking.

Hayley poured herself a cup, sat down across from her, and sipped it a few times. Merle waited for her to speak. She took her time, sipping and staring at the table.

"I've really enjoyed living here with you and Arthur," she said.

"We like having you. After all the nightmare stories I heard about roommates, you were a dream come true."

Hayley raised an eyebrow and looked at her doubtfully.

That comment was somewhat over the top, Merle realized. Also, Hayley had said "enjoyed"—past tense.

"Thanks." Hayley took another drink of coffee, a big one.

"Look. I think it's better if I move out."

Merle's stomach turned over and her anxiety shot through the roof. This wasn't unexpected, but it still hit her hard. Her left brain said it was a good idea, and she agreed. But her right brain screamed, "No. No. No." This was crazy.

"Why?" Merle asked.

"I think you know, but I'll say it anyhow. I've got feelings for you, but you don't feel the same about me. I'm not prepared to keep sharing this home with you. It wouldn't be good for either of us."

"Right," Merle said, but that wasn't what she was thinking.

Hayley drained her coffee cup and nearly slammed it on the table. She stood up.

"I'll need some time to find a new place to live. But I'm going to leave as soon as I can."

She rinsed her cup and put it in the dishwasher as Merle watched her silently. "I'll see you later," she said and walked out of the kitchen.

❖

Hayley went to her bedroom and sat on the bed, proud of herself for executing that conversation unemotionally. It was one of the toughest things she'd ever had to do. She just had to follow through and get a new place to live.

She wanted to return to the kitchen and tell Merle she'd made a big mistake, but she steeled herself and fought back the tears. She'd made the right decision, the mature choice. That was who she was, not some lovesick teenager, never mind how she felt at the moment. She needed to start going through her possessions and look online at rental listings. But she did neither of those things. She lay down on her bed and thought fleetingly of her night with Angie. It wasn't the sex that lingered in her mind. It was Angie's question.

She supposed Merle did care for her but not in the right way, not the way she wanted. There was no way to change that. She gave up and gave in to her tears then.

❖

The next week she went to the coming-out support-group meeting, and when her turn came around, she said, "I've made up my mind. I've got to move. It's killing me to be around Merle and not be with her."

"Oh, my God!" Amy said, "Have you told her?"

"What did she say?" Betty asked.

"Yes, I told her. She didn't say much."

"How do you feel?" Diane asked.

Yes, that was the question, wasn't it? Hayley didn't know how she felt other than very sad and very silly at that same time.

"I don't like feeling like a teenager, but I'm willing to accept that. I don't have to act like one. I don't want to hang around someone mooning over her like a lovesick schoolgirl, so I'm going to split." She took a swig of water. She was acting a whole lot more together than she felt.

It was Amy once again who waylaid her after the meeting. "Come on, let's go have coffee."

Hayley agreed.

"So what's the real story?" Amy asked.

"You know it. I fell in love with her."

"Did you tell her?"

"Of course not. That would be a mistake." *Angie thought I should tell her as well. I can't face the rejection. I just can't.* "She's made it super clear she can't get involved with anyone right now. After we had sex, she backed off so quick it was like I had a social disease."

Amy chuckled. "You're funny, but maybe you could try to be honest with her about why you're moving out."

"I guess," Hayley said uncertainly. It couldn't hurt for Merle to hear the whole truth. She was getting tired of pretending to be okay. "I'll think about it."

❖

At work, Merle turned over the page on her wall calendar. In spite of using her electronic calendar to actually keep track of things, she still liked the old-fashioned calendars with pictures...if they were free. She was too cheap to buy a fancy wall calendar. This year's was from a company that made antibodies.

It was November first. Which week did Thanksgiving fall in? She supposed she'd spend it with Clea and Sigrid. They always cooked a big dinner. She wondered about Hayley's plans. They hadn't spoken for a few weeks and had stopped having meals together. It was time to fully disengage, and this saddened Merle profoundly.

She sat at her desk staring at the calendar display of little dancing cartoon antibodies looking for antigens. The captions proclaimed the company's efficiency in manufacturing antibodies avid for their antigens. Merle shook her head and tried to focus on her work. She thought about the upcoming weekend with its two days of nothing that needed to be filled. This never used to be the case. When had she lost the ability to make plans? Right around the time Kay left, probably.

She had to stay out of the house and away from Hayley as much as possible. She was going to move so Merle had to get used to not being around her.

Then she remembered a task she'd been putting off for weeks. Her nephew was getting married next month and she needed to buy a wedding gift. She might as well just head downtown to Union Square Macy's store and get it done. Pick them out a nice chafing dish or something. Whatever. She wasn't much of a shopper, but if she saw something *she* wanted, she'd buy herself a gift.

Then she'd go to a meeting—anything to avoid seeing Hayley. How immature and silly. No, it was really self-preservation. She had to get over her.

On Sunday afternoon, Merle wandered through the housewares department in the basement of the big Macy's store. She'd printed out the bridal registry list for Holmes-Sinclair. It was simply a question of picking something up and having it shipped to them with a card and she'd be done. Then she could see if any good clothes were on sale. Winter was coming; maybe she should buy a new sweater.

She stood in front of a dish display. If the list from the registry was correct, one place setting cost fifty bucks. Did her nephew and his fiancé have overly expensive tastes, or had china become outrageously expensive since the last time she'd bought some?

Then she checked the list again and saw that three had already been bought of the four they'd requested. Dynamite, she'd be the last. The kids would have service for four and her obligation would be fulfilled. She double-checked the make of the place setting to be sure she had the right one. There were so many choices. She started looking for the right brand name, tapping the touch screen impatiently.

Then she heard a very familiar voice behind her say, "It's up to you. I don't care what we get."

Even if she hadn't recognized who was speaking, the next moment, she heard the response that confirmed her thought.

"I get that, Kay. If you're okay with it, I like this one best."

It was definitely her ex, but who did the other voice belong to? It might be someone she knew, but she wasn't sure. Should she announce her presence or not?

"Oh my God, Merle?" *Too late.*

She turned around and there stood Kay, looking greatly alarmed. Behind her loomed a very tall woman that Merle recognized as someone she'd met before, but she couldn't place where or what her name was.

"Hello, Kay."

"What a surprise to run into you in Macy's, of all places." Kay's voice was quite tense, and she glanced back at the tall woman nervously.

The woman raised her eyebrows and stepped forward with her hand out. "Hi. I'm Dana."

"Hi, Dana, nice to meet you." Merle knew she knew this woman, but she was willing to go along with the charade that they were unacquainted.

She turned back to Kay. "I'm here shopping for a wedding gift. How have you been?"

And Kay looked at Dana again. Something was going on with them. *Oh, shit.* This was her new lover. Right.

"Good. Say, Dana, I haven't seen Merle in quite a while. How about you finish your shopping and we'll go have coffee at the café?" She turned to Merle and asked, "If you've got the time?"

Why not? She was deeply curious about what and who Dana was. "Sure, I got a couple minutes."

"Great. I'll text you. Half an hour?"

Dana nodded and looked relieved, then turned and walked away.

As Merle and Kay made their way through the store, Merle asked Kay, "So who's that?"

"Oh, you remember Dana. She's one of the assistant city attorneys. You met her at that Christmas party? The one we had at the Gift Center?" Kay was trying valiantly to sound casual and easygoing, but Merle knew her so well. Something was going on.

"Maybe. How come you're shopping at Macy's with her?" Merle couldn't keep the sarcasm out of her voice.

"I'll explain everything once we sit down." Good old Kay. The reveal would always be in her time frame, not Merle's. Good to know she was still the same.

They each fetched a coffee and found a table. Since it was Sunday, Macy's café was crowded with shoppers. Not the ideal place for an intimate chat.

"So?" Merle twirled her coffee cup and fixed Kay with a questioning stare, cocking an eyebrow.

"I wanted to tell you at the right time, but I guess this is as good a time as any. How are you, by the way?"

"Like I said, I'm fine. Tell me what, exactly? That you're with her now? So what?" Kay was unquestionably very nervous for some reason. Merle feigned a nonchalance she didn't actually feel. She felt more like strangling someone. Like Kay, for instance.

"Well. Yes. I wanted to explain it to you."

"Explain? What's to explain? You've moved on. That's great." It wasn't really. Merle realized at that moment that she harbored a deeply buried hope that somehow she and Kay would reconcile. After Kay had gone through whatever she was going through, she'd see how they belonged together, in the end. She would come back to Merle and Arthur and the comfy Craftsman house in Bernal Heights. Clea had been right after all. She hadn't let go of Kay.

Kay looked great. She *always* looked great. Her curly mane of hair was well styled. The little spray of freckles across her nose that gave her that sweet, innocent look was still there. So were her nicely shaped pink lips and sharp cheekbones. She was still beautiful. In spite of her pique, Merle's palms started to sweat and she visualized making love to Kay like she used to way back when.

"I wanted to explain about Dana and me." Kay looked more uneasy than ever.

"I'm listening."

"We'd talked and talked about when it would be okay to tell you. Dana wanted to a long time ago, but I refused. I knew you wouldn't take it well."

"A long time ago? How long ago? What are you saying?" Merle was beginning to understand precisely what Kay was saying, and it infuriated her.

"Last year."

"Last *year*?" Last year they were going to therapy every week and talking about what to do so they could stay together.

"Merle. Sweetie. This is so hard. I knew this would be—"

"Wait just a fucking minute here, Kay. You were seeing Dana while we were still together? Were you fucking her?"

Kay glanced around to see if anyone had heard that pointed question and also to buy herself some time, no doubt.

"No, I mean, not really."

"Which was it? Is this why you broke up with me?"

"I don't know. It wasn't really. Sort of. I just knew we weren't working." Typical Kay. She wouldn't commit to a straight answer. She was always so vague, it was maddening. Merle glared at her. Kay looked away, then back at Merle. Merle watched her gather herself and move from nervousness to defiance.

"Dana and I worked together."

As if that explained everything! "Yeah. I know, but so what?"

"Well. One thing led to another." Kay was an investigator with the city attorney's office. Her job was doing the footwork that attorneys didn't have time for when they were putting together a case, and she sometimes worked long hours. Obviously, she'd spent some of those hours in extracurricular sex. Why had this *never* occurred to her? She recalled Sigrid asking the question. Good grief, she was a nitwit.

"Yeah. I'll bet. So you were cheating on me the whole time."

"Merle. I wanted to stop seeing Dana. I wanted us to stay together. I really did. That's why I didn't tell you, because I knew it would devastate you. I wanted us to work! I went to all those frigging therapy sessions with you. Didn't that prove I was trying? It wouldn't have helped if I'd told I was sleeping with Dana."

"The only thing any of this crap proves is you're a good liar and major codependent freak. Devastate me? How could it *not* devastate me? You could have been honest and saved us a buttload of money." Merle hated that she used so much foul language when she was angry, but too bad.

"I knew you'd be mad. Anyone would be. You wanted us to make it so badly. I couldn't face your disappointment."

"Nope. You were never any good at facing *anything*, were you? You couldn't decide what brand of dishwashing liquid to buy, let alone whether you wanted to spend the rest of your life with me!"

"Now you're just being mean." Here came the petulance, right on time.

"I suppose Dana came along at just the right time when you were hovering on the cusp of indecision, and she scooped you right up." Kay's lovely face darkened and her lips curled.

"However it helps you to think about it Merle, feel free. I wanted us to be friends, but—"

"I get why you gave me so much time to buy you out of the house: you were feeling guilty. *I* started to feel guilty because I wasn't paying you back fast enough. Sheesh. Oh no. There's no 'let's be friends with the ex' here. Not going to happen. Thanks for filling me in on the details. I'll keep up with payments. Don't worry. Bye." She stood up and walked away. She refused to let Kay see her tears.

Unfortunately, she had to pull herself together and go back to finish the wedding-gift transaction. She went on autopilot—made her purchase, then caught the underground and bus home.

The trip gave her plenty of time to go over the whole miserable scenario once again. She guessed that all cheated-on lovers picked apart the past looking for the telltale signs they'd missed. She was no different, and as she thought about the last year of their relationship, a lot of it made much more sense.

She supposed she was grateful. She was *not* crazy, at least not too crazy. And she wasn't stupid either. Trusting someone isn't stupid, it's essential. That your trust is violated sometimes is the price of admission to intimacy. She had no future with Kay. She never had, and it was senseless to regret the past. She'd tried and she'd failed, but it wasn't her fault. It was time to let go.

Merle looked out the window of the Muni bus chugging its way through the Mission to her home and remembered her other heartache. Hayley was probably seeing someone now. She hoped it was someone nice, unlike her other dates. And, she was going to move out.

Merle ought to get off her ass, buck up, and start diving into the dating pool. Waiting wasn't really going to make any difference. It was amazing, but after Kay's revelation, something had cleared in her mind. She was done with Kay—finally, completely, and forever.

She got home in time to let Arthur out, but just barely. She was going to have to drive to the Sunday third-step meeting to make it on time. Oh, well. The environmental gods wouldn't strike her down.

Merle grabbed her car keys and drove like a madwoman. She slid into a seat just in time for the meeting to begin, and as she listened to the speaker, she thought about willingness in its many forms. Or its opposite: unwillingness. Stubbornness. Kay had handed her a gift. She was ready to think of it in that fashion. She *had* to view it that way. She raised her hand.

"My name is Merle and I'm an alcoholic." The chorus of "Hi, Merles" was so comforting, so routine, and so reliably encouraging.

"It's great to be at a meeting of Alcoholics Anonymous and to be sober. Thank you for your share." This was for the speaker, whom she'd thought adequate but not especially inspiring. She needed to say aloud what had happened to her and how it affected her so that she could make it real. That was one of the ways recovery helped.

"I learned a huge lesson about unwillingness today." She heard some scattered giggles, not of derision but of recognition. In an AA meeting, everyone identified with what everyone else went through, both the terrible darkness of alcoholic behavior and during the ups and downs in recovery.

"I don't like to be wrong. I mean, who does, right?" Again some murmurs of assent.

"Nor do I ever want to look like I don't have it together. *Ever*. Well, good luck with *that*." She paused.

"I found out today that the woman I loved and thought I knew had successfully fooled me about everything. We broke up a few months ago after ten years together."

Lots of groans greeted that sentence.

"But I found out the real reason today. It wasn't because I was screwed up or didn't love her well enough. I did. It really was her fault all along." Everyone in the room was silent. One of the many wonderful things about AA was that you could say *anything*, and Merle had heard so many things over the years. But no one could judge you, at least out loud. It was your experience, your feelings. No one would dispute that or try to change your interpretation of your life.

"My part was my unwillingness to let go of my hope that it would all be okay and that somehow we'd get back together. It's not going to happen, and I'm glad because I know what the truth was. I always thought she was indecisive and that she might make up her mind to come back to me. I cannot hang on to magical thinking. I have to be a grown-up and accept reality. We're not getting back together. She came clean about some stuff today that I don't need to tell you in detail. It was rough to hear but gave me the ability to let go. I don't want her back. My unwillingness is broken. I'm willing to see reality, and I'm willing to get on with my life, whatever that may end up being. I'm glad to be here today. Thanks."

After the meeting she spoke to a few people, including young Alec, who came over and hugged her.

"You're amazing," he said. "A couple weeks ago, you were just like me. A wreck."

Merle chuckled. It was true after all. Leave it to a newbie to see the truth about her and state it baldly. You couldn't fool people in AA, no matter how hard you tried. AAs weren't into sugarcoating stuff to save face. The AA wisdom said you could save your face or you could save your ass. Pick one.

"How about you?" she asked Alec.

"Oh, man. History. She's history. No use in trying to hold on, like you say. We're better than that and better than them."

"We are, certainly. It takes a while to get there, but once you do, you're there."

"You're right. I got there and I didn't drink. I thought about it a couple times, but I didn't."

"Nope. That's the miracle. Shit happens and you don't have to drink. You just have to move through the pain to the other side. Have a good week and take care, Alec."

"You too. Thanks so much, Merle." They hugged again.

"Thank you!" she whispered in his ear.

Chapter Sixteen

As Merle drove home, she enjoyed the feeling of relief. She was also extremely hungry and wished Hayley had cooked something. Ah, Hayley. What a gal. Merle hoped she was doing okay. When they ran into one another, Hayley looked shell-shocked. Since Merle had had her breakthrough about Kay, it would be nice if Hayley's life and feelings could be synched up with hers and they could be together, but that wasn't going to happen.

It was sad, but Merle had to be okay with that too. She needed to stop wishful or magical thinking about everything and everyone. She'd find a way to deal with her feelings for Hayley. She had to start her life again. Besides, Hayley was moving out.

As she walked into the house she could smell something good. It would be hard to not have someone to cook with or eat with. She'd have to go through the whole annoying search for a roommate. Again. *Whatever.*

Arthur stood in front of her, his tail going a hundred miles an hour. He needed a walk for sure, and she'd do that after dinner. Hayley wasn't in the kitchen, but a pot of chili and a pan of cornbread sat on the stove. God bless her. She lifted the lid and took a good whiff, then found a bowl and plate and sat down at the kitchen table.

Hayley appeared in the doorway.

"Oh, hey," Merle said. "Thanks for making dinner."

"No problem." She fell silent.

"You okay?" Merle asked. Hayley had an odd look on her face. Merle automatically wanted to take care of her. She could endure it if Hayley wanted to talk about her new girlfriend—or that she didn't have a new girlfriend. In spite of her resolve, she wanted there to be a new girlfriend. To make it easier to let go.

"Yeah. I'm fine. Do you have time to talk now? I don't want to bother you…"

"No, not at all. Sit down. You ate already, I assume?"

"Not really. I wasn't hungry."

"Wow. You made dinner anyhow. That was really sweet." Merle definitely didn't want Hayley to move out and take her cooking skills with her. Or for that matter her plumbing skills. They would certainly come in handy at some point in the future. She silently ordered herself to let it go.

Hayley poured herself a glass of water and took a big gulp. Her throat muscles moved in an attractive way, but Merle reprimanded herself again for noticing. She waited for Hayley to start talking.

"I wanted to discuss something with you, because, well. Shit, this is hard." Hayley took another drink. She looked spooked, as though she'd rather be gulping whiskey than water. Merle could relate to that. What in the world was going on? Surely it wasn't another stalker. That would be too weird.

"What's the matter?" Merle asked, just to help her get started with saying what she wanted to say.

Hayley didn't answer right away. She poured another glass of water and stared at her hands, then at Arthur, who was panting hopefully in the doorway.

"Hi, guy," she said to Arthur. "Poor fellow. You know you're not allowed in the kitchen when we're eating."

Jesus Fucking Christ, she was taking her time. Merle told herself to be patient.

Hayley took her usual seat at the kitchen table. "Ah shit!" she said to the table. "I'm not good at this at all. I need to tell you something I should have told you before, but I couldn't."

"It's fine, Hayley. I'm not going to be upset."

"What? You don't know what I'm going to say!" She sounded angry.

"No, but I have an idea—"

"You've got no idea!" Hayley nearly shouted. Merle was taken aback.

"Oh, sorry. Let me just let you talk."

"Thanks," Hayley mumbled, then took another deep breath and turned to lock eyes with Merle.

"I'm in love with you. I think I fell in love with you the first time I came over here to interview with you. But I know it's not going to work. You've told me so."

"You're, uh—" Merle was flummoxed. This wasn't at all what she'd expected.

"I know it's maybe not what you want to hear. If you don't feel the same, I get it, but I wanted to tell you the truth—"

Merle stopped her outpouring with a kiss.

It was a twin of the kiss they'd shared after they'd booted Sherrie out of the house. It was a superb kiss. As soon as her lips met Hayley's, Merle knew it was right. It was perfect. She was there, Hayley was there. She felt a whole lot of love, an enormous amount of caring, and massive, overpowering lust. The kiss went on and on until they had to stop or risk asphyxiation.

"You're okay with my being in love with you?" Hayley asked, somewhat suspiciously. She looked at Merle closely. "What about all your talk about me needing to get experience?" She used the air quotes around "experience." "And what about all that stuff you said about you're not ready for a relationship again?"

It was a fair question. "Um. I think I'd better stick to my own feelings and not analyze yours. I had a breakthrough today. An epiphany."

"So did I!" Hayley beamed. "What was yours?"

So Merle told her about Kay and Dana. "I was still stuck in the past, and I'd put you in a box as untouchable because you'd just come out. It was silly, but it was more about my issues than about you. I was unconsciously thinking I was going to get back with Kay. And it took finding out the truth about her for me to be able to let her go. Ahem, I also had to stop assuming I knew what you were thinking or that I knew what was good for you. I started falling for you right after you moved in." She stopped. Hayley was looking at her, her expression relieved but with a hint of a smile.

"Yeah. Uh-huh. You're the big lesbian expert. I get it. But you hadn't gotten over Kay. I suppose that's understandable."

Merle had one lingering doubt so she asked Hayley, "What about that woman you're seeing?"

Hayley looked confused. Then the light dawned. "Oh. Yeah. Angie. I'm not seeing her."

"But you…?"

"Slept with her, yes. I did. And it was nice, but it wasn't you."

Hayley told her about Angie and what they'd discussed. "It seems I can't come unless I'm with someone with whom I'm in love."

"No shit." That was all Merle could think of to say.

"So all this BS about me needing to date a lot of people so I can enjoy being a lesbian is, well, BS. If you remember, I did go out on some dates. The walker, the talker, the stalker, remember?"

"Well. True. But that doesn't mean that—"

"Shut up, Merle Craig. Will you please stop bossing me around?" Hayley had her hands on her hips, and her glare would melt steel. "Stop trying to protect me, just stop."

"I'm sorry!" Merle couldn't seem to avoid putting her foot in it. She slumped back in her chair, hands at her sides. Hayley grabbed one of them in both of hers and held on tight, forcing Merle to make eye contact.

"Good. Now I'm telling you. I don't have time to waste trying to figure out if this woman or that woman or some mythical woman I've yet to meet is the 'right one.' You're the right woman." She stopped speaking to let that statement sink in.

"Can I tell you 'you need to come to bed with me right this instant'?" Merle asked in a small, acquiescent voice.

"Oh. Sure. That's okay." They laughed, then kissed again.

Hayley drew away suddenly with a hand on Merle's chest.

Merle gaped at her, befuddled by sexual arousal. "What? Something wrong?"

"Yes, there is! Isn't there something you want to tell me?"

"I don't know? Is there?" Merle was at a loss.

"Think, my dear!"

Then the light dawned. "Oh, yes. Hayley, I love you!"

"That's much better. We can proceed. Your place or mine?" She giggled. "I've wanted to say that for a long time."

"*Our* place. My bed?"

"Works for me."

❖

It took them a little longer to really get started this time, but Hayley wasn't complaining. When Merle started removing her clothes, she said, "You know there's something I've always wanted to do?"

Merle was kissing her neck and her ears and her shoulders and taking her shirt off.

"What's that, sweetie? Anything you want! I can't get too gymnastic, but within reason…"

"I want us to take a shower. For starters. Then I want you to go down on me, and then I want you to fuck me with a dildo. You've got one, haven't you? Then—"

Merle's eyes glittered. "Whoa, whoa. Take it easy, love. We'll get to everything."

"See. I can have as much experience as I need with just you."

"I see that. Okay. Let's get the rest of your clothes off."

Hayley leaned against her and said in her ear, "What about yours?" and nipped her earlobe.

Merle gasped and stuttered, "Oh yeah, mine too." They finally got naked and jumped into the bigger shower, which happened to be the one across the hall from Hayley's room.

Under the warm spray, they soaped each other all over, and Hayley marveled at the way their slick soapy bodies slid against each other. She'd never had a shower like this one. Merle pushed her against the wall and shoved her thigh between her legs. She reached between them to pull her nipples and bit her neck until Hayley wanted to scream.

"More." She moaned into Merle's mouth. Merle used her leg to support Hayley and her fingers to stoke her clit. The orgasm buildup started in her feet and traveled up her legs.

After she came, she exhaled deeply. "You're—"

Merle said, "I'd like to be dried off and in between soft sheets, and then you may do with me what you will." They rubbed themselves and each other dry.

In bed, Merle kissed her gently everywhere. "These are called rose-petal kisses." She kissed lightly, just the barest touch on hundreds of spots. Each one was like a butterfly had flapped its wings on her flesh.

Hayley was in a waking-dream state, but she dimly recalled that she'd wanted to do something specific to Merle that she hadn't gotten around to the other time.

"Merle?" Merle stopped kissing her and looked up, her eyes soft and loving.

"Yes, love?"

"Come hold me."

Merle dutifully stretched out next to her and wrapped her up in a snug embrace. "Like this?"

"Yes. Like this."

"I'll do anything you want, but I really want to make love to you again."

"Shh. Don't be greedy. You just did a few minutes ago in the shower."

"I'm very greedy. And relentless. You'll find that out."

"Oh, I've no doubt, but before you do, I've something important to tell you. Then I get my turn with you, and boy are you going to get it."

"Bring it on, but what do you have to tell me first?"

Hayley turned on her side so their gazes locked. Merle's grayish-blue eyes were grave and attentive.

"I was married when I was twenty-two years old. I had no idea what I was about, what he was about, or what love was about. Clueless doesn't even begin to describe it."

Hayley put her hands on either side of Merle's face and spoke with as much sincerity as she could possibly muster.

"I thought I was in love, but I know I was nowhere close to it. I learned what women in love do by watching videos and reading books, but I couldn't really appreciate what it's like or what it means until I was with you. I get what all the excitement's about. The only resemblance between what it's like with you and what it was like with him is that both involve two human beings and sexual organs. That's it. I never had an orgasm with him."

Merle's eyes widened. "Never? Not once?"

"*Nada.* I gave them to myself. But it's more than that, much more. When you touch me, I feel in my soul that we're deeply connected. I experienced that the first time and thought it was just me."

Merle smiled ruefully and rubbed her arm. "I feel that too, but I didn't want to believe it. I'm sure now."

Hayley melted at her expression. "Okay. I just had to get that out. I'm ready to keep going."

"Yay!" Merle started to roll them over so that Hayley was under her, but Hayley stopped her.

"Nuh-uh. Just settle down, lover." She pushed Merle onto the bed, none too gently, and knelt over her. "You'll do it *my* way."

"Righto. I'm all yours. Do with me what you will. You're very cute when you're being dominant." Merle grinned and stretched out to her full height, put her hands behind her head, and closed her eyes.

Hayley fell on her, jamming her thighs open with her leg and pushing against her. Merle embraced her and rubbed her ass. Hayley wanted to make love to Merle while she was close enough to sense her every movement and tremor. Oral sex was sexy and sensual, but she was too far away from the rest of Merle's body.

She whispered into Merle's ear as she stroked her all over. "Can I go inside you?"

"Yes, please."

She entered her with one finger, then with two, and pushed as far as she could. Merle's body jerked.

"Oh. Yes. Keep doing that."

Hayley obliged.

"Wait. Sorry. Just stop for one sec."

Hayley, alarmed, obeyed her.

Merle rolled over and opened a drawer on her nightstand and took out a small plastic bottle. "Hold out your hand."

Hayley did and Merle poured some fluid into it. "Lube. Sometimes, I get a little dry. This will help."

They resumed what they were doing. The silky feeling of the lubricant was surprisingly nice, and its effect on Merle was miraculous. Her labia and vagina grew soft and squishy. She arched her body into Hayley's hand.

Hayley kept an arm around her and asked softly, "Will you come this way?"

"Rub my clit with your thumb," she said. "Like this." She guided Hayley's hand to the right position.

Hayley experimented until she could keep her fingers in place and the back of her thumb hard against Merle's clitoris. The results were amazing. When she came, Hayley could feel everything: the pelvic thrusts, the contractions of her muscles as they closed around her fingers. She'd never felt so powerful, nor had she ever experienced such profound sexuality. Causing and then witnessing and experiencing a woman's deep pleasure was transcendent. Nothing in her life compared to it.

Merle stopped moving and released a deep, satisfied sigh. Hayley kissed her face, then her lips. She was limp in her arms. The whole thing awed Hayley.

❖

Hayley wasn't sure how the group would receive her news about Merle. Some of them had been looking for love for years, yet she'd found it in a mere five months. It might strike some women as too good to be true. Hayley felt that way herself sometimes, but the thought disappeared when she looked into Merle's eyes. Merle was no longer opaque or withdrawn. She was totally there, physically and emotionally. It was a marvelous transformation.

Hayley took her seat in the familiar circle, thinking it might be her last meeting. She couldn't see the need for the group any longer. This was going to be good-bye.

When her turn came, she said simply, "I've fallen in love with Merle and she has with me. We're together." A lot of gasps and a few claps filled the room.

Sheila, the incurable romantic said, "Aww. That's so nice. Congratulations."

Diane, the skeptic, said, "Well, that was fast."

Amy tilted her head and looked at Hayley for a moment. "I'm not surprised. What now?"

"That's a good question. On one level, I feel like I'm out, but my work isn't done. I haven't come out at work yet, and Mom hasn't fully reconciled herself to my 'decision.' When I introduce her to Merle, I hope that will change."

The women laughed.

Betty said, "You're never really done, you know. It's a lifelong process. If you want to continue to come and share your experience, it would be great."

Hayley thought about the invitation. "Maybe I will. I have a lot of fun with you guys, and I've learned a lot. Maybe it would be good to stay."

Everyone but Diane said, "Oh, yeah, please stay!" or something similar.

❖

One evening, Merle and Hayley forced themselves to forgo sex for a short time in order to discuss their new status and what it meant. It was Hayley who suggested they have a talk, and Merle agreed.

"I have no desire to see other people, but I don't know how you feel. Is it weird that we're already living together?"

Merle chuckled because it was so Hayley—the questions, the need to nail down all relationship parameters explicitly. Merle didn't mind. After years of Kay's maddening endless ambiguity and elusiveness, the request was refreshing.

"It's kind of strange that we're already living together, but at least we know we're compatible."

"Yeah, that's true. It's kind of the reverse of how it usually happens, isn't it? Usually people fall in love, find out their sexual compatibility, and *then* move in."

"Right. So we did it backward. Who cares?"

"Not me, but I still have my original question." Hayley fell silent, looking intently at Merle.

"I can't see any circumstances where I'd want to see other women. I'm too old for that. I don't have the time or patience. It's actually quite nice that the universe kind of dumped you into my lap. Very convenient. I don't have to go through that messy and annoying process of dating."

Hayley shoved her but laughed.

"What about you, missy?" Merle asked.

"What about what? I told you already. I can get all the experience I need with you. But, come to think of it, you haven't dug out any of your toys. What's up with that? I said I wanted to try a dildo. Maybe even a strap-on. Ooh, just thinking about it makes me wet, and—"

"Hayley, I've got some bad news. I don't have any toys."

Hayley's shoulders drooped and her face fell. "Why not? You don't like them? What?"

"Kay got them in the divorce. I was so distracted, I didn't question why she'd want them. I just let it go. Now I know why." She grimaced.

"Oh, right, the other woman."

Merle put an arm around Hayley and squeezed her shoulders and nuzzled her hair. Hayley relaxed into her and they kissed.

Merle leaned back and touched Hayley's adorable nose. "Besides, it's the height of tackiness to use sex toys from your ex-lover on your new lover."

"Eww. Yeah. You're right." She wrinkled her nose.

"So that means we get to go shopping."

Hayley squealed and jumped on Merle's lap.

Hayley tore herself away from kissing her and said, "There's something else I wanted to ask you."

Merle kissed her neck and said, "Mmm. Whatever it is, the answer is yes."

Hayley pulled back to make eye contact with her and said, "You might rethink that when you hear what it is."

Merle raised her eyebrows. "Okay."

"I want you to meet my mother."

Merle started laughing and said, "Sorry. Love. I'm not laughing at you. Well, I kind of am. That's not what I thought you were going to say. Never mind." She shrugged. "Sure. Whenever you want."

Hayley said, "I'm not sure. I'm nervous about it."

"Of course. It's a big deal."

"She wasn't exactly positive when I first told her."

"So you said. It'll take some time."

"I don't want to make you uncomfortable."

"No worries. I'll be fine."

"I am really concerned, and I want it to go well." Hayley had worked herself into a full-fledged case of anxiety.

"Of course you do, but you can't control the whole scenario or your mom's reactions."

"She's got all these preconceived ideas. She probably doesn't know any gay people. She lives in Concord and she's—"

"Hayley, sweetheart. Calm down. It'll be fine."

Hayley took a deep breath and concentrated on Merle's encouraging smile and the feel of her hands. She exhaled. "Yes. I think so. I hope so."

❖

Hayley was grateful that Merle offered to drive them across the Bay to visit Ellie. She assumed she wouldn't be able to concentrate properly on driving. Instead her mind was free to roam and come up with all kinds of unpleasant possibilities. She'd asked ahead of time if she could bring Merle, and Ellie had agreed, but to Hayley's ears, her mother's assent sounded begrudging, though that was possibly her imagination.

Merle told her, "Try to be cool about it. The more calm and matter-of-fact you are, the more relaxed she'll be. This is just part of normal life. You take your beloved to meet your parents. It's what people do."

"I know, I know." Merle's advice both reassured and annoyed her. Merle didn't know Ellie.

Hayley bristled, thinking about the thoughtlessly homophobic comments Ellie might make and hurt Merle's feelings. Protectiveness and defiance fought for dominance in Hayley's psyche. She struggled to focus on being positive and remaining calm. If nothing else, Ellie had to be curious about what sort of woman Hayley might end up with. That was the key to the success of the whole thing. Hayley had to let Ellie get to know Merle and replace vague stereotypes with a living, breathing human. They had to start the process sometime, and the sooner the better.

When they walked into the old-fashioned suburban ranch home, Hayley called loudly, "Mo-om, we're here." She heard a faint answer from the back of the house. Soon enough, they stood in the dining room face-to-face.

Hayley made her introduction, and Merle solemnly shook Ellie's hand and favored her with a restrained but sincere smile. "I'm very pleased to meet you, and thank you for inviting me to your home."

Hayley couldn't divine what was going on in Ellie's mind. She seemed almost like a youngster struggling to be on her best behavior for her parents' important company. She was a little overformal and much less talkative than usual. As agreed, Hayley kept quiet and let Merle converse with Ellie, which she did in a series of innocuous and polite comments on the house, the lunch, the weather in Concord versus San Francisco, and Ellie's garden. Hayley had fed her information she could use, and Ellie started to thaw a bit and stop appearing as though she expected the roof to fall at any moment. Hayley should have known Merle would be expert at putting someone at ease. She was actually content to observe.

They'd finished their lunch and sat on the deck, drinks in hand. Merle and Ellie spoke at length about gardening and the various seasonal plants, pesky insect invaders, and how to cope with drought.

There was a pause, and Ellie beamed at both of them and asked, "So do you girls think you'll be getting married soon?"

Merle's genial expression faltered. Clearly she didn't expect *that* question to come up. Hayley was floored as well.

"Mom. I just got divorced, I don't think I want to rush into anything that soon."

"Oh, I know, dear. I hear so much about it on the news, it made me wonder."

Merle cleared her throat. "I can remember back when I was young and no one who was gay had the slightest inkling that marriage would be possible. We all said, 'who needs marriage?' It was easier to just not care about it."

"The world has changed, hasn't it?" Ellie asked. "We've all learned to think about these things differently."

"I believe so. In answer to your question, I wouldn't presume to rush Hayley into anything, but yes, it's something I've thought about. Something I hope she might consider. In the future."

Hayley looked at Merle closely and reached for her hand. "I would. Really."

Ellie caught the gesture and smiled. "I look forward to it. Now. Do you want more iced tea?"

❖

"Okay, okay. You can say I told you so. You're allowed."

They were on their way home, and Hayley was surprised it had gone so smoothly. She wasn't exactly disappointed, but she felt silly for having blown it up into a big drama in her head.

"Not at all, sweetheart. You were right to be nervous. It's a big step. It went well and we were fine. It's all good."

"I never in a million years thought she would mention marriage. That was unbelievable."

"Well. It's not out of the question, is it?" Merle turned briefly to make eye contact.

"No. It's not. Not at all." Hayley paused.

"It's crazy, but I think I may be still having a hard time accepting that I'm a lesbian so I think everyone else in my life is going to not be supportive. No one at work but Britt knows. Still. I've got to do something about that soon."

Merle patted her leg. "Honey, you're not crazy. Don't worry, and yes, you're going to have some unconscious negative feelings. It's called internalized homophobia. We all go through it. The culture sends us too many bad messages. Things are so much better now, but they're not perfect. You'll get more used to your new life. You'll gradually come out. It's a process, you know, not an event. A lifelong process, actually."

"Oh, Merle, love, you're so smart. I sometimes forget you've gone through all of this already. I couldn't do this without you."

"Good news, you don't have to." Merle squeezed her thigh and Hayley tingled, happy they'd be home soon. She picked up Merle's hand and rubbed it on her cheek.

❖

A couple of weeks later, Merle and Hayley sat on the couch in Sigrid and Clea's living room. Their first visit to Clea and Sigrid as a couple was for Thanksgiving dinner. Things had gotten complicated when Ellie had invited them for dinner after they'd accepted Sigrid and Clea's invitation. Ellie was disappointed, but she asked them to come for dessert.

Arthur was invited as well, and Clea and Sigrid's two cats were sequestered in a bedroom. Arthur seemed to sense his privilege. He sat erect next to the couch, his head swiveling from Merle and Hayley to Sigrid and finally to Clea, who was setting the dining room table, and then back to Merle again.

Hayley was nearly sitting in Merle's lap. Merle kept an arm around her, slowly moving her hand from Hayley's neck to her butt. Hayley had her head on Merle's shoulder and kissed her cheek or nuzzled her neck every so often. Her soft breaths tickled, and Merle shivered. She couldn't stop smiling.

"If you two weren't so cute, you'd be disgusting," Sigrid said with an insufferable air of self-satisfaction. Merle was happy to let her enjoy her unspoken, but quite obvious, "I told you so."

Clea said, "You having fun with the weather? Getting out on Bernal Hill? Girl, it's way too warm for November." They'd had an unexpected heat wave the last week: the last gasp of summer.

"Yep. We walk the dog every day. He loves it…It sure as heck is warm. *Very* warm." Hayley discreetly stuck her tongue in Merle's ear, making her jump.

Sigrid noticed and grinned and shook her head.

"May all our Novembers be warm," Merle said. "And all our other months too." Hayley kissed her as Clea and Sigrid laughed.

About the Author

Kathleen Knowles grew up in Pittsburgh, Pennsylvania, but has lived in San Francisco for more than thirty years. She finds the city's combination of history, natural beauty, and multicultural diversity inspiring and endlessly fascinating. Her first novel, *Awake Unto Me*, won the Golden Crown Literary Society award for best historical romance novel of 2012.

She lives with her spouse and their three pets atop one of San Francisco's many hills. When not writing, she works as a health and safety specialist at the University of California, San Francisco.

Books Available From Bold Strokes Books

The Chameleon's Tale by Andrea Bramhall. Two old friends must work through a web of lies and deceit to find themselves again, but in the search they discover far more than they ever went looking for. (978-1-62639-363-9)

Side Effects by VK Powell. Detective Jordan Bishop and Dr. Neela Sahjani must decide if it's easier to trust someone with your heart or your life as they face threatening protestors, corrupt politicians, and their increasing attraction. (978-1-62639-364-6)

Autumn Spring by Shelley Thrasher. Can Bree and Linda, two women in the autumn of their lives, put their hearts first and find the love they've never dared seize? (978-1-62639-365-3)

Warm November by Kathleen Knowles. What do you do if the one woman you want is the only one you can't have? (978-1-62639-366-0)

In Every Cloud by Tina Michele. When Bree finally leaves her shattered life behind, is she strong enough to salvage the remaining pieces of her heart and find the place where it truly fits? (978-1-62639-413-1)

Rise of the Gorgon by Tanai Walker. When independent Internet journalist Elle Pharell goes to Kuwait to investigate a veteran's mysterious suicide, she hires Cassandra Hunt, an interpreter with a covert agenda. (978-1-62639-367-7)

Crossed by Meredith Doench. Agent Luce Hansen returns home to catch a killer and risks everything to revisit the unsolved murder of her first girlfriend and confront the demons of her youth. (978-1-62639-361-5)

Making a Comeback by Julie Blair. Music and love take center stage when jazz pianist Liz Randall tries to make a comeback with the help of her reclusive, blind neighbor, Jac Winters. (978-1-62639-357-8)

Soul Unique by Gun Brooke. Self-proclaimed cynic Greer Landon falls for Hayden Rowe's paintings and the young woman shortly after, but will Hayden, who lives with Asperger syndrome, trust her and reciprocate her feelings? (978-1-62639-358-5)

The Price of Honor by Radclyffe. Honor and duty are not always black and white—and when self-styled patriots take up arms against the government, the price of honor may be a life. (978-1-62639-359-2)

Mounting Evidence by Karis Walsh. Lieutenant Abigail Hargrove and her mounted police unit need to solve a murder and protect wetland biologist Kira Lovell during the Washington State Fair. (978-1-62639-343-1)

Threads of the Heart by Jeannie Levig. Maggie and Addison Rae-McInnis share a love and a life, but are the threads that bind them together strong enough to withstand Addison's restlessness and the seductive Victoria Fontaine? (978-1-62639-410-0)

Sheltered Love by MJ Williamz. Boone Fairway and Grey Dawson—two women touched by abuse—overcome their pasts to find happiness in each other. (978-1-62639-362-2)

Searching for Celia by Elizabeth Ridley. As American spy novelist Dayle Salvesen investigates the mysterious disappearance of her ex-lover, Celia, in London, she begins questioning how well she knew Celia—and how well she knows herself. (978-1-62639-356-1).

Hardwired by C.P. Rowlands. Award-winning teacher Clary Stone and Leefe Ellis, manager of the homeless shelter for small children, stand together in a part of Clary's hometown that she never knew existed. (978-1-62639-351-6)

The Muse by Meghan O'Brien. Erotica author Kate McMannis struggles with writer's block until a gorgeous muse entices her into a world of fantasy sex and inadvertent romance. (978-1-62639-223-6)

Death's Doorway by Crin Claxton. Helping the dead can be deadly: Tony may be listening to the dead, but she needs to learn to listen to the living. (978-1-62639-354-7)

No Good Reason by Cari Hunter. A violent kidnapping in a Peak District village pushes Detective Sanne Jensen and lifelong friend Dr. Meg Fielding closer, just as it threatens to tear everything apart. (978-1-62639-352-3)

Romance by the Book by Jo Victor. If Cam didn't keep disrupting her life, maybe Alex could uncover the secret of a century-old love story, and solve the greatest mystery of all—her own heart. (978-1-62639-353-0)

The 45th Parallel by Lisa Girolami. Burying her mother isn't the worst thing that can happen to Val Montague when she returns to the woodsy but peculiar town of Hemlock, Oregon. (978-1-62639-342-4)

A Royal Romance by Jenny Frame. In a country where class still divides, can love topple the last social taboo and allow Queen Georgina and Beatrice Elliot, a working-class girl, their happy ever after? (978-1-62639-360-8)

Bouncing by Jaime Maddox. Basketball coach Alex Dalton has been bouncing from woman to woman because no one ever held her interest, until she meets her new assistant, Britain Dodge. (978-1-62639-344-8)

Same Time Next Week by Emily Smith. A chance encounter between Alex Harris and the beautiful Michelle Masters leads to a whirlwind friendship and causes Alex to question everything she's ever known—including her own marriage. (978-1-62639-345-5)

All Things Rise by Missouri Vaun. Cole rescues a striking pilot who crash-lands near her family's farm, setting in motion a chain of events that will forever alter the course of her life. (978-1-62639-346-2)

Riding Passion by D. Jackson Leigh. Mount up for the ride through a sizzling anthology of chance encounters, buried desires, romantic surprises, and blazing passion. (978-1-62639-349-3)

Love's Bounty by Yolanda Wallace. Lobster boat captain Jake Myers stopped living the day she cheated death, but meeting greenhorn Shy Silva stirs her back to life. (978-1-62639334-9)

Just Three Words by Melissa Brayden. Sometimes the one you want is the one you least suspect…Accountant Samantha Ennis has her ordered life disrupted when heartbreaker Hunter Blair moves into her trendy Soho loft. (978-1-62639-335-6)

Lay Down the Law by Carsen Taite. Attorney Peyton Davis returns to her Texas roots to take on big oil and the Mexican Mafia, but will her investigation thwart her chance at true love? (978-1-62639-336-3)

Playing in Shadow by Lesley Davis. Survivor's guilt threatens to keep Bryce trapped in her nightmare world unless Scarlet's love can pull her out of the darkness back into the light. (978-1-62639-337-0)

Soul Selecta by Gill McKnight. Soul mates are hell to work with. (978-1-62639-338-7)

Shadow Hunt by L.L. Raand. With young to raise and her Pack under attack, Sylvan, Alpha of the wolf Weres, takes on her greatest challenge when she determines to uncover the faceless enemies known as the Shadow Lords. A Midnight Hunters novel. (978-1-62639-326-4)

Heart of the Game by Rachel Spangler. A baseball writer falls for a single mom, but can she ever love anything as much as she loves the game? (978-1-62639-327-1)

Prayer of the Handmaiden by Merry Shannon. Celibate priestess Kadrian must defend the kingdom of Ithyria from a dangerous enemy and ultimately choose between her duty to the Goddess and the love of her childhood sweetheart, Erinda. (978-1-62639-329-5)

The Witch of Stalingrad by Justine Saracen. A Soviet "night witch" pilot and American journalist meet on the Eastern Front in WWII and struggle through carnage, conflicting politics, and the deadly Russian winter. (978-1-62639-330-1)

boldstrokesbooks.com

Bold Strokes Books
Quality and Diversity in LGBTQ Literature

victory EDITIONS

Drama

MATINEE BOOKS

E-BOOKS

SCI-FI

BSB SOLILOQUY

MYSTERY

HE erotica

YOUNG ADULT

BOLD STROKES BOOKS

EROTICA

LIBERTY EDITION

Romance

W·E·B·S·T·O·R·E
PRINT AND EBOOKS